The DUCHESS RANCH *of* OLD JOHN WARE

WRITTEN BY JAMES DAVIDGE

DRAWN BY BOB PRODOR

BOOK DESIGN BY FIONA STAPLES

ROSENCRANTZ COMICS
A DIVISION OF BAYEUX ARTS

THE DUCHESS RANCH OF OLD JOHN WARE
Copyright © 2010 James Davidge, text; Bob Prodor, illustrations

Published by: Bayeux Arts, Inc., 119 Stratton Crescent SW, Calgary, Canada T3H 1T7, www.bayeux.com

Cover image: Bob Prodor

Library and Archives Canada Cataloguing in Publication

Davidge, James, 1973-
The duchess ranch of old John Ware / James Davidge ; Bob
Prodor, illustrator.

ISBN 978-1-897411-18-6

I. Prodor, Bob, 1971- II. Title.

PN6733.D38D83 2010 j741.5'971 C2010-900537-6

First Printing: October 2010
Printed in Canada

Books published by Bayeux Arts/Rosencrantz are available at special quantity discounts to use as premiums and sales promotions, or for use in corporate training programs. For more information, please write to Special Sales, Bayeux Arts, Inc., 119 Stratton Crescent SW, Calgary, Canada T3H 1T7.

The publishing activities of Bayeux/Gondolier are supported by the Canada Council for the Arts, the Alberta Foundation for the Arts, and by the Government of Canada through its Book Publishing Industry Development Program.

 Canadian Heritage Patrimoine canadien   Alberta Foundation for the Arts   Canada Council for the Arts   Conseil des Arts du Canada

I would like to dedicate this to my parents, Gary and Marilyn Davidge, for instilling in me an earnest appreciation for history and for helping me through many of my mercurial attempts at figuring out right from wrong.

- James Davidge

This book is dedicated to my Nana, Josephine Prodor, whose kindness and strength is an inspiration to me every day.

- Bob Prodor

THANK YOU

For their help on this project, I would like to thank Christa Mayer, Ella Davidge, Jesse Davidge, Natalie Norcross, Brad Meadows, Dr. Leslie Robertson, Jason Mehmel, Toby Malloy, Con Loree, Harry Sanders, Cheryl Foggo, George Lane, Dan Balkwill and Shawn Canning.

- JAMES

I would like to thank my mom Joann, my sister Jane, my nephews Mike and Nick and especially Corissa, for giving me nothing but positive encouragement always.

I would also like to give a special thanks to my dad Gerry for helping me get certain parts right and for his never ending support.

I'd also like to thank Corb for extra help and James for hiring me for this project.

- BOB

Introduction

By Cheryl Foggo

Here in Alberta, we like to attach numbers to our founding trailbreakers – the Big Four, the Famous Five. If you had asked me during my cowboy-obsessed childhood days, I would have assigned John Ware Number One. Stumbling upon the Ware display on a field trip to the Glenbow Museum marked the first time I saw a person of African descent reflected in the wider culture of the place that many generations of my family had been calling home.

James Davidge and Bob Prodor's careful research, insightful and compelling drawings and fresh and accessible language beautifully fuse the struggles and joys that were the pieces of John Ware's life. On these pages they introduce a legendary man to a generation that otherwise may never have known how he galloped our prairies and helped to sculpt the landscape that shaped our culture.

Award-winning author and historian Cheryl Foggo has been published and produced extensively as a journalist, young adult novelist, screenwriter, poet, playwright, and writer of fiction, and has also written extensively on the history of Black pioneers on the prairies. A recent recipient of the Harry Jerome Award for Excellence in the Arts, she is looking forward to the publication of two new books.

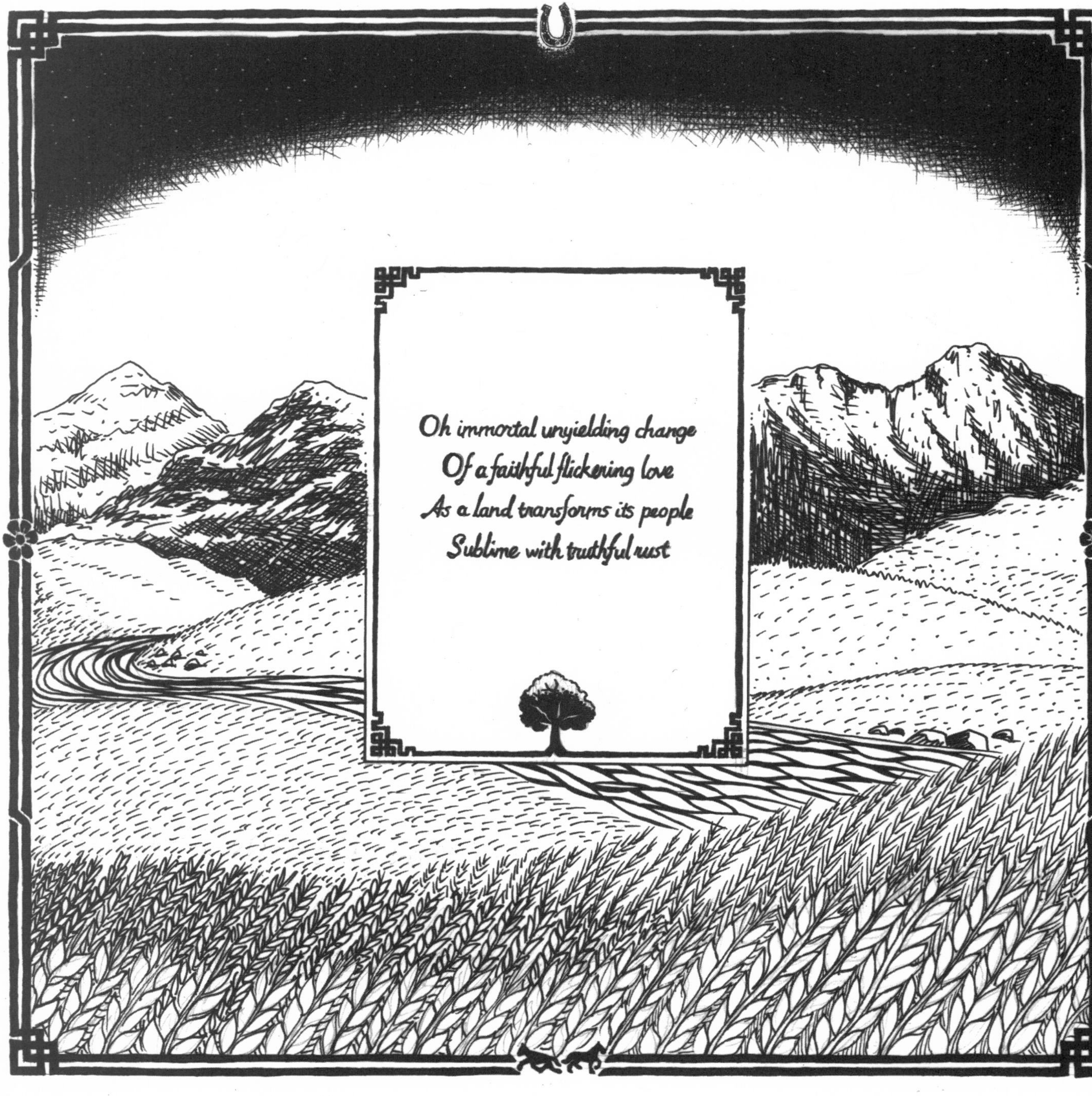
Oh immortal unyielding change
Of a faithful flickering love
As a land transforms its people
Sublime with truthful rust

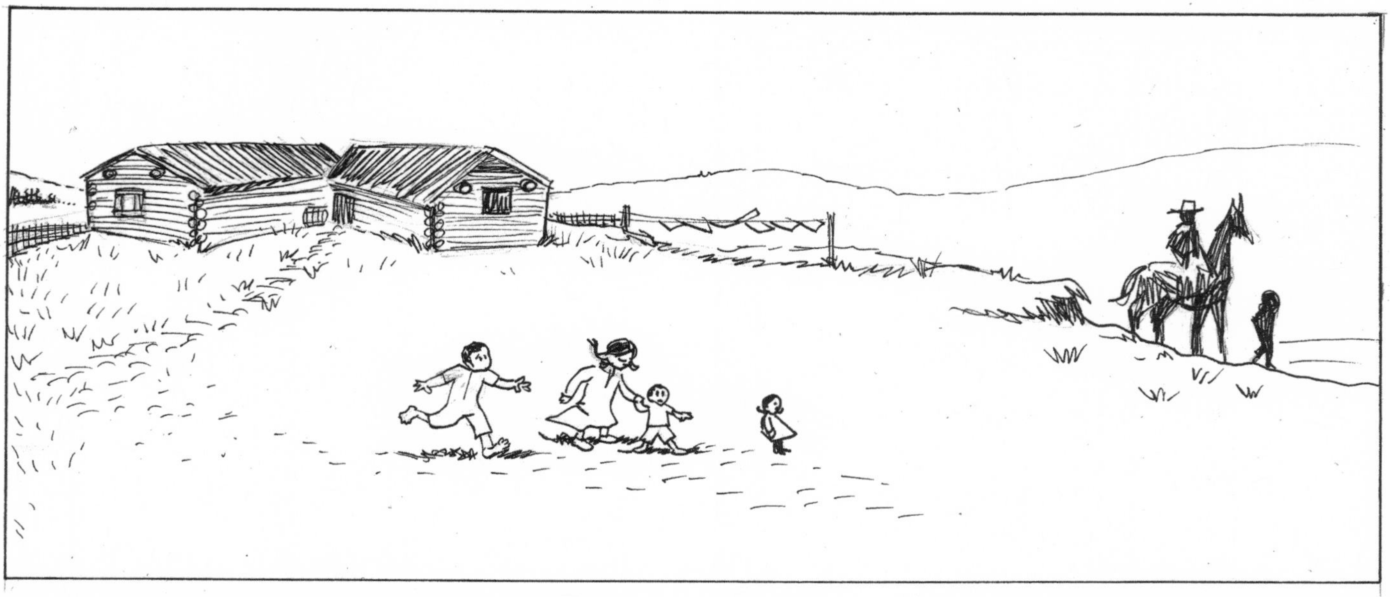
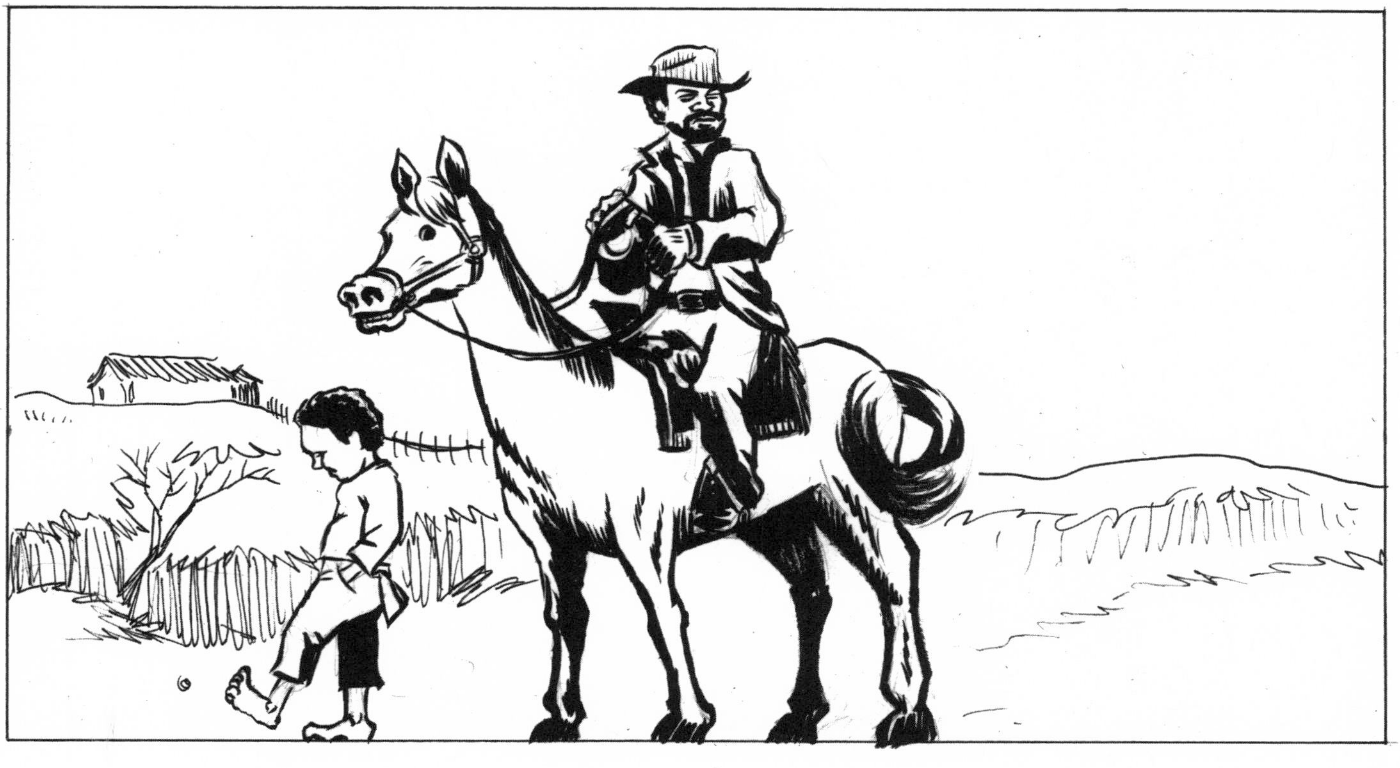

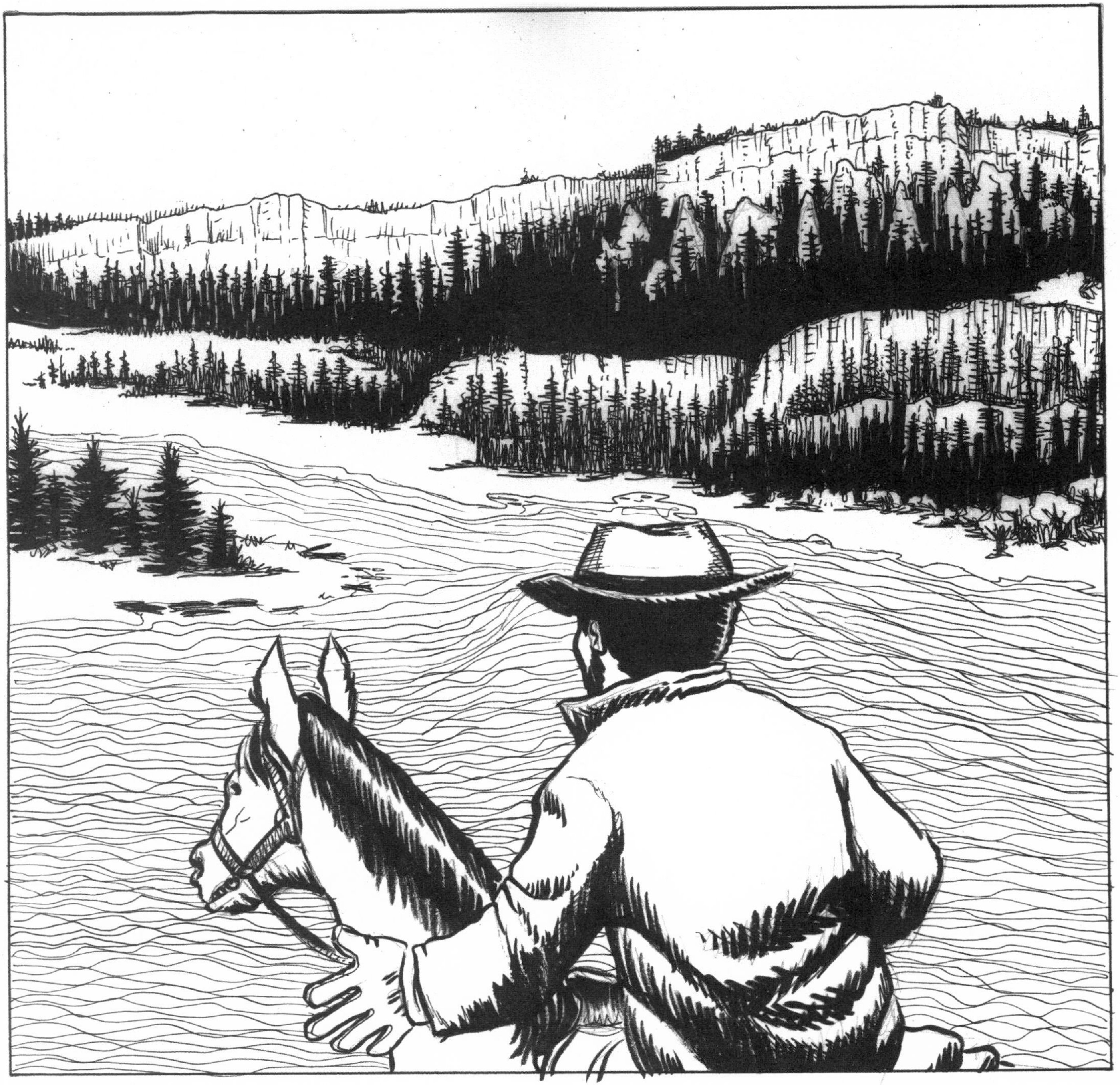

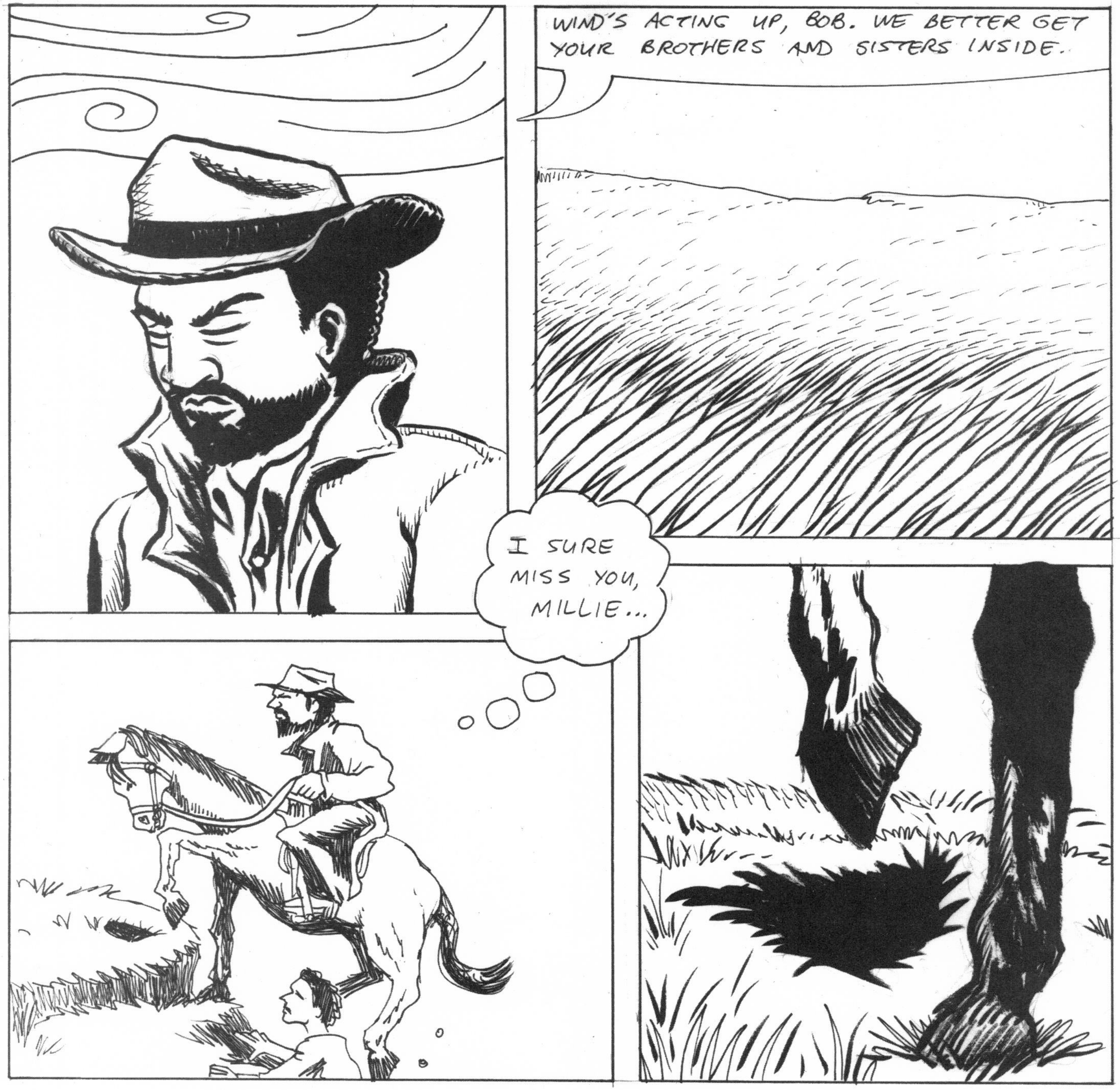
WIND'S ACTING UP, BOB. WE BETTER GET YOUR BROTHERS AND SISTERS INSIDE.
I SURE MISS YOU, MILLIE...

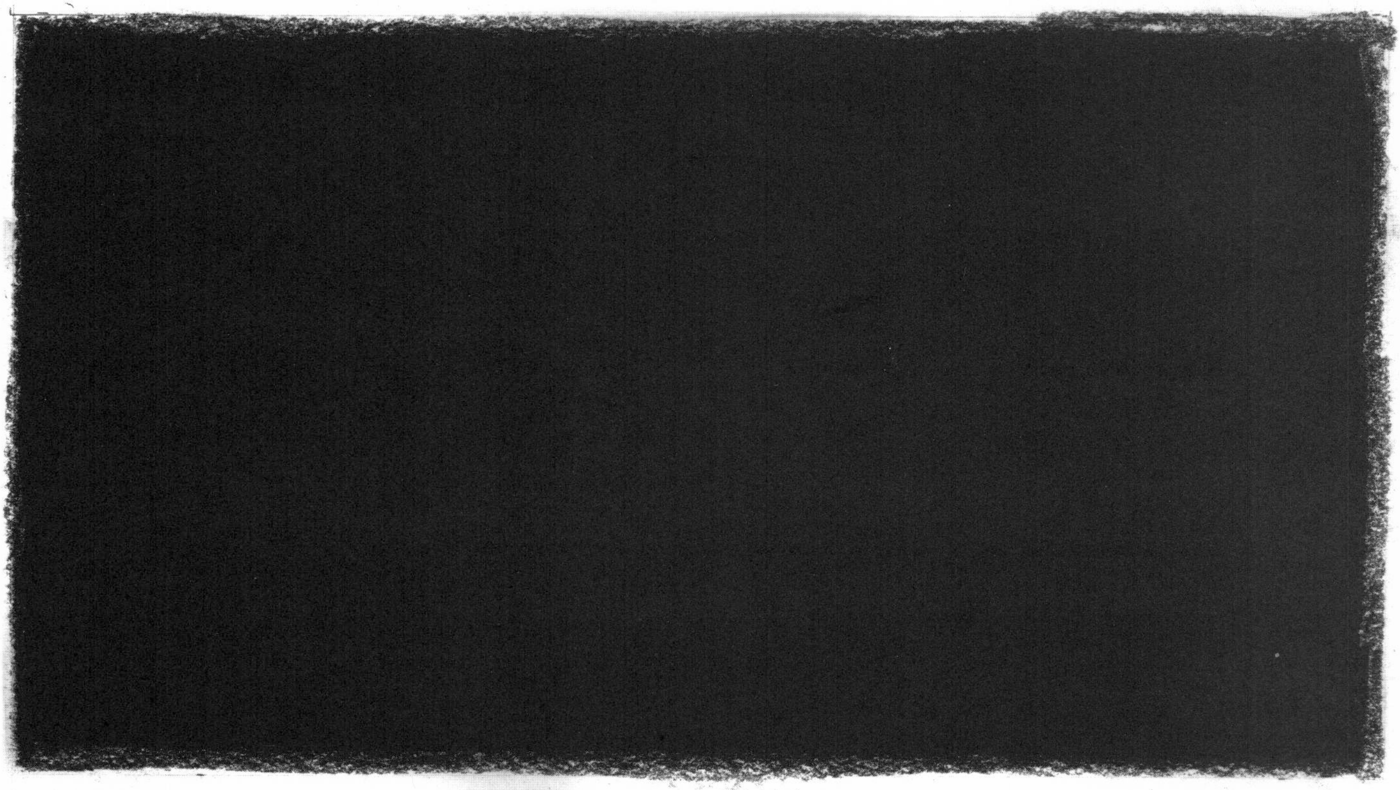

Wide eye to the universe
Astute ear to the dawn
Imagine and conceive
Time's earliest explosion

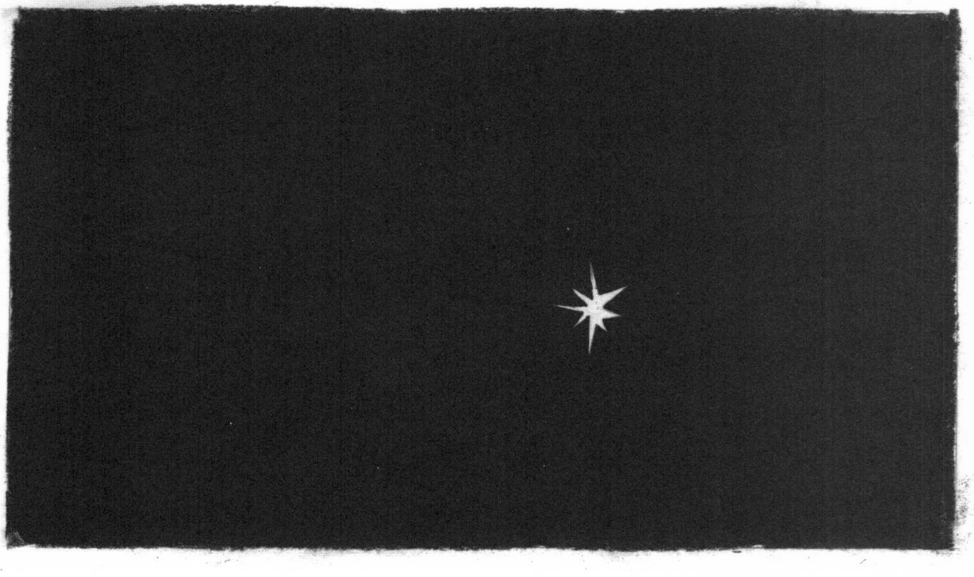

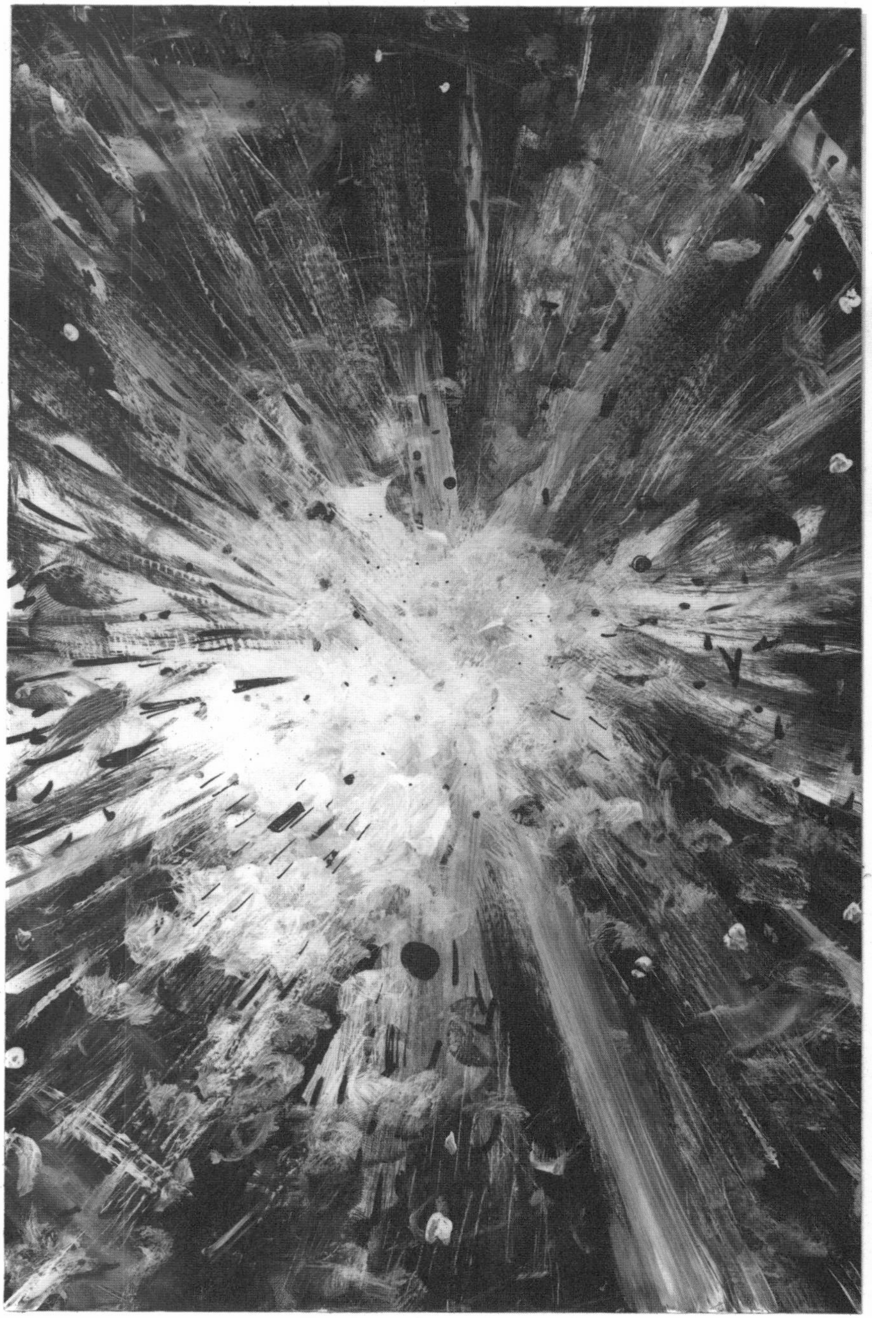

Expelled from contracting heat and light
Boundaries both dissolved and determined
Matter diversified into form
To be cooled, curved and spun

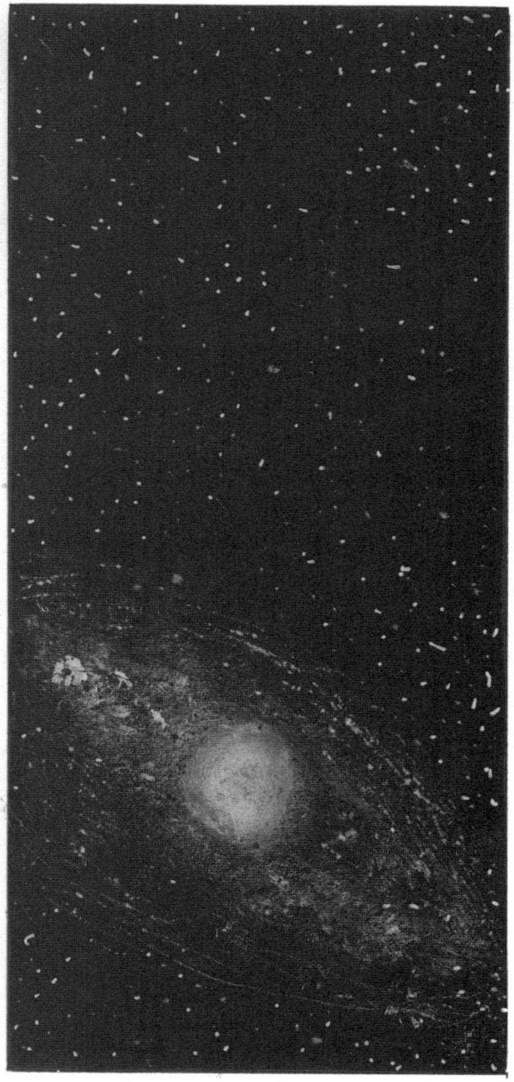

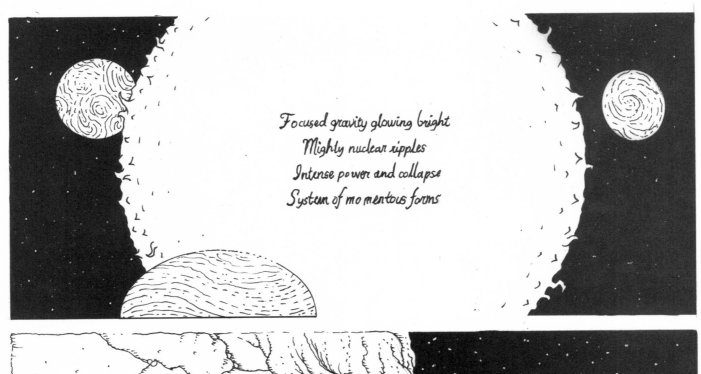

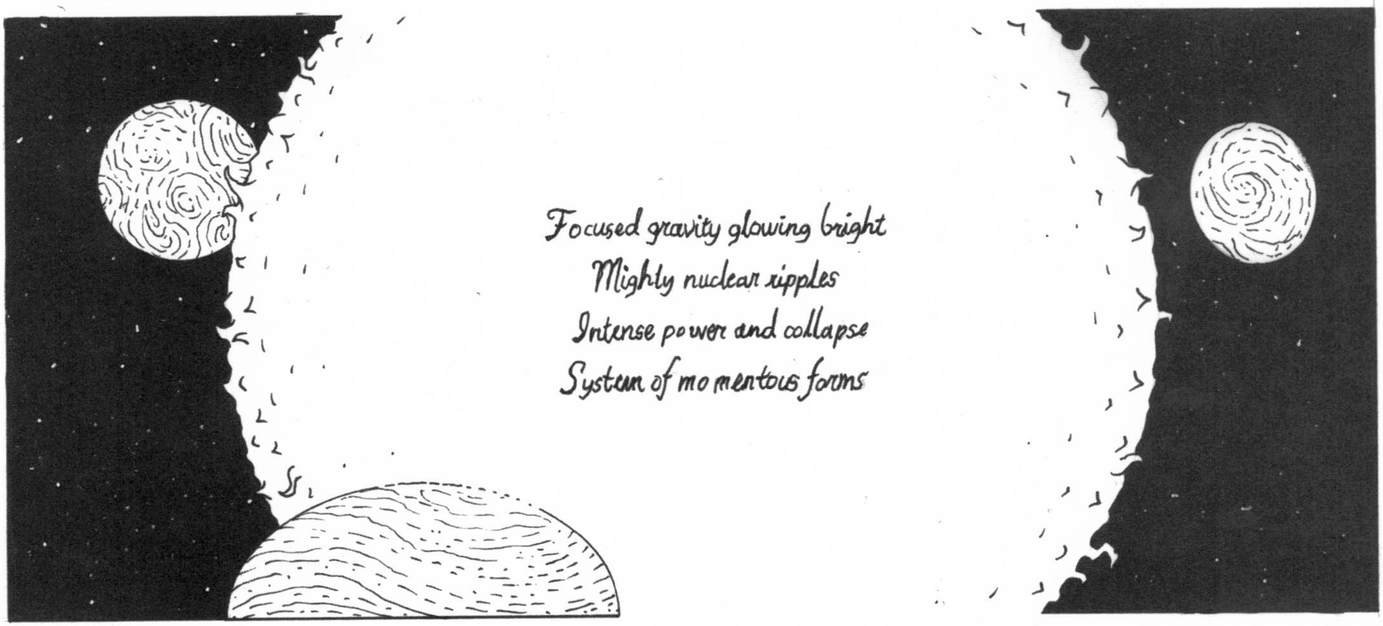
Focused gravity glowing bright
Mighty nuclear ripples
Intense power and collapse
System of momentous forms

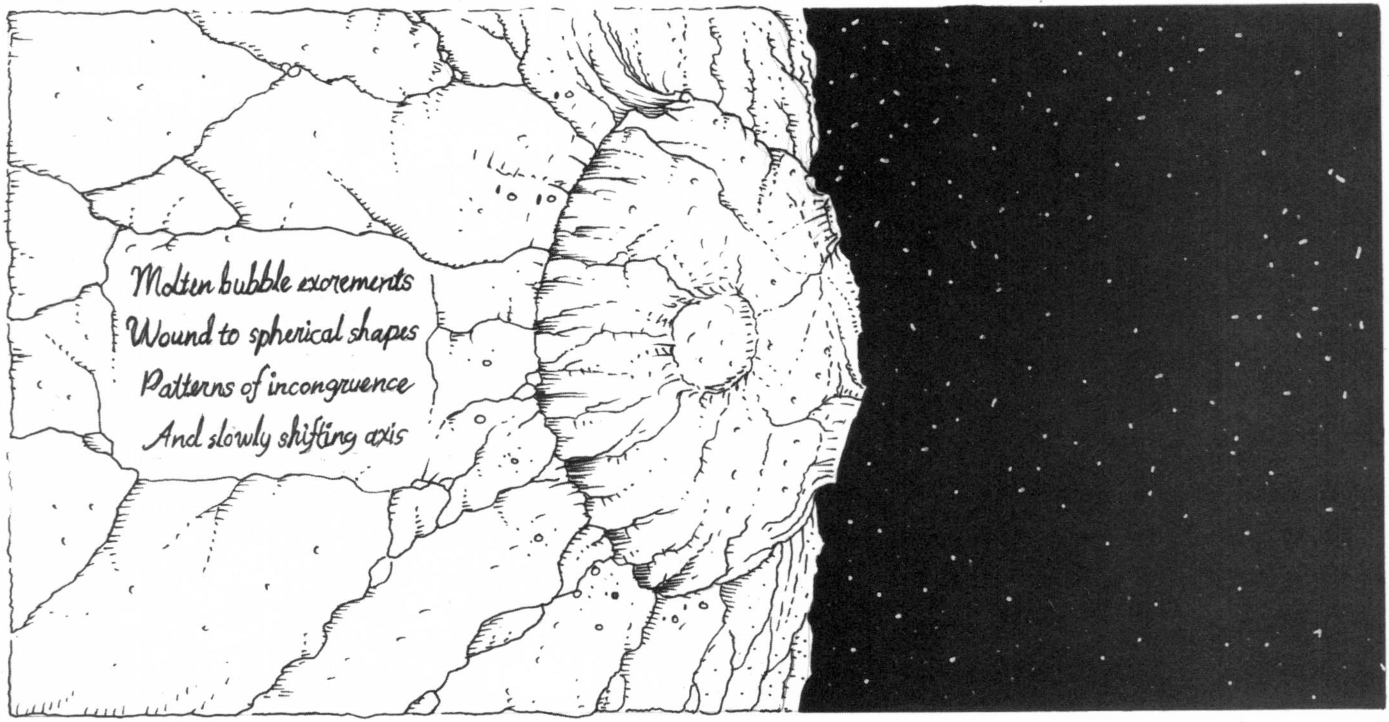
Molten bubble excrements
Wound to spherical shapes
Patterns of incongruence
And slowly shifting axis

Clay, fluid and gas
Uneven combinations
Of opulent clouds
And mystical rock

Wind is prime
Pushing water Rising dust
Challenging densities
Flights of falter and freedom

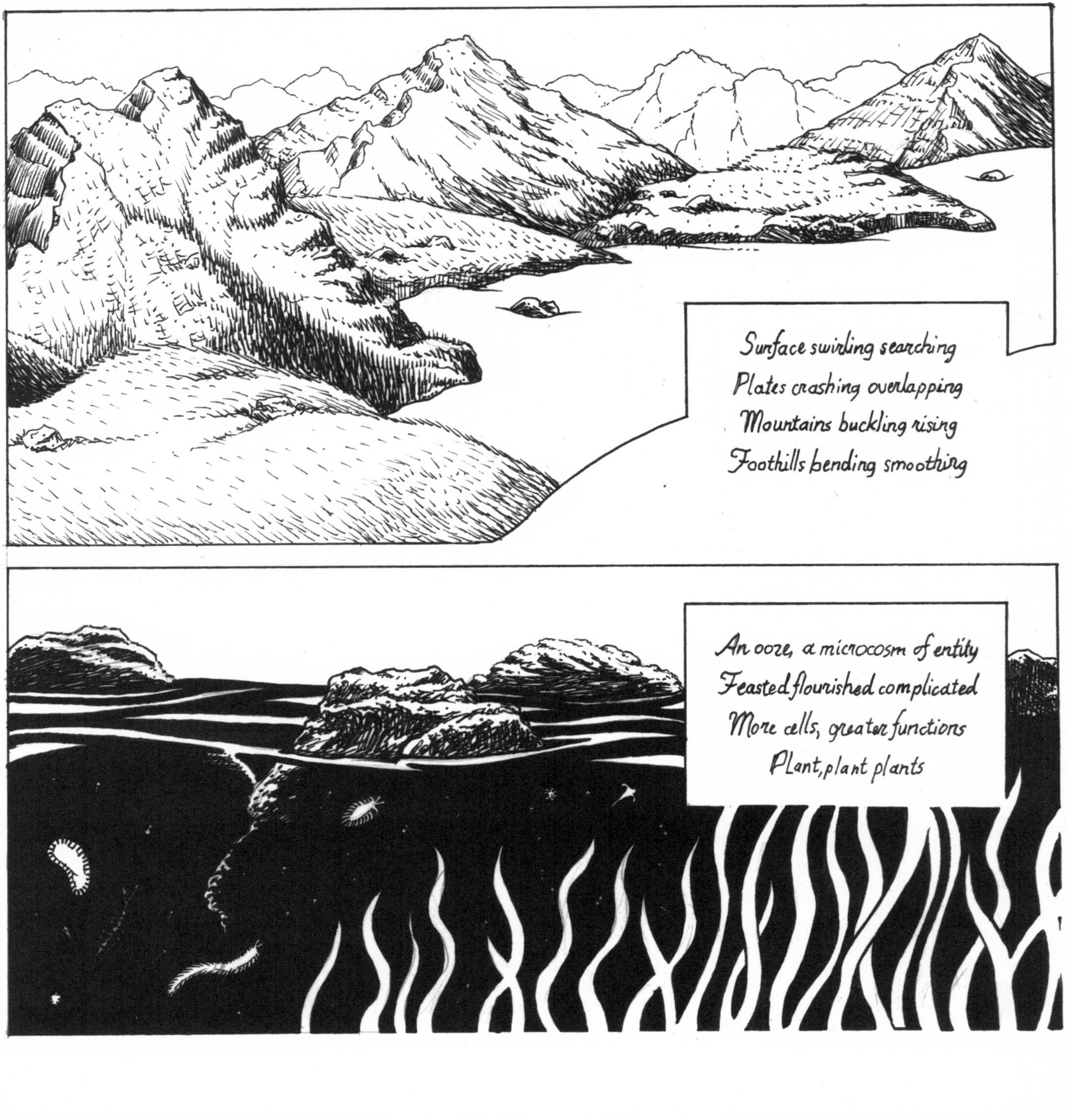
Surface swirling searching
Plates crashing overlapping
Mountains buckling rising
Foothills bending smoothing
An ooze, a microcosm of entity
Feasted flourished complicated
More cells, greater functions
Plant, plant plants

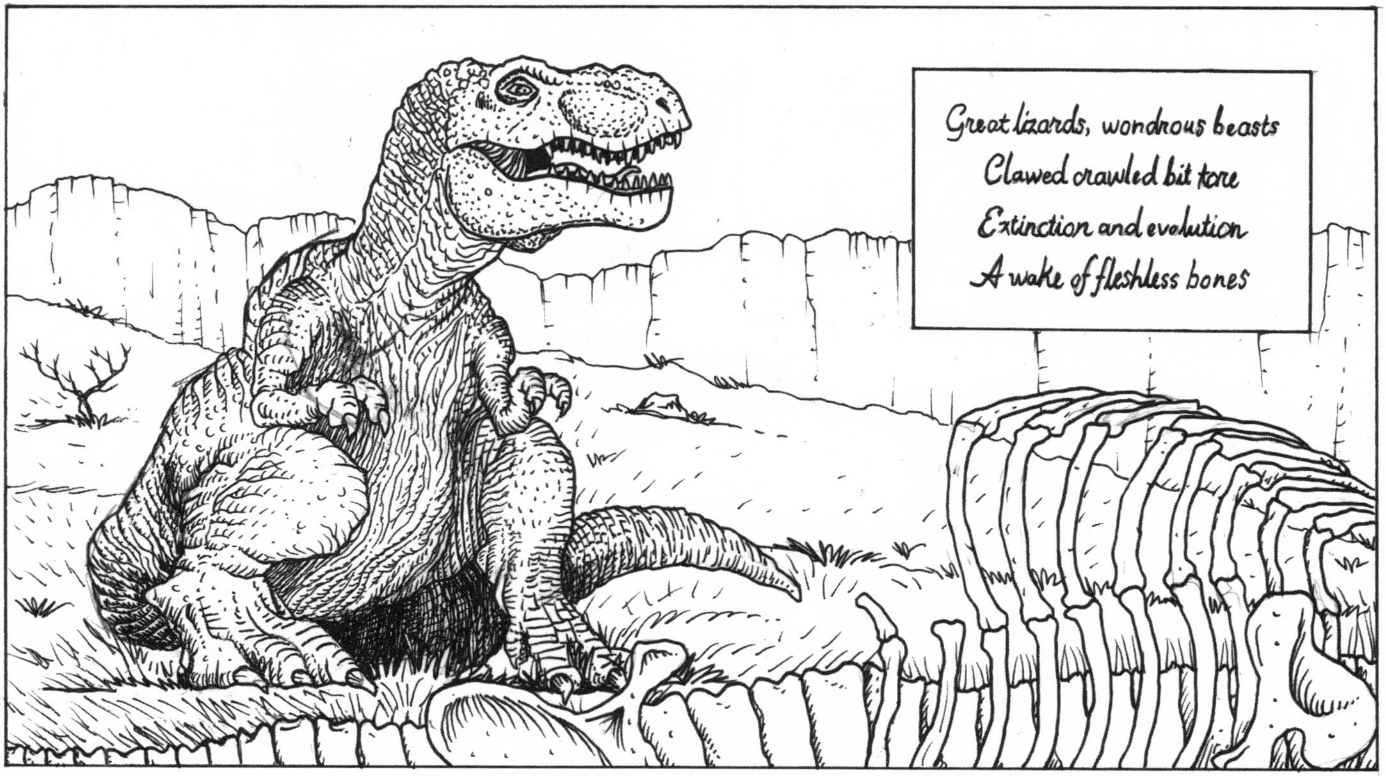
Great lizards, wondrous beasts
Clawed crawled bit tore
Extinction and evolution
A wake of fleshless bones

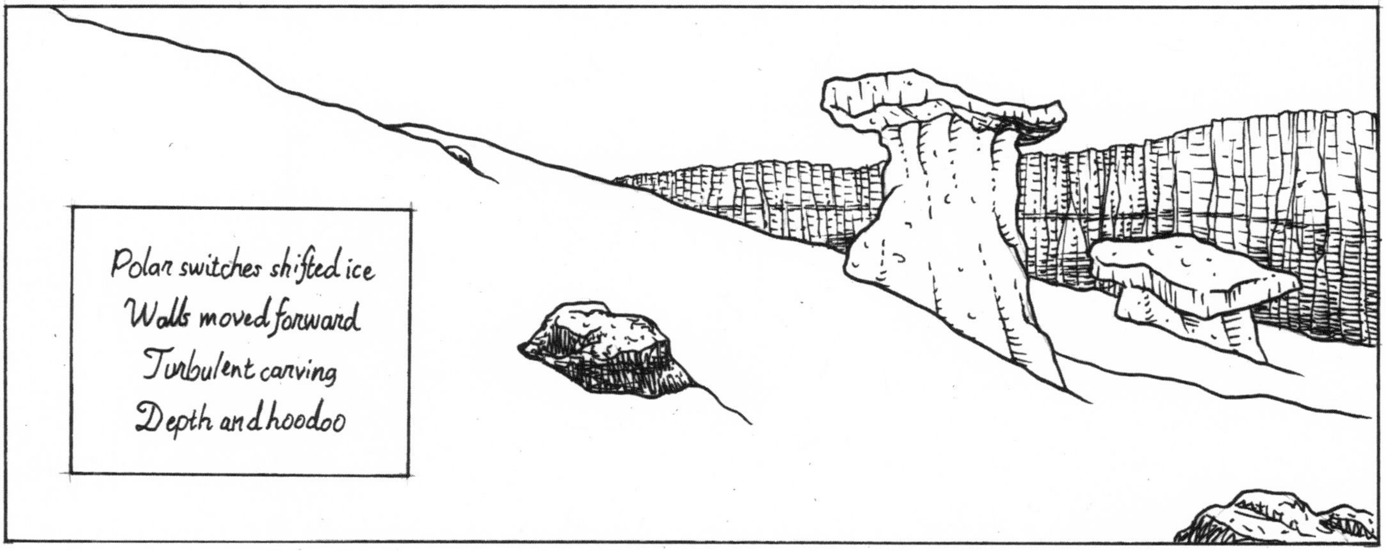
Polar switches shifted ice
Walls moved forward
Turbulent carving
Depth and hoodoo

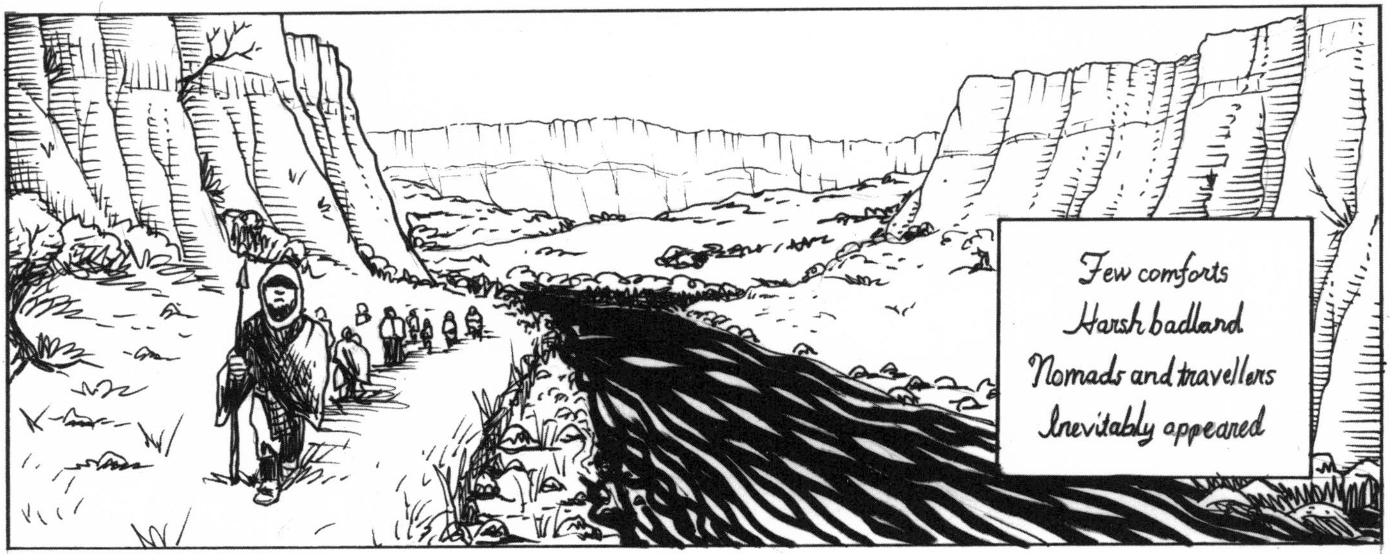
Few comforts
Harsh badland
Nomads and travellers
Inevitably appeared

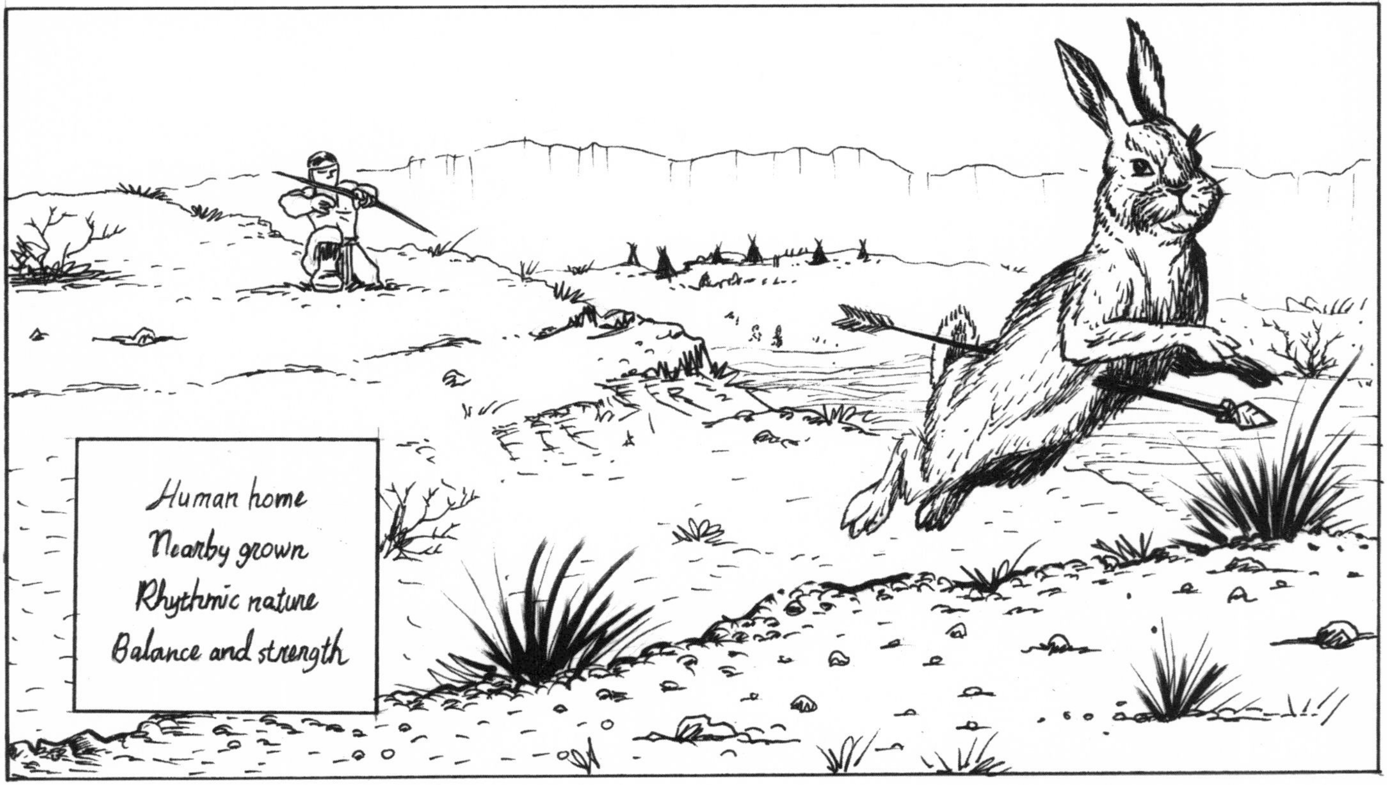
Human home
Nearby grown
Rhythmic nature
Balance and strength

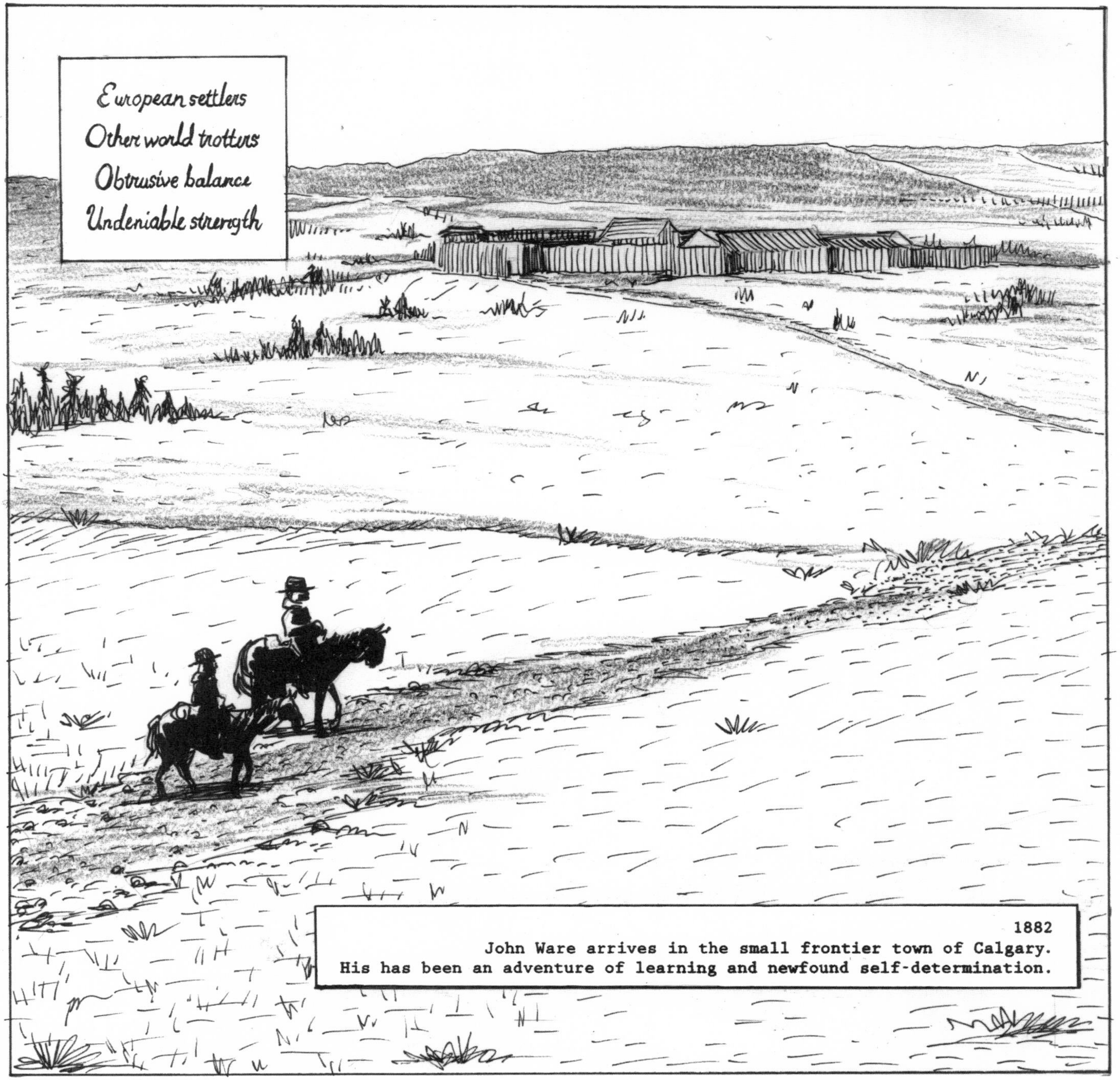
European settlers
Other world trotters
Obtrusive balance
Undeniable strength
1882
John Ware arrives in the small frontier town of Calgary.
His has been an adventure of learning and newfound self-determination.

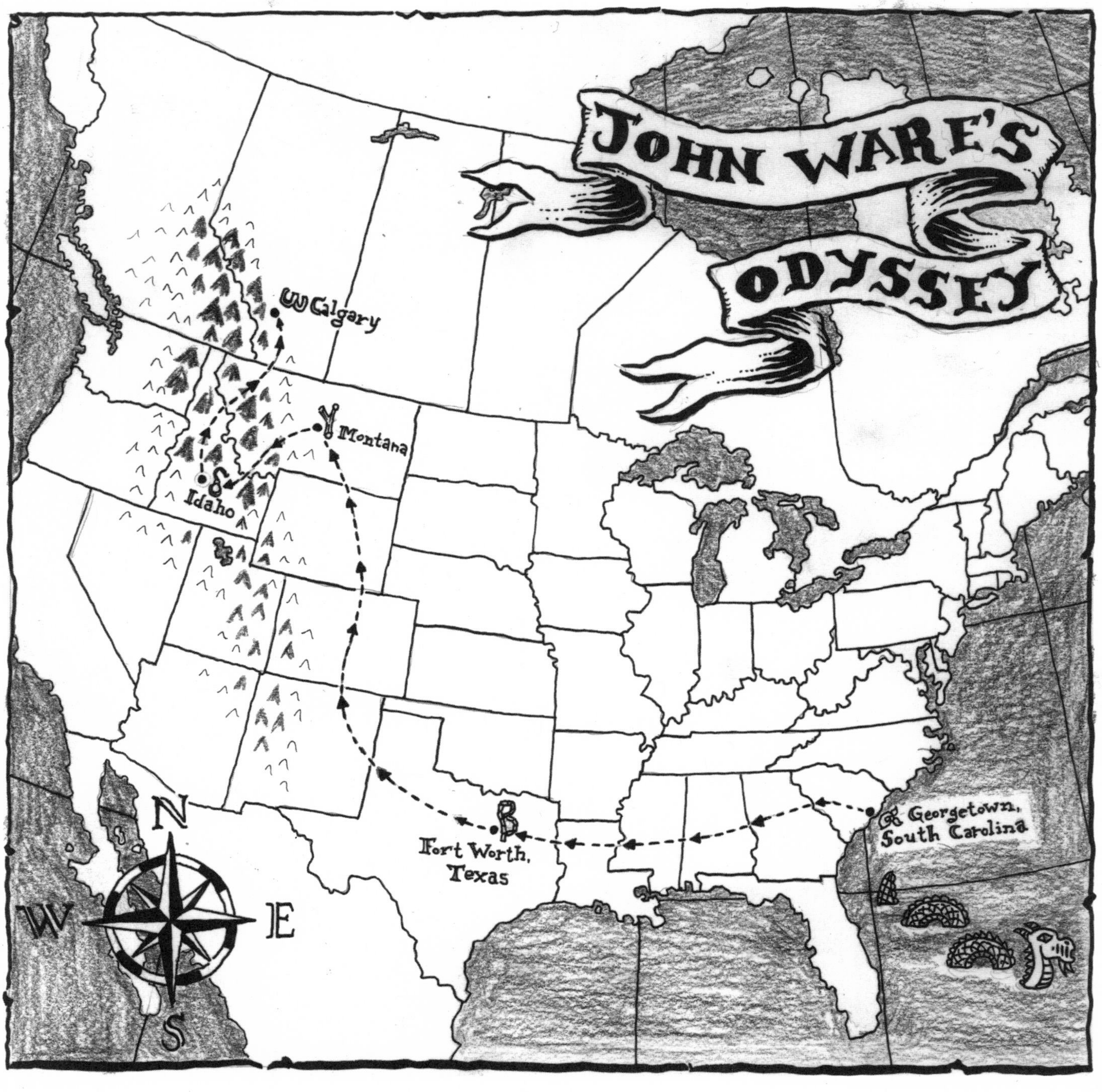

JOHN WARE'S ODYSSEY
Calgary
Montana
Idaho
Fort Worth, Texas
Georgetown, South Carolina
N
W
E
S

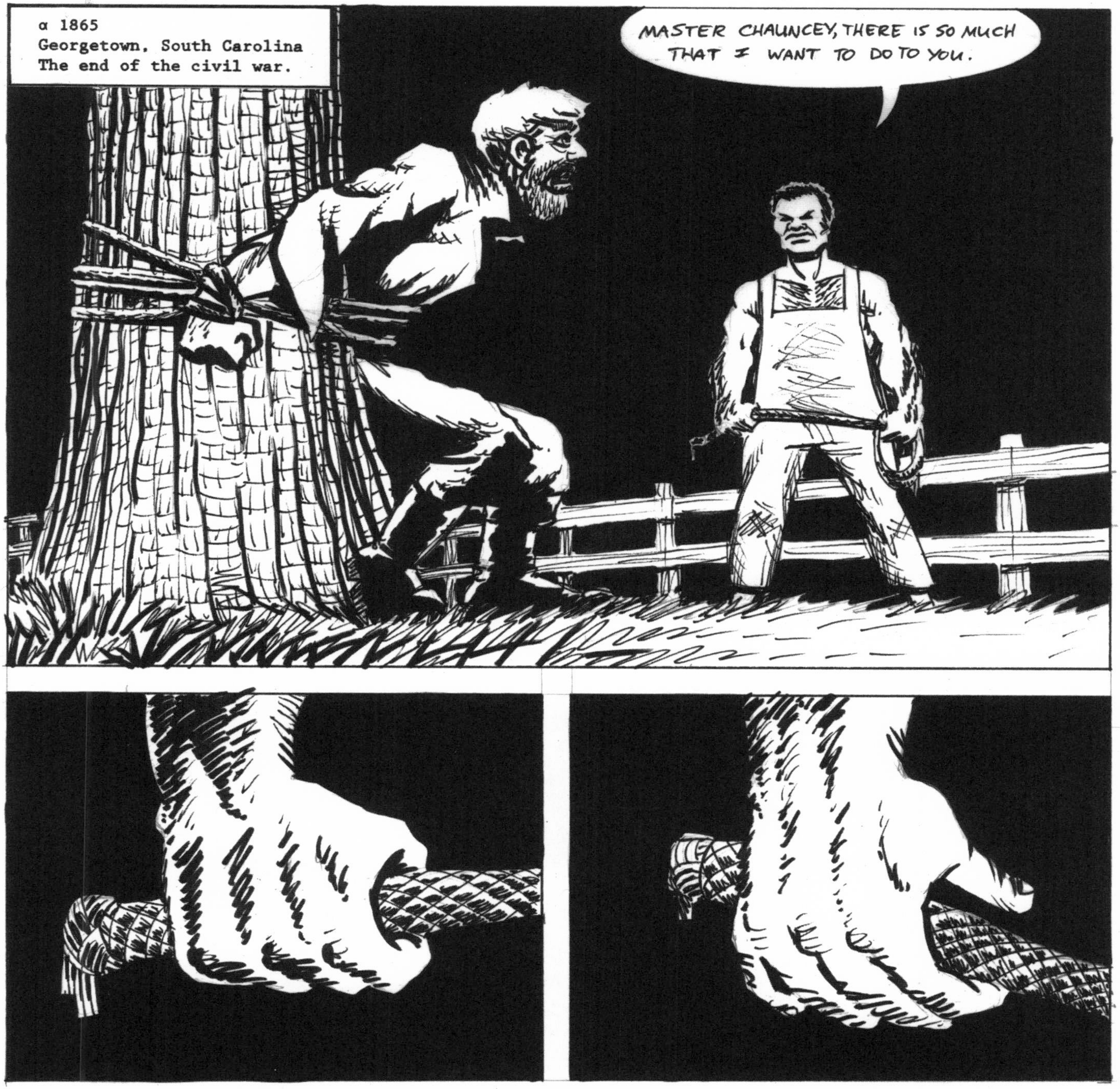
α 1865
Georgetown, South Carolina
The end of the civil war.
MASTER CHAUNCEY, THERE IS SO MUCH THAT I WANT TO DO TO YOU.

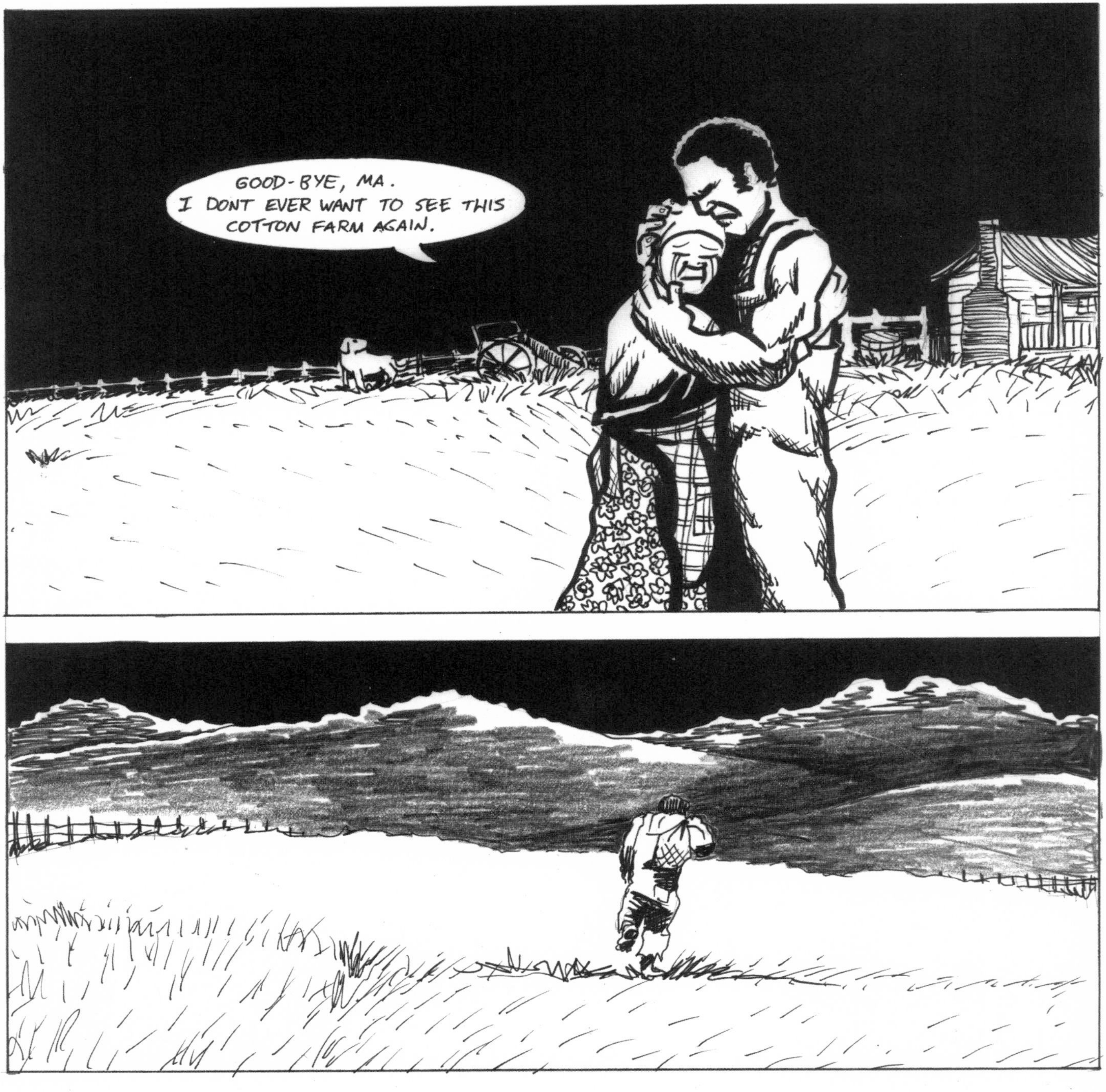
GOOD-BYE, MA. I DONT EVER WANT TO SEE THIS COTTON FARM AGAIN.

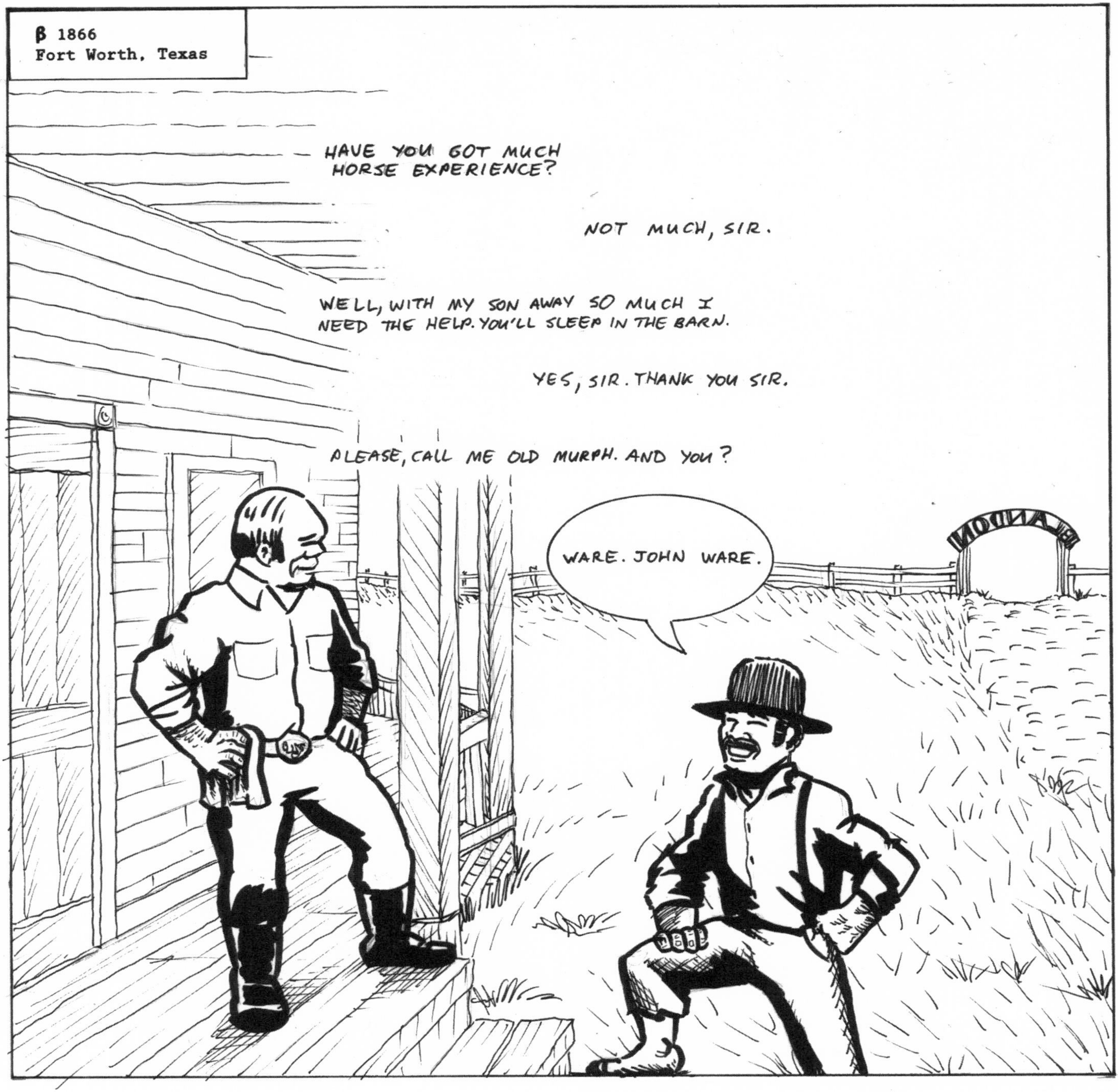
β 1866
Fort Worth, Texas
HAVE YOU GOT MUCH HORSE EXPERIENCE?
NOT MUCH, SIR.
WELL, WITH MY SON AWAY SO MUCH I NEED THE HELP. YOU'LL SLEEP IN THE BARN.
YES, SIR. THANK YOU SIR.
PLEASE, CALL ME OLD MURPH. AND YOU?
WARE. JOHN WARE.

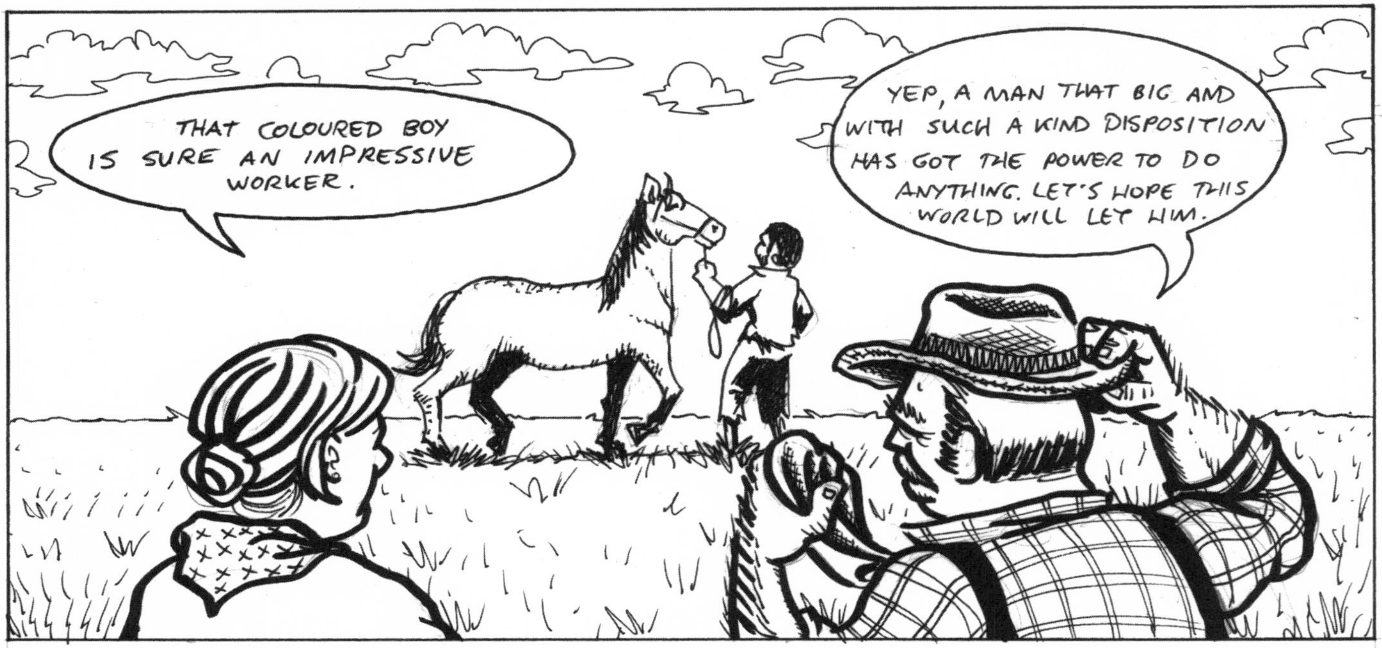
THAT COLOURED BOY IS SURE AN IMPRESSIVE WORKER.
YEP, A MAN THAT BIG AND WITH SUCH A KIND DISPOSITION HAS GOT THE POWER TO DO ANYTHING. LET'S HOPE THIS WORLD WILL LET HIM.

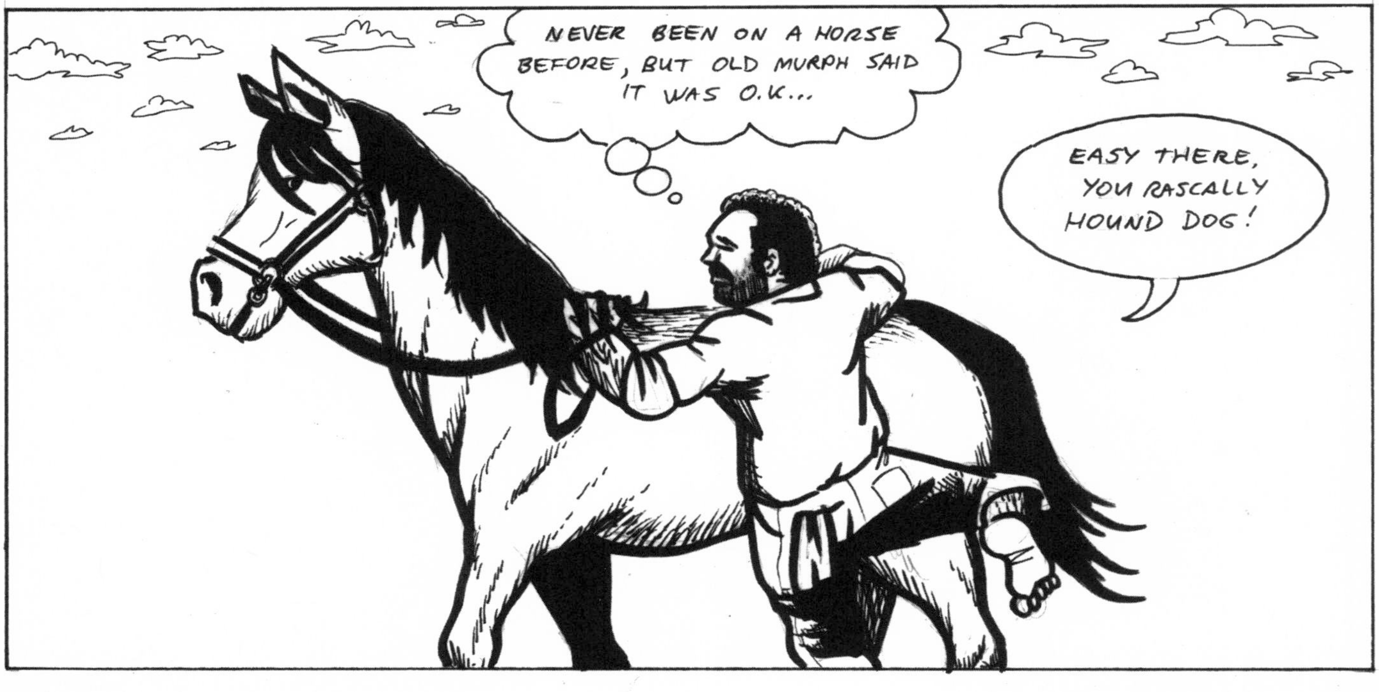
NEVER BEEN ON A HORSE BEFORE, BUT OLD MURPH SAID IT WAS O.K...
EASY THERE, YOU RASCALLY HOUND DOG!

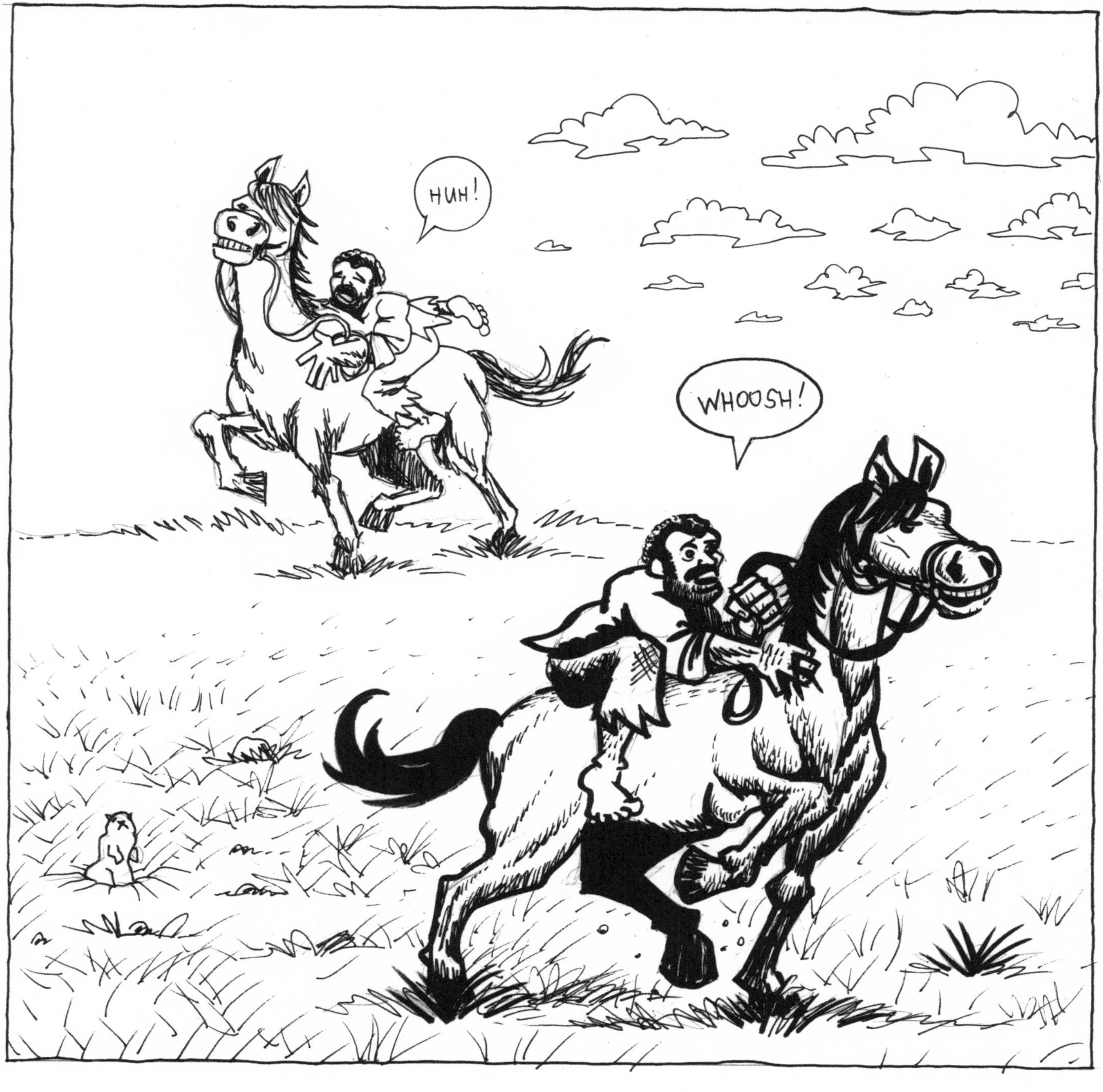
HUH!
WHOOSH!

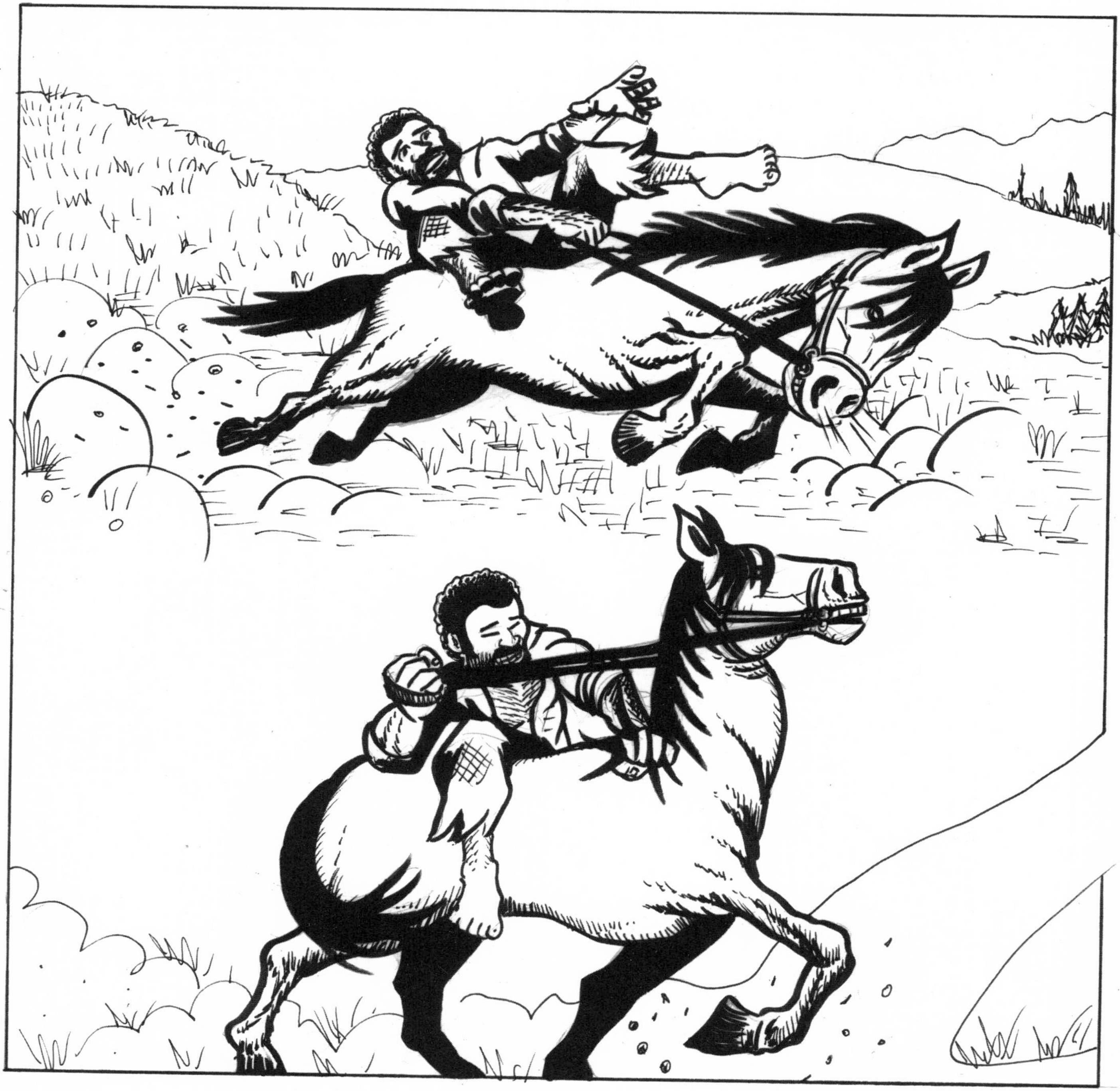

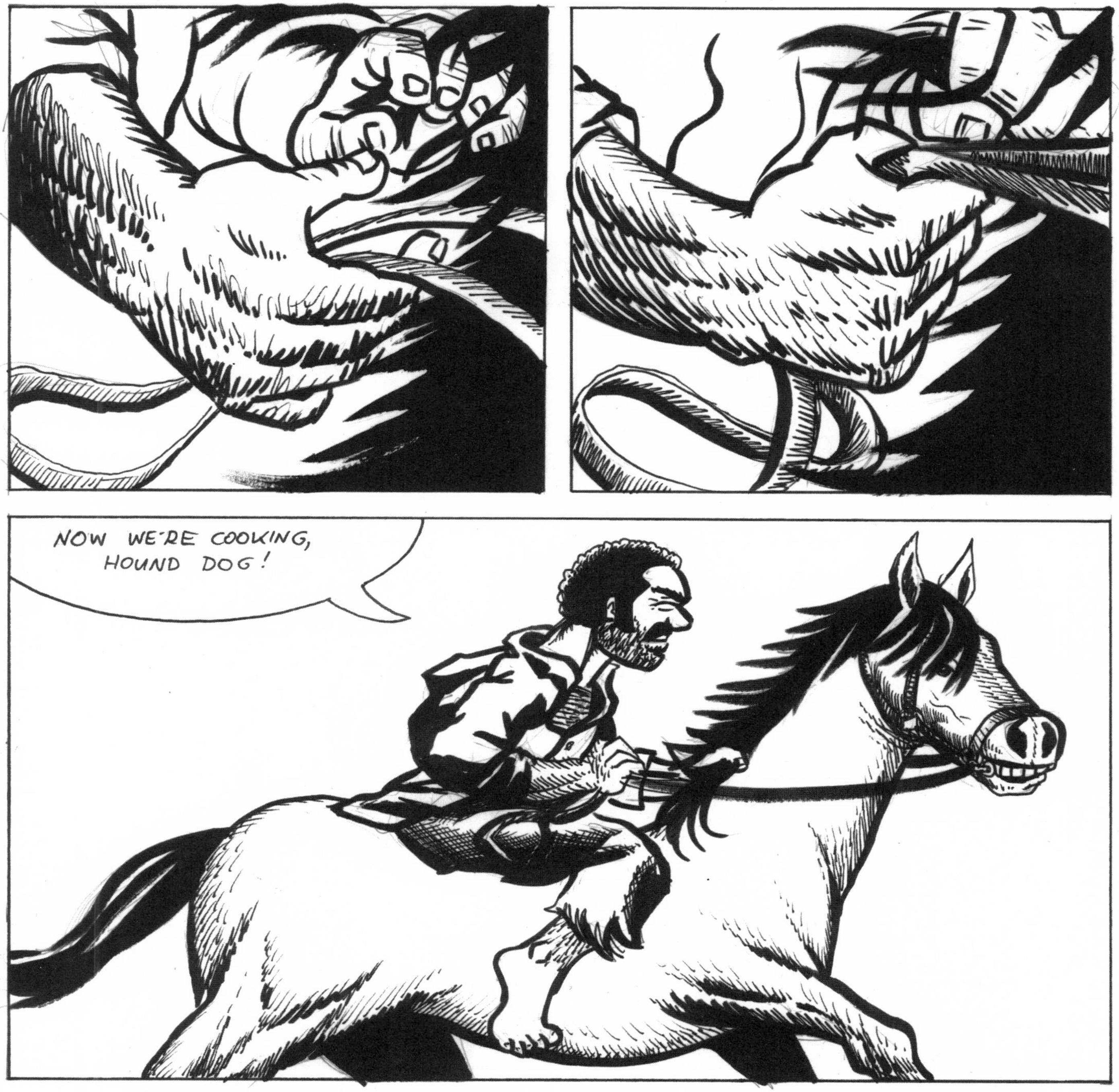
NOW WE'RE COOKING, HOUND DOG!

HOUND DOG ENDS RACE-DAY WITH SURPRISE WIN

HORSE WAS LAST-MINUTE ENTRY

Old Murph was as caught unaware as anyone when his new horse Hound Dog won the final Free-For-All at the September Racing Day. He wasn't even riding it! John Ware, a cowhand that works at Murph Blandon's Ranch acted as the spontaneous jockey. Previously, Hound Dog had come in second in the buggy race and the dejected Old Murph was ready to call it a day. John suggested that Blandon enter Hound Dog, a gray colt of three years, in the final race and let Ware ride it. Murph agreed having witnessed John handle himself well on an impressive back woods gallop with the gelding. However, out of the gate Hound Dog and Ware both revealed their inexperience as they merely trotted in the rear. Moment's later Ware seemed to show greater command of the reins and Hound Dog surged with a burst of speed. With a sprint that had the whole crowd on its feet the duo lunged to the front of the pack to cross the finish line ahead of any opponent by at least half a length. The most startling thing is that John was not wearing shoes as he doesn't own any! Murph Blandon has made a public proclamation that the horse is not for sale.

The Students' Herald

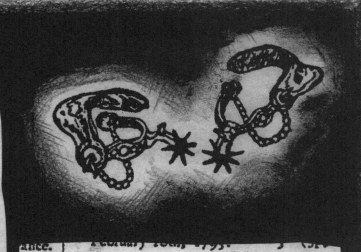

HOUND DOG RETIRES FROM RACING

WILL JOURNEY TO MONTANA WITH WARE

After a dozen years of racing at the Fort Worth Track, Murph Blandon's Hound Dog is retiring from the sport. There were many wins in the horse's career but none were ever as memorable as the "Shoeless Shoot" in which John Ware, a freed slave from South Carolina, road the gray colt to an unexpected victory. As a thank you for years of steadfast service, Old Murph has given Ware the horse along with a saddle. The Fort Worth Frontier wishes to extend their best wishes to both John Ware and Hound Dog as they journey with Nelson Storey on the next cattle ride to Montana in the northwest of the United States.

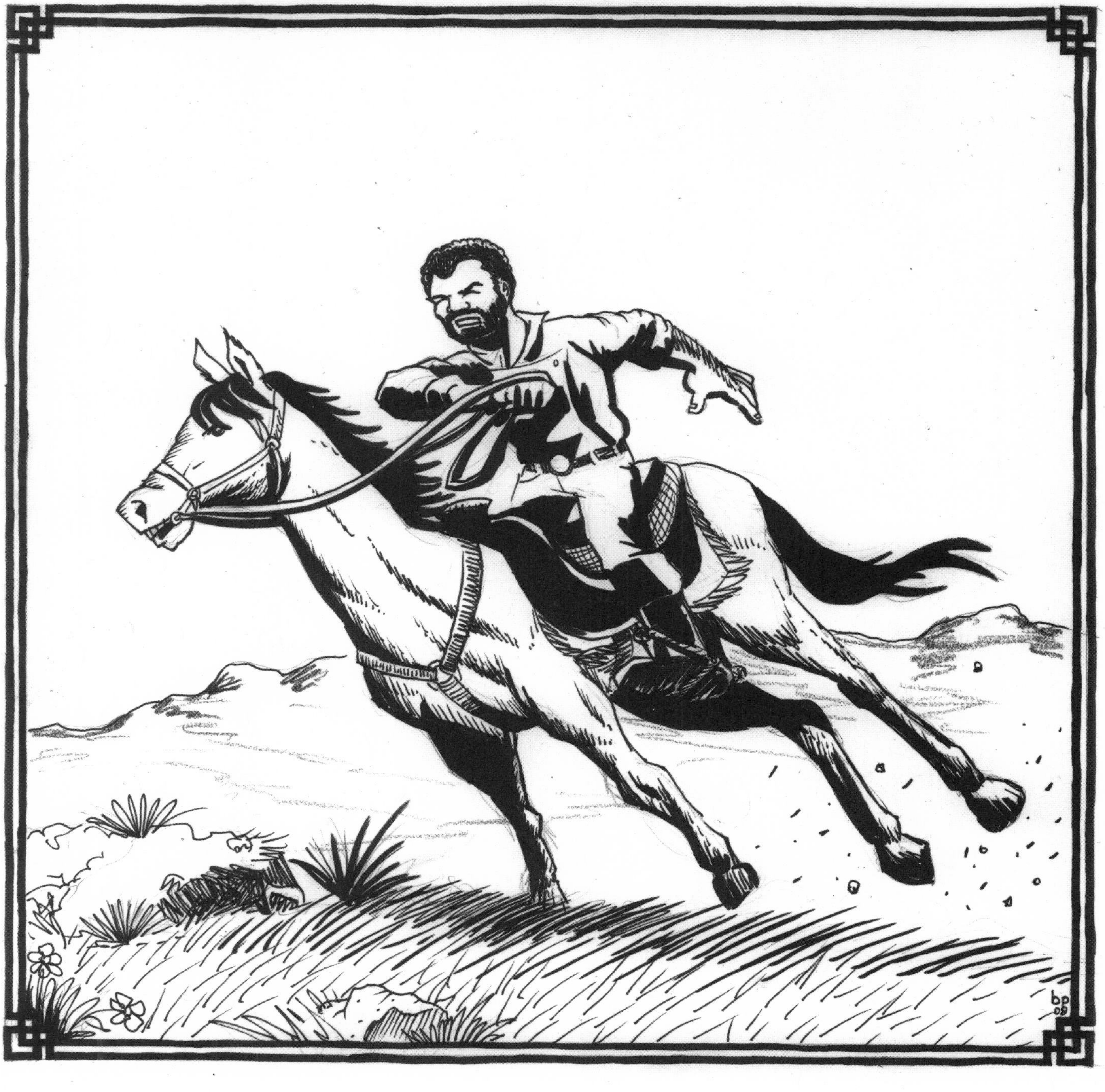

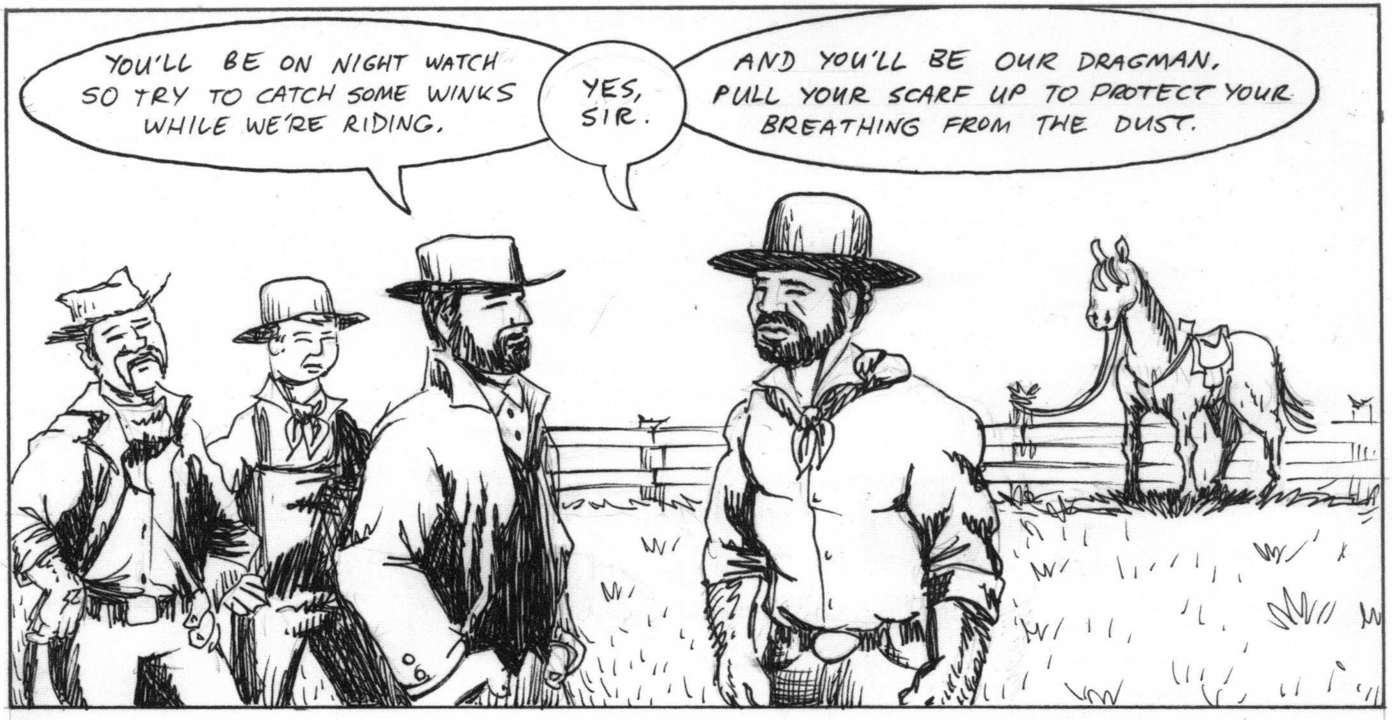
YOU'LL BE ON NIGHT WATCH SO TRY TO CATCH SOME WINKS WHILE WE'RE RIDING.
YES, SIR.
AND YOU'LL BE OUR DRAGMAN. PULL YOUR SCARF UP TO PROTECT YOUR BREATHING FROM THE DUST.

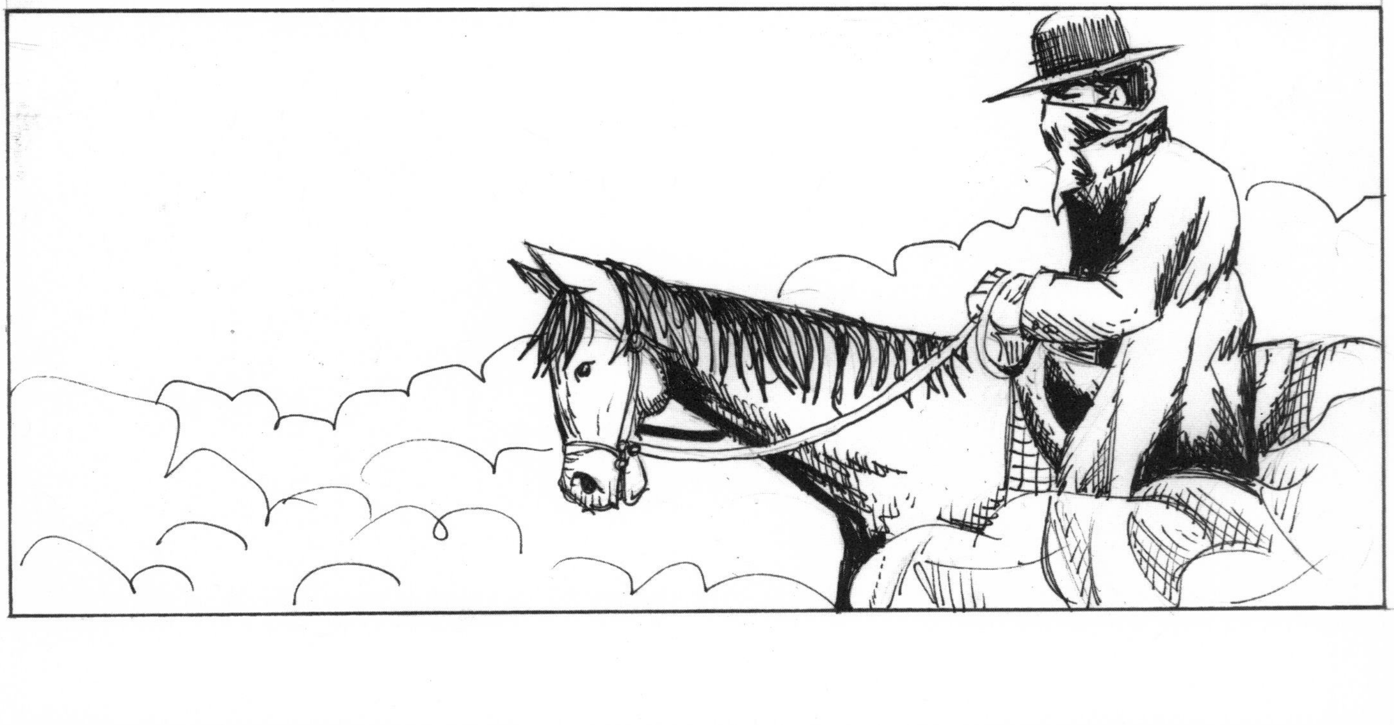

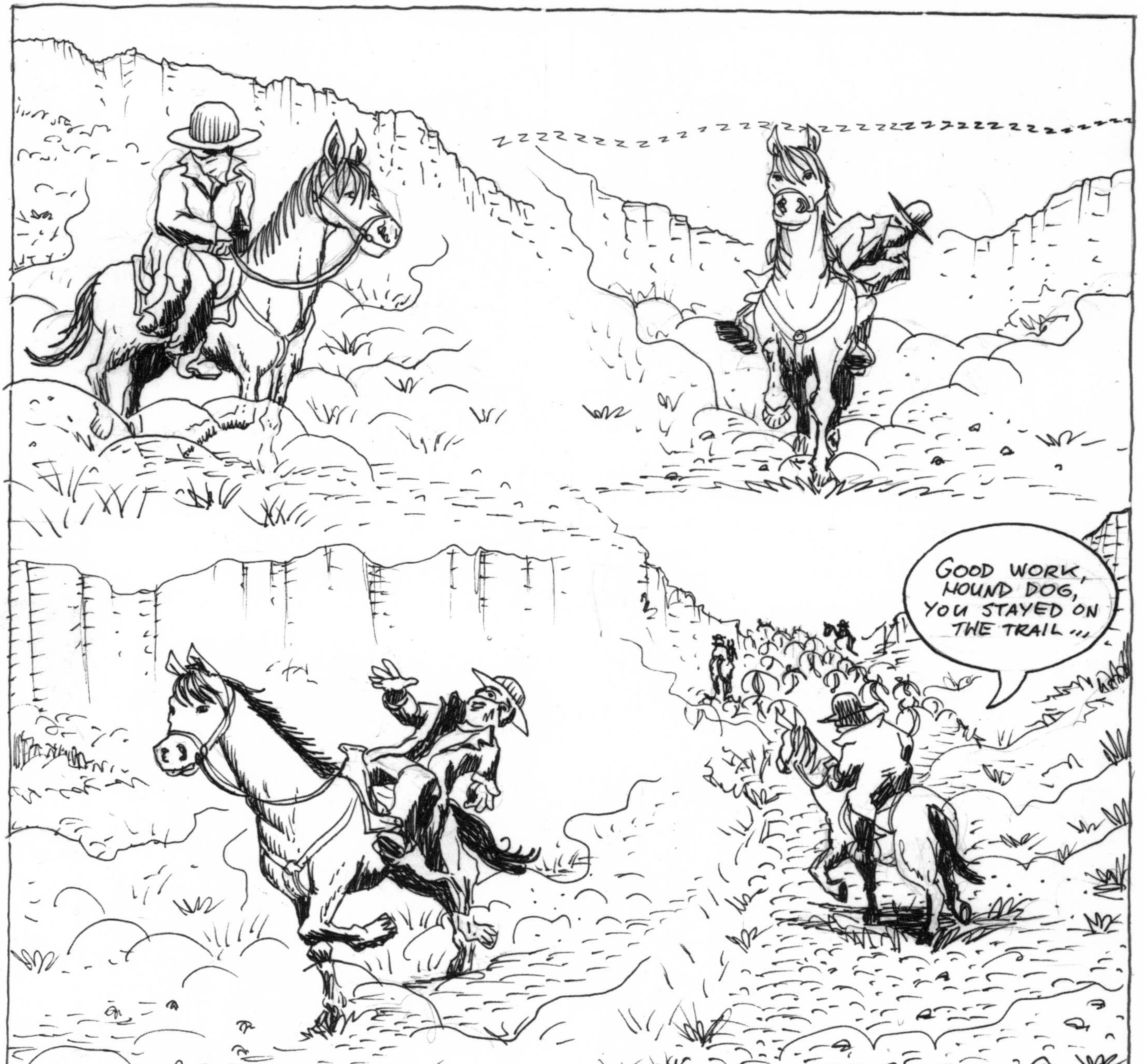
ZZZZZZZZZZZZZZZZZZZZZZZZZZZZZZZZZZZZ
GOOD WORK, HOUND DOG, YOU STAYED ON THE TRAIL...

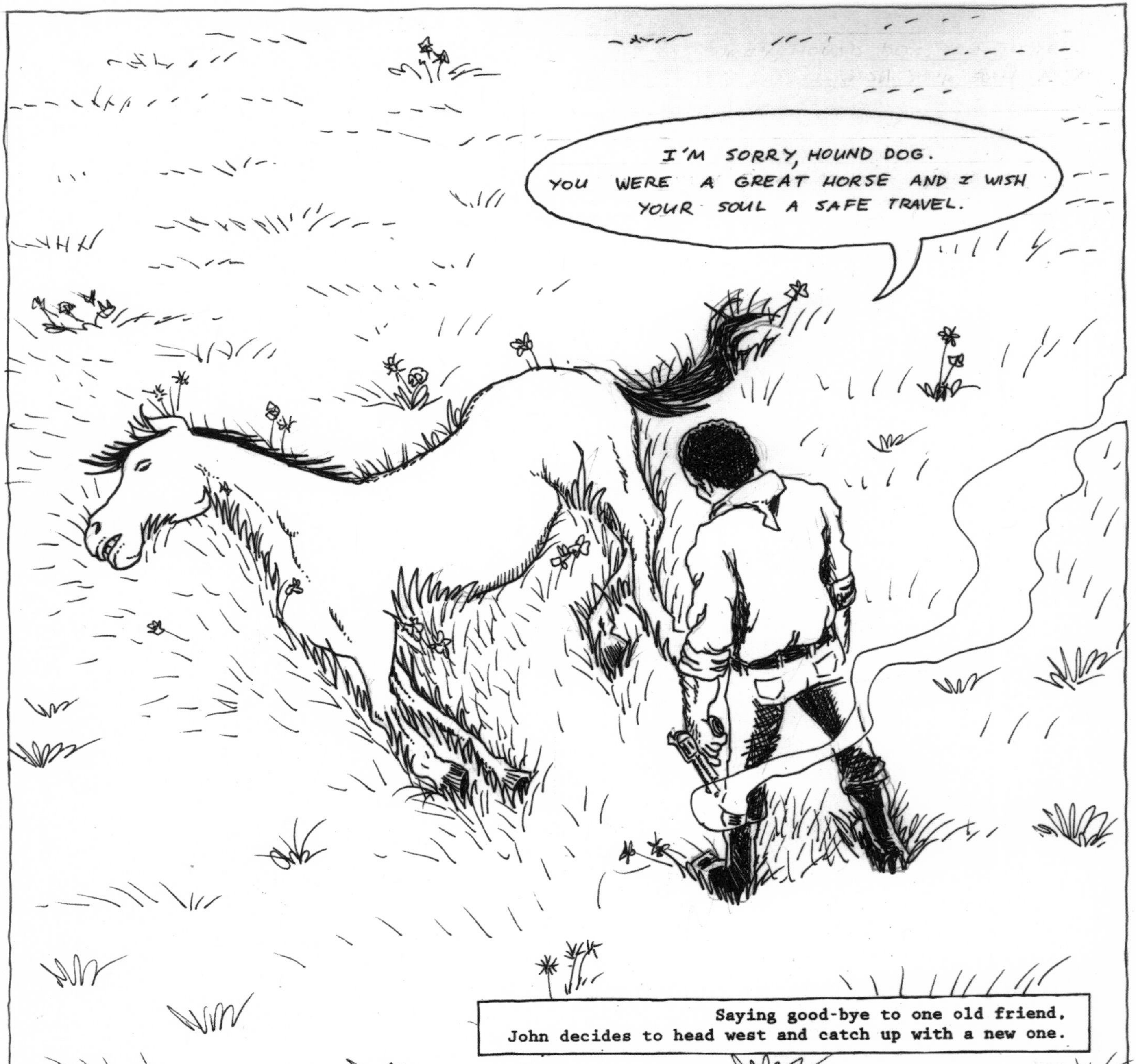
I'M SORRY, HOUND DOG. YOU WERE A GREAT HORSE AND I WISH YOUR SOUL A SAFE TRAVEL.
Saying good-bye to one old friend. John decides to head west and catch up with a new one.

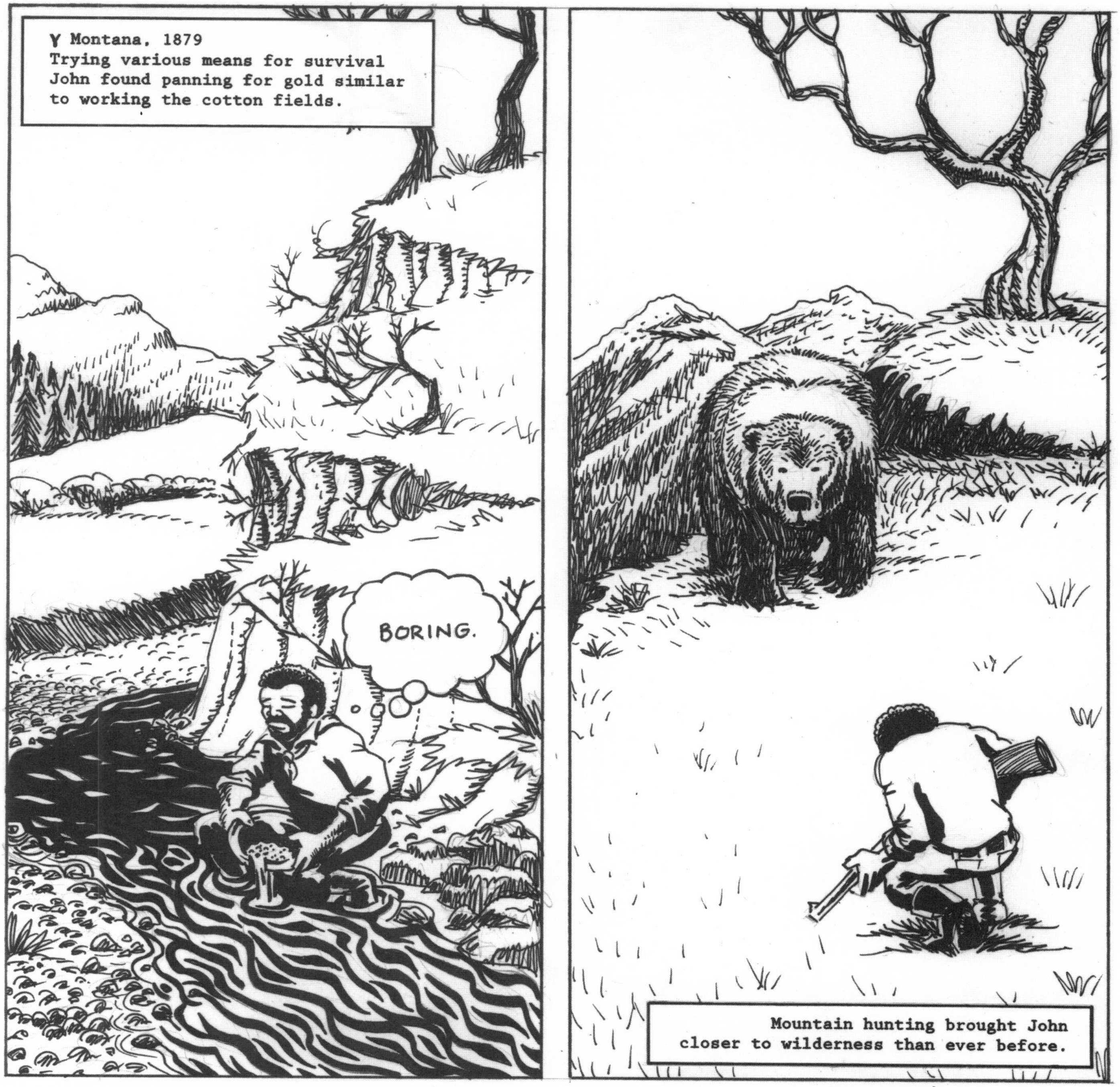
Y Montana, 1879
Trying various means for survival
John found panning for gold similar
to working the cotton fields.
BORING.
Mountain hunting brought John
closer to wilderness than ever before.

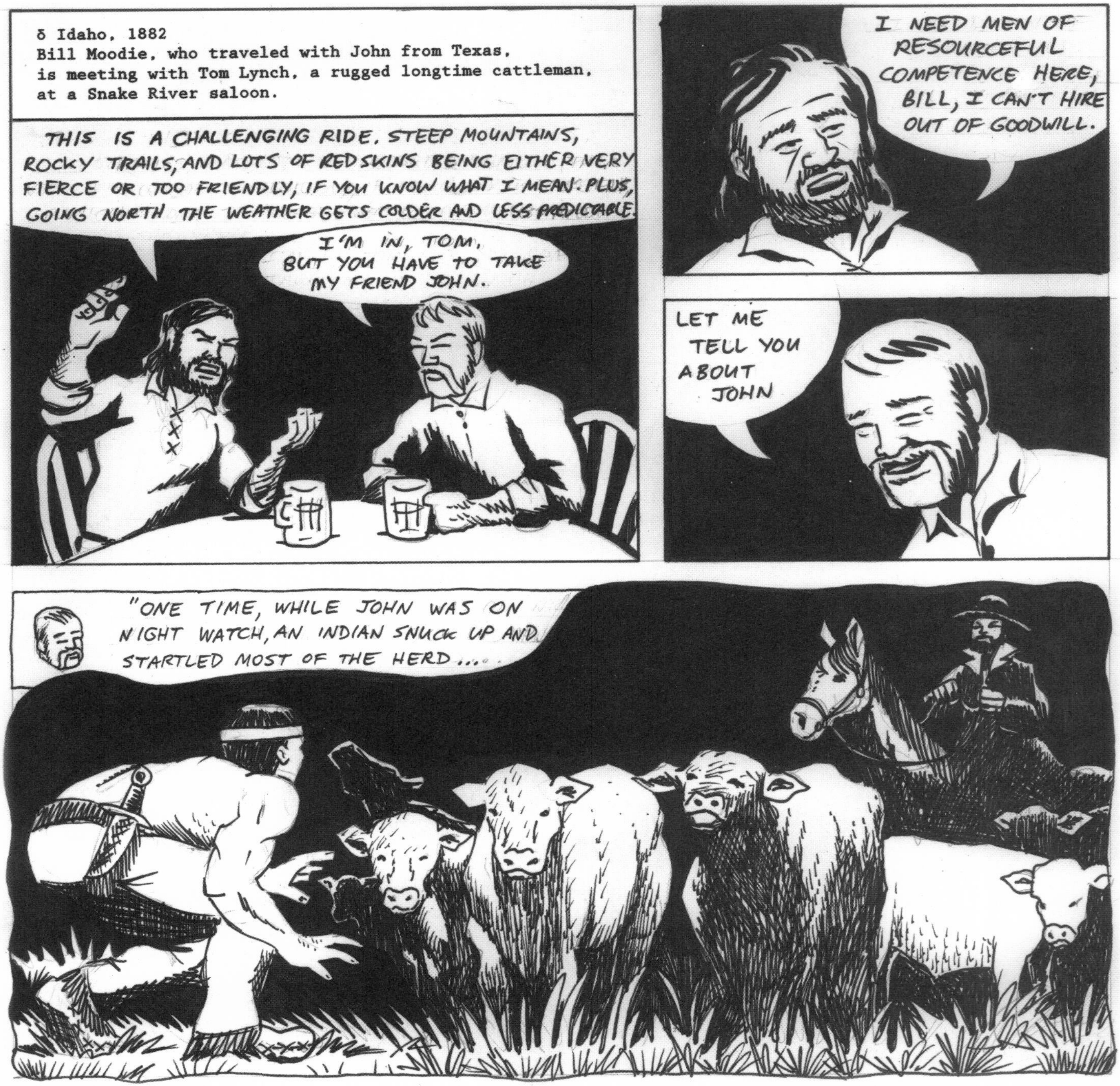
δ Idaho, 1882
Bill Moodie, who traveled with John from Texas, is meeting with Tom Lynch, a rugged longtime cattleman, at a Snake River saloon.
THIS IS A CHALLENGING RIDE. STEEP MOUNTAINS, ROCKY TRAILS, AND LOTS OF REDSKINS BEING EITHER VERY FIERCE OR TOO FRIENDLY, IF YOU KNOW WHAT I MEAN. PLUS, GOING NORTH THE WEATHER GETS COLDER AND LESS PREDICTABLE.
I'M IN, TOM, BUT YOU HAVE TO TAKE MY FRIEND JOHN.
I NEED MEN OF RESOURCEFUL COMPETENCE HERE, BILL, I CAN'T HIRE OUT OF GOODWILL.
LET ME TELL YOU ABOUT JOHN
"ONE TIME, WHILE JOHN WAS ON NIGHT WATCH, AN INDIAN SNUCK UP AND STARTLED MOST OF THE HERD....

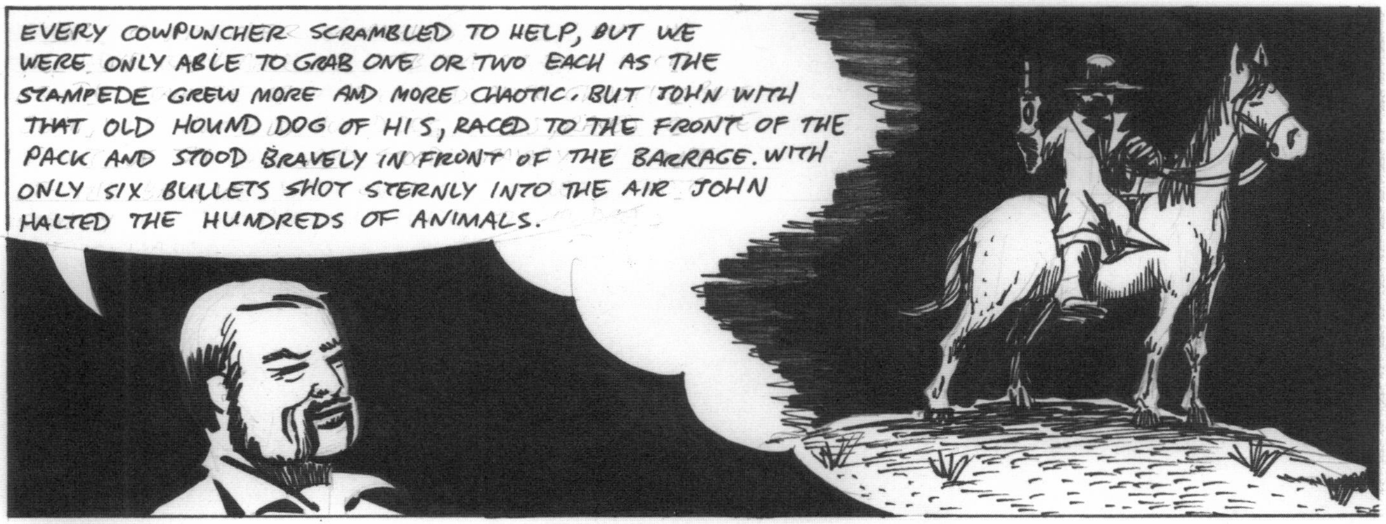
EVERY COWPUNCHER SCRAMBLED TO HELP, BUT WE WERE ONLY ABLE TO GRAB ONE OR TWO EACH AS THE STAMPEDE GREW MORE AND MORE CHAOTIC. BUT JOHN WITH THAT OLD HOUND DOG OF HIS, RACED TO THE FRONT OF THE PACK AND STOOD BRAVELY IN FRONT OF THE BARRAGE. WITH ONLY SIX BULLETS SHOT STERNLY INTO THE AIR JOHN HALTED THE HUNDREDS OF ANIMALS.

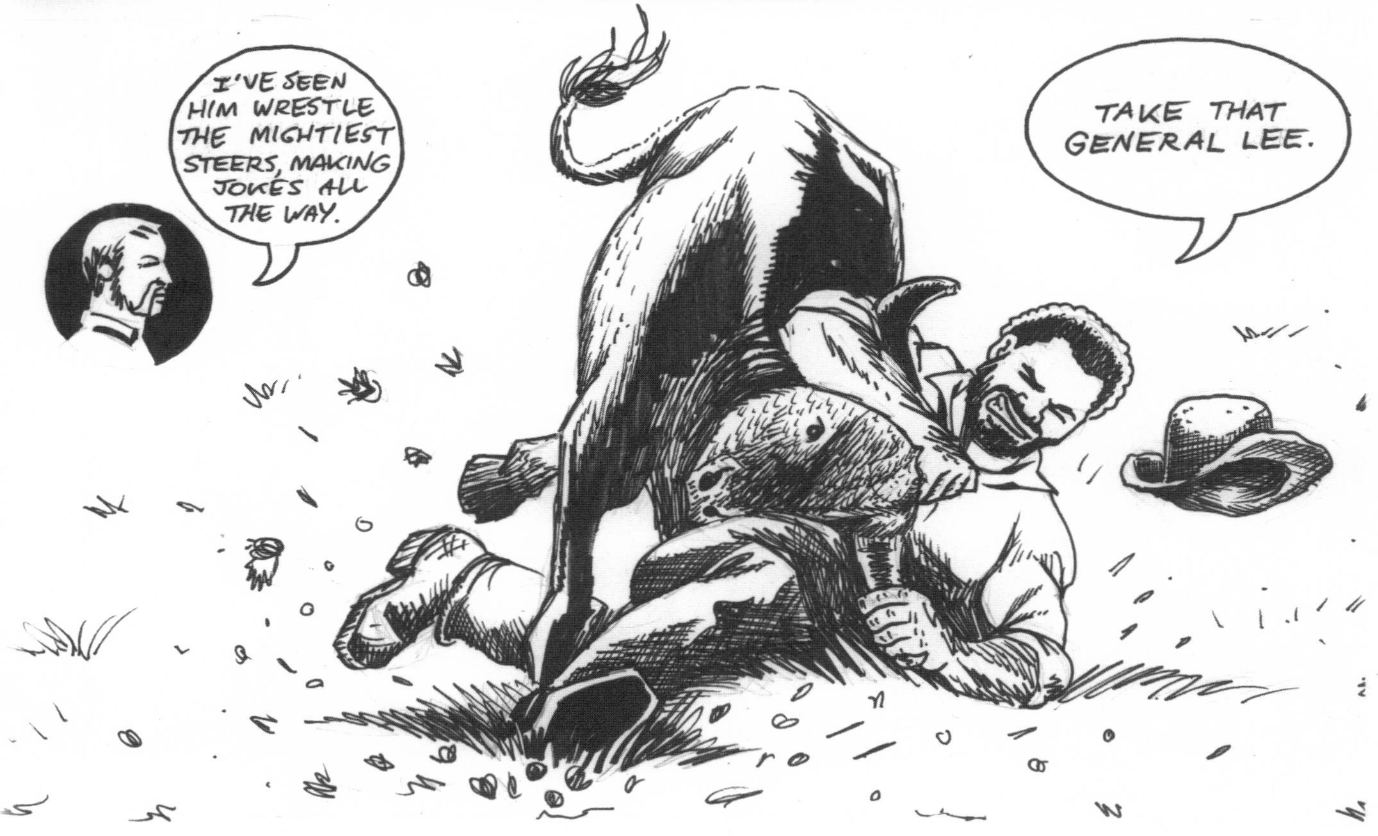
I'VE SEEN HIM WRESTLE THE MIGHTIEST STEERS, MAKING JOKES ALL THE WAY.
TAKE THAT GENERAL LEE.

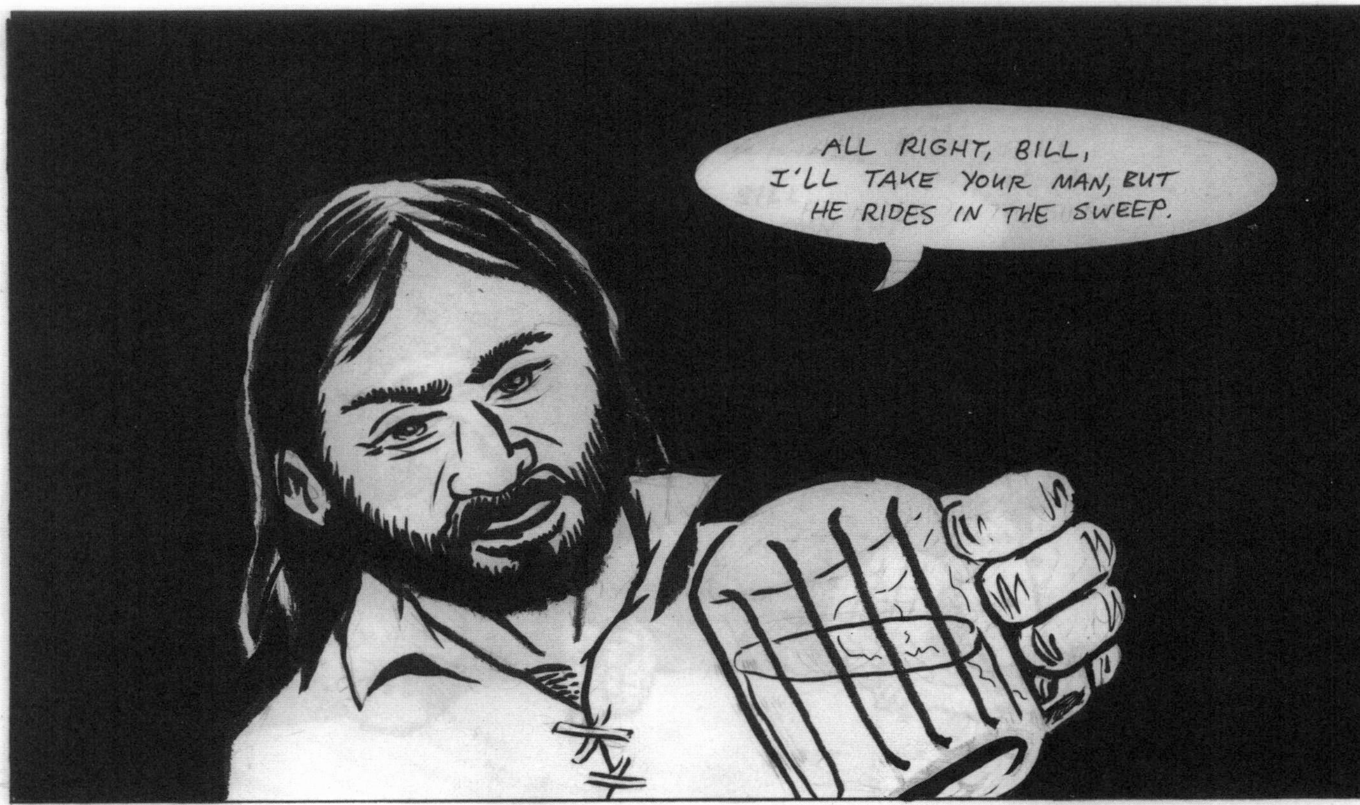
ALL RIGHT, BILL, I'LL TAKE YOUR MAN, BUT HE RIDES IN THE SWEEP.

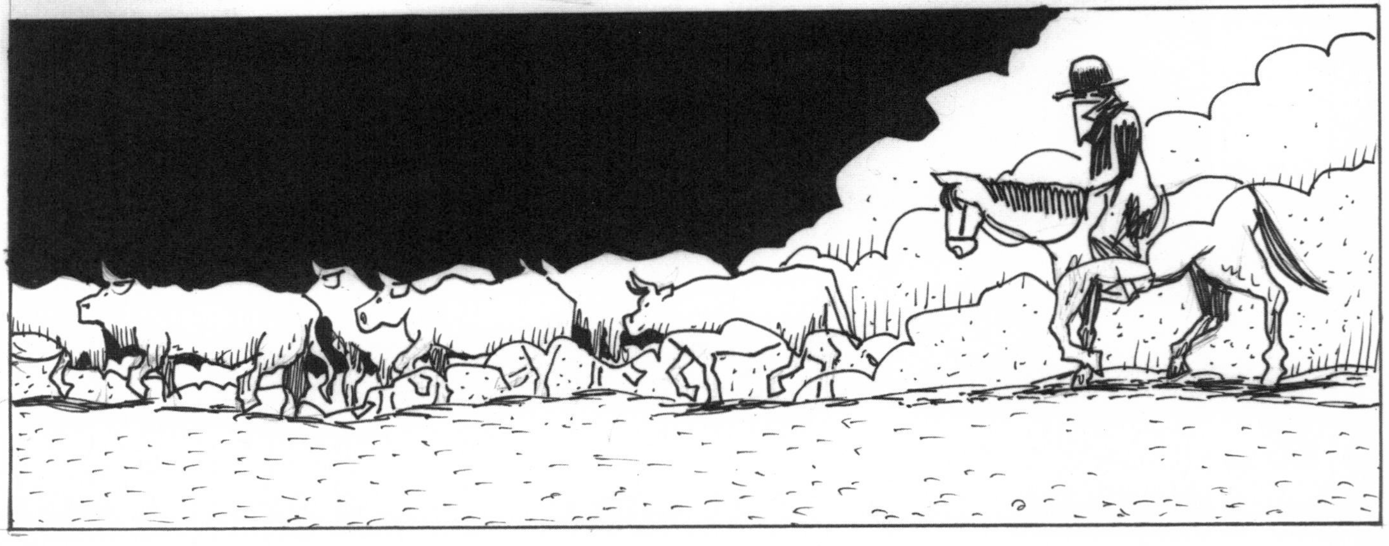

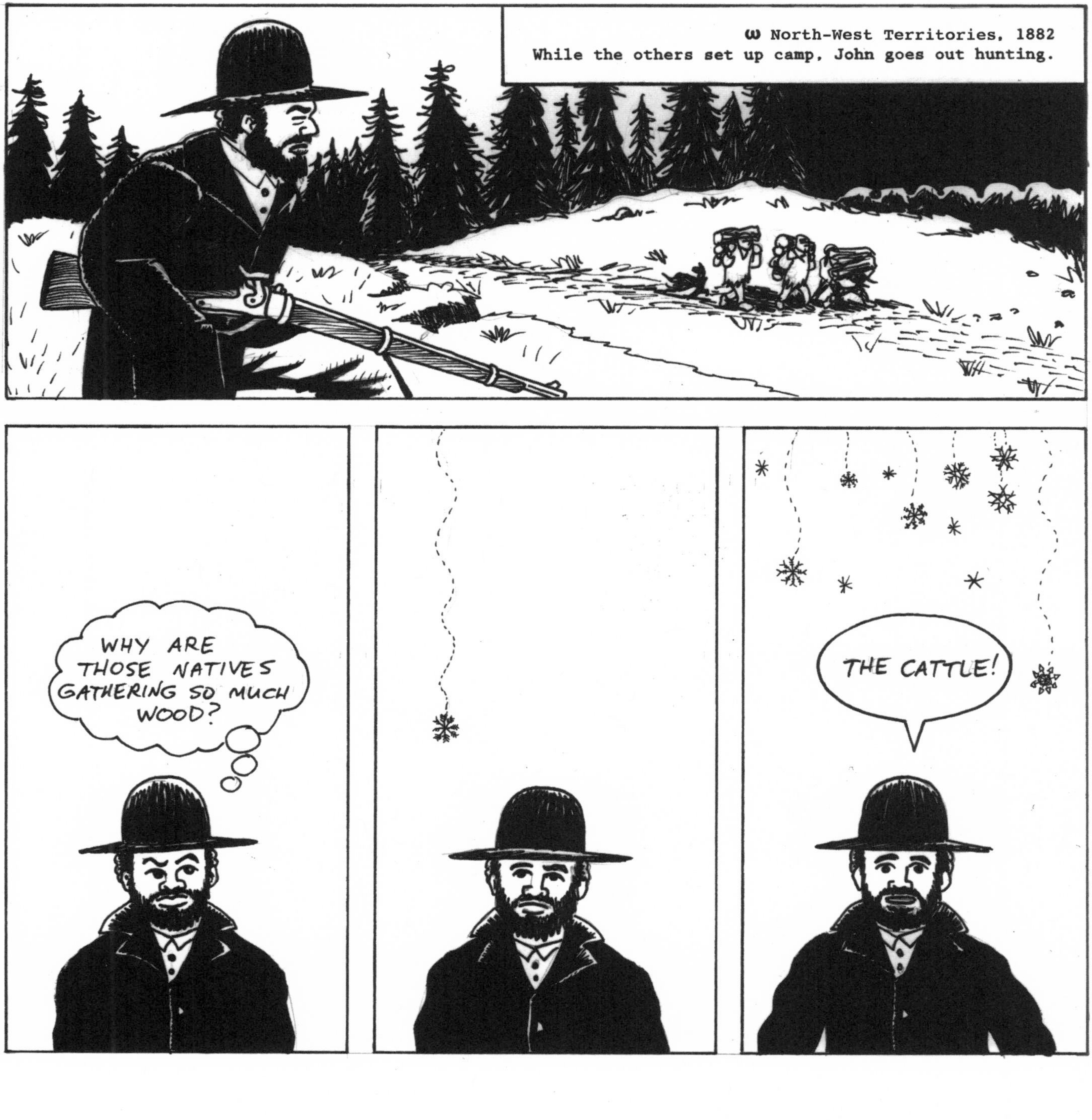
ω North-West Territories, 1882
While the others set up camp, John goes out hunting.
WHY ARE THOSE NATIVES GATHERING SO MUCH WOOD?
THE CATTLE!

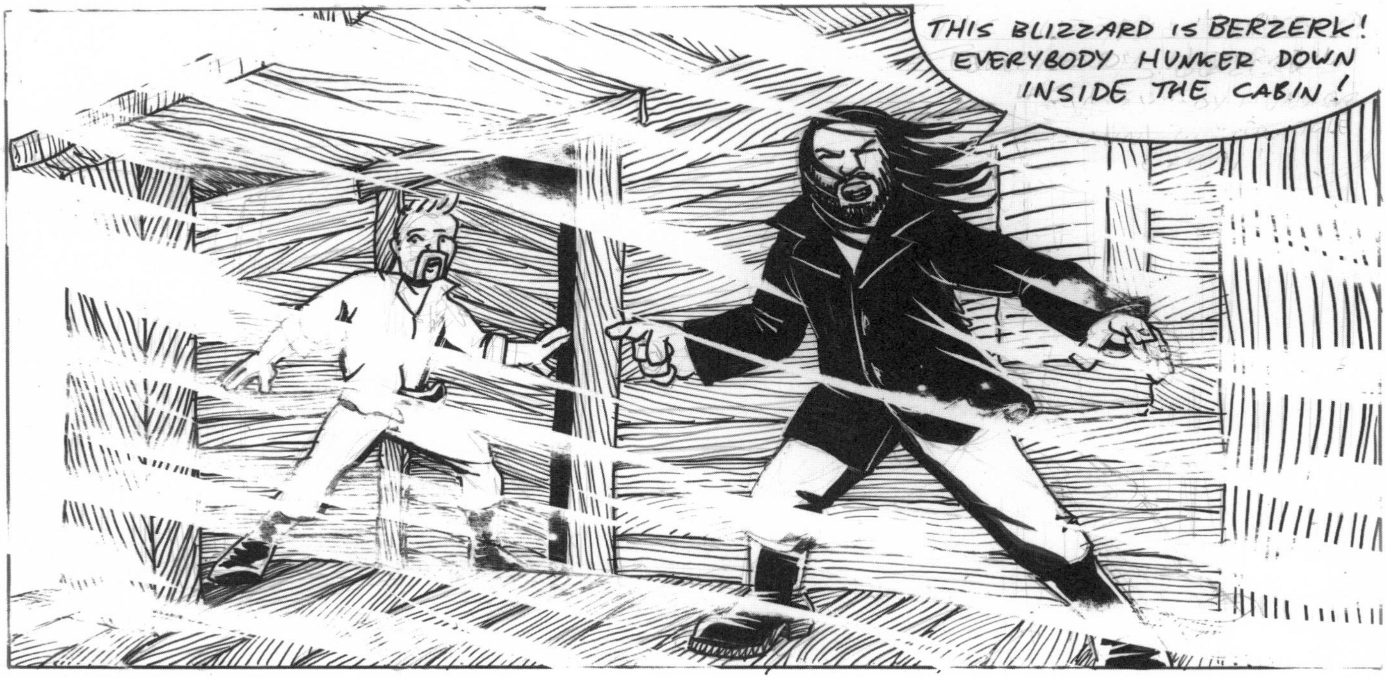
THIS BLIZZARD IS BERZERK! EVERYBODY HUNKER DOWN INSIDE THE CABIN!

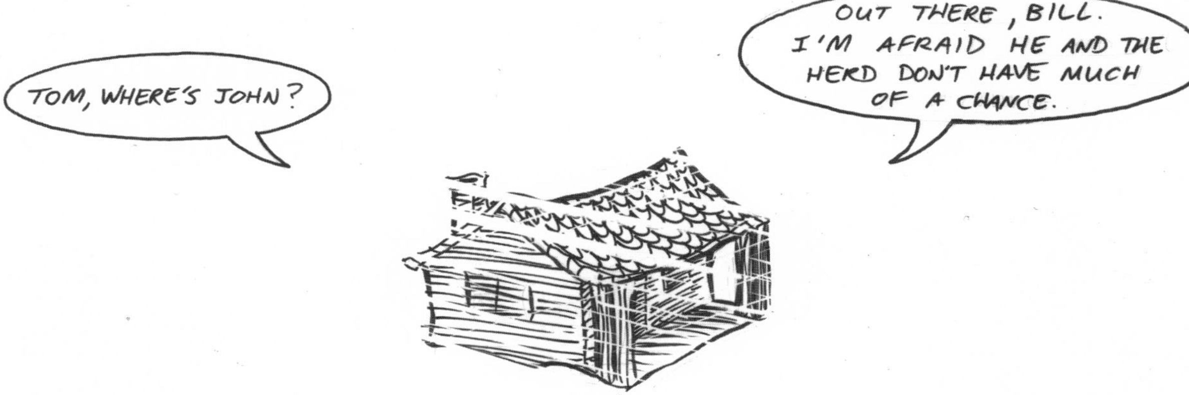
TOM, WHERE'S JOHN?
OUT THERE, BILL. I'M AFRAID HE AND THE HERD DON'T HAVE MUCH OF A CHANCE.

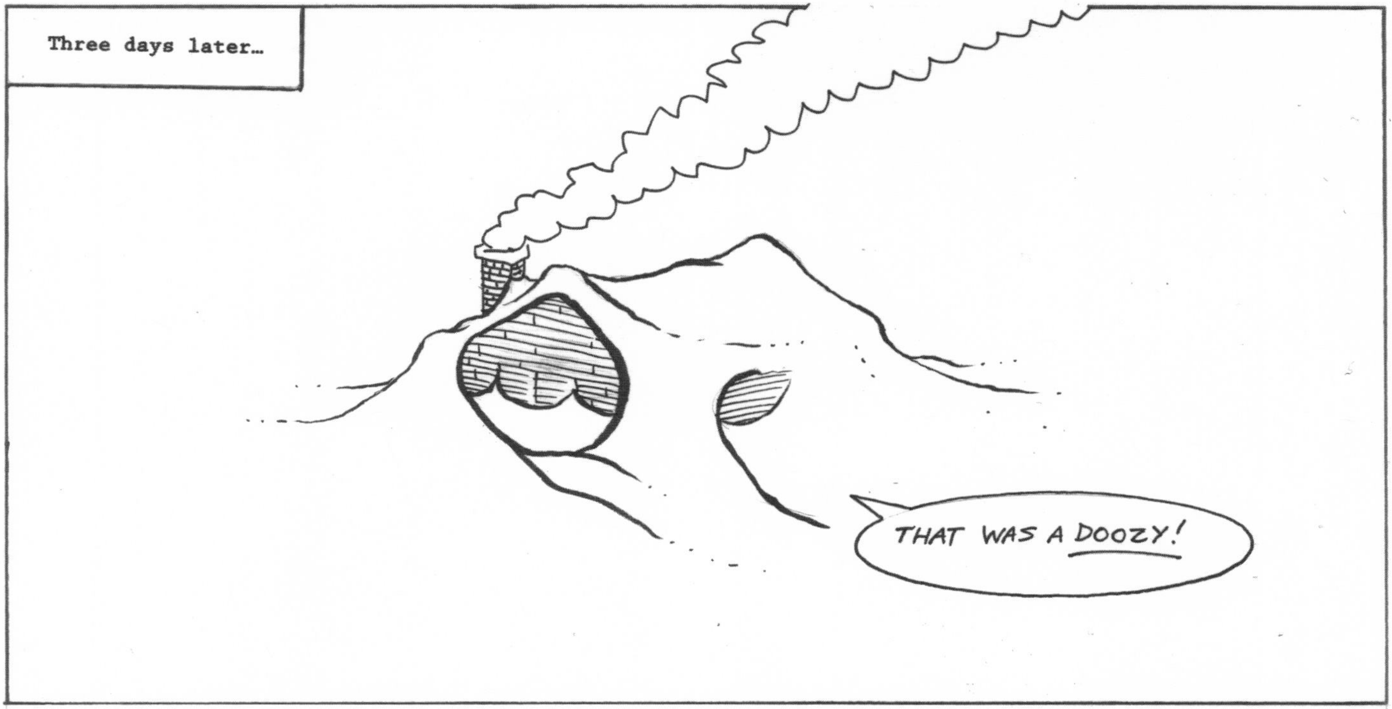
Three days later…
THAT WAS A DOOZY!

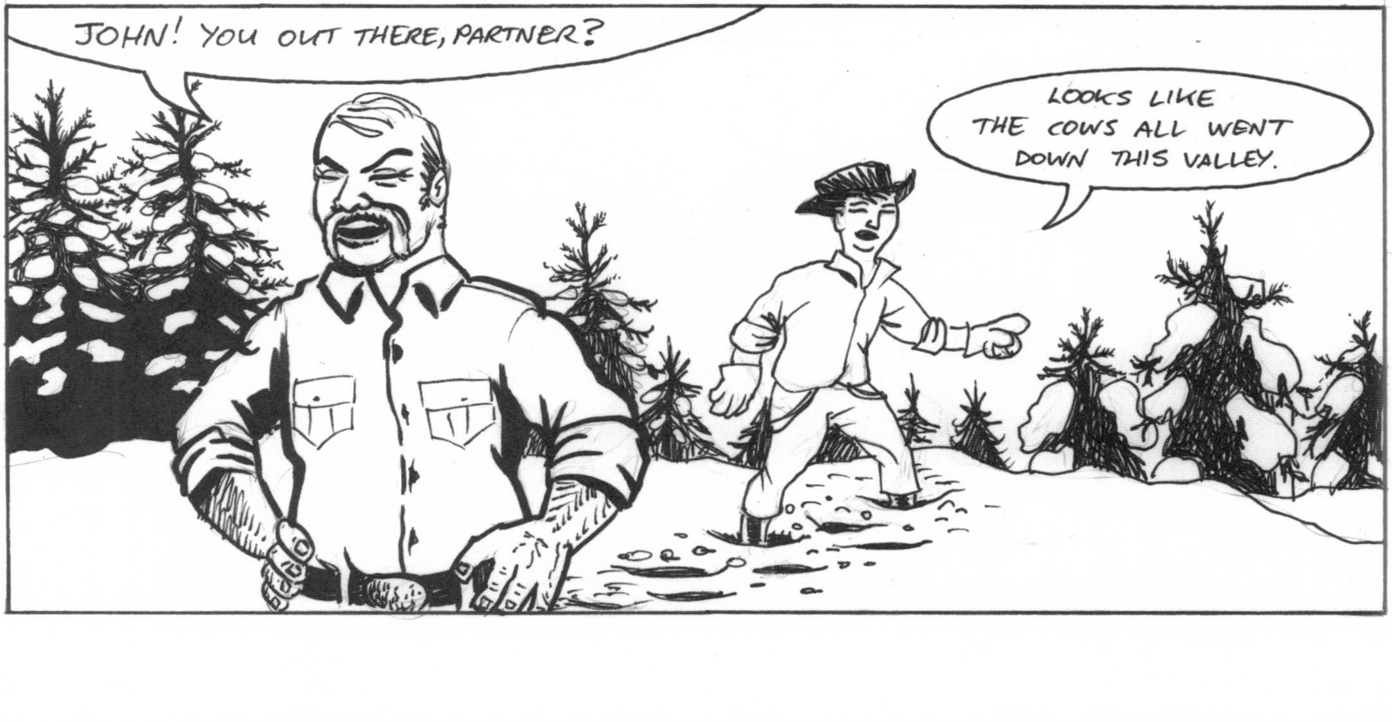
JOHN! YOU OUT THERE, PARTNER?
LOOKS LIKE THE COWS ALL WENT DOWN THIS VALLEY.

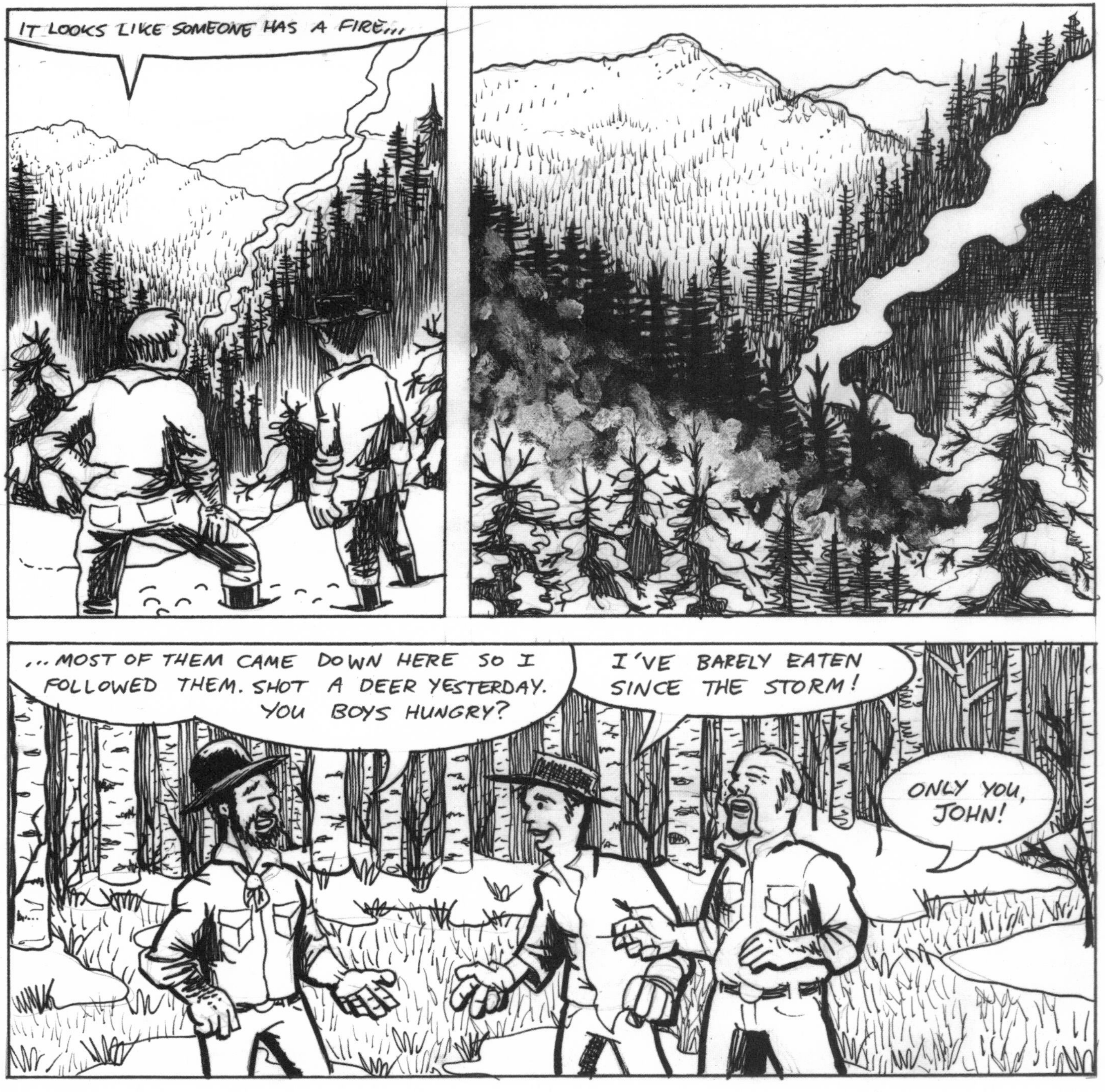

IT LOOKS LIKE SOMEONE HAS A FIRE...
...MOST OF THEM CAME DOWN HERE SO I FOLLOWED THEM. SHOT A DEER YESTERDAY. YOU BOYS HUNGRY?
I'VE BARELY EATEN SINCE THE STORM!
ONLY YOU, JOHN!

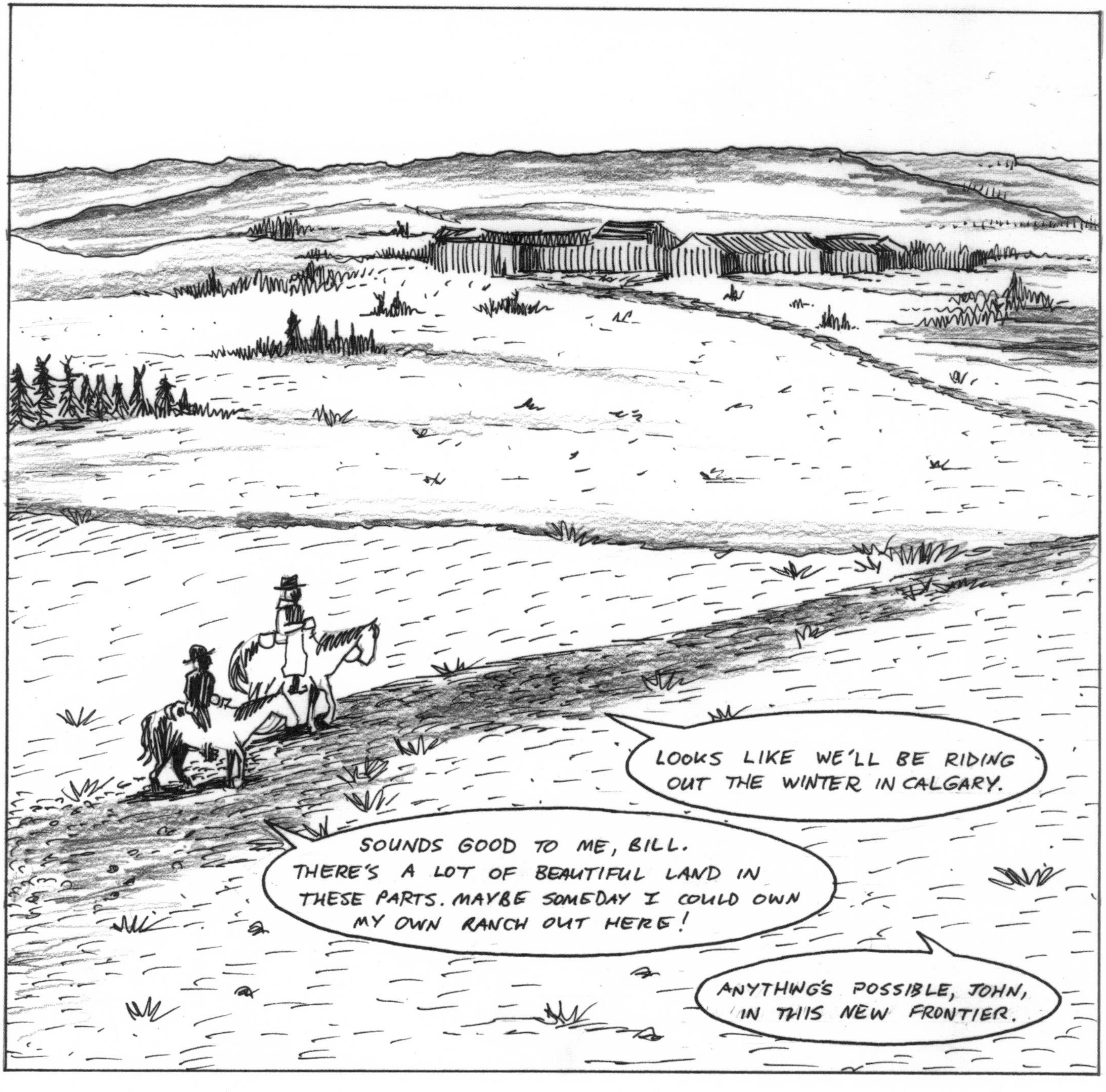
LOOKS LIKE WE'LL BE RIDING OUT THE WINTER IN CALGARY.
SOUNDS GOOD TO ME, BILL. THERE'S A LOT OF BEAUTIFUL LAND IN THESE PARTS. MAYBE SOMEDAY I COULD OWN MY OWN RANCH OUT HERE!
ANYTHING'S POSSIBLE, JOHN, IN THIS NEW FRONTIER.

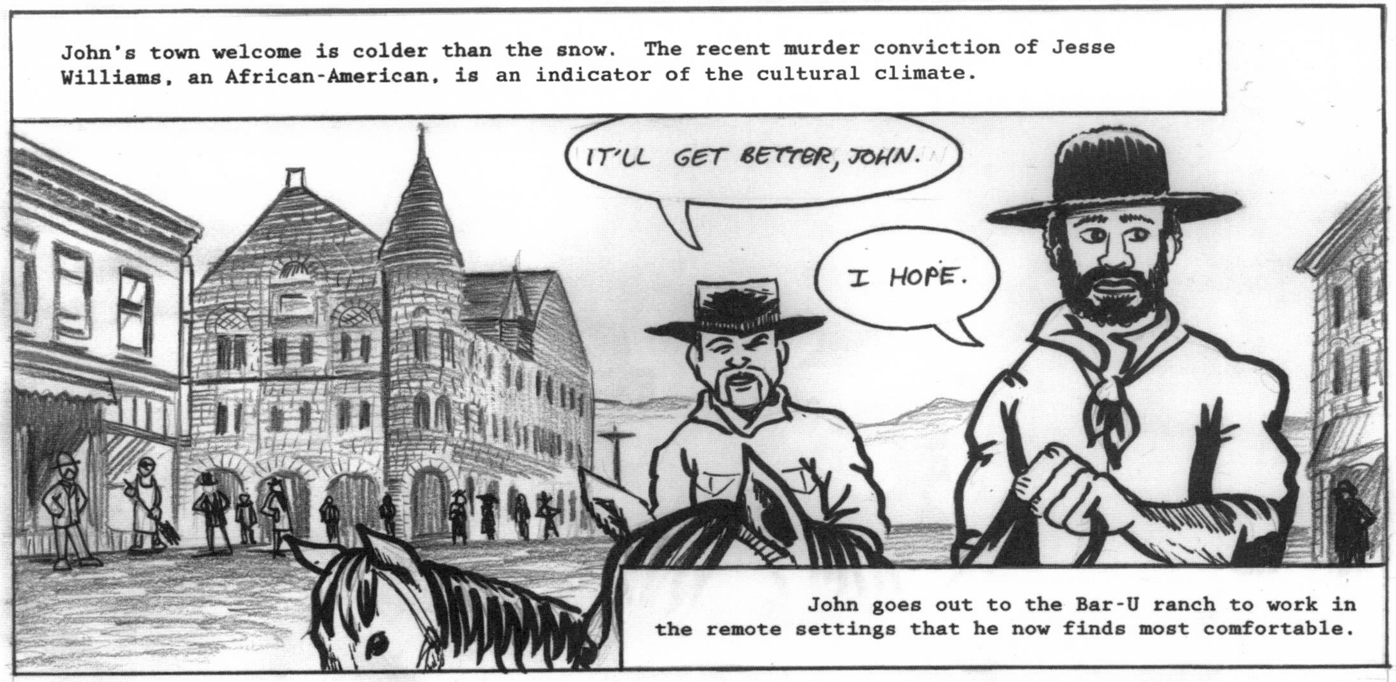
John's town welcome is colder than the snow. The recent murder conviction of Jesse Williams, an African-American, is an indicator of the cultural climate.
IT'LL GET BETTER, JOHN.
I HOPE.
John goes out to the Bar-U ranch to work in the remote settings that he now finds most comfortable.

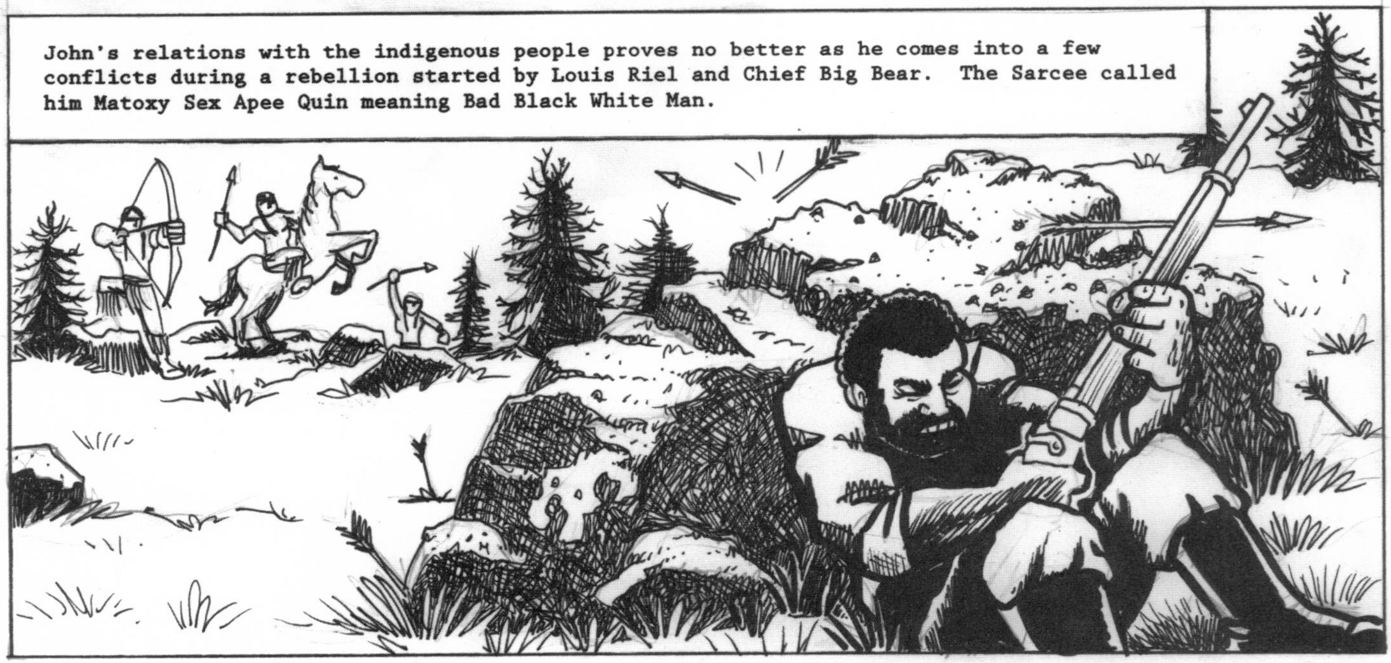
John's relations with the indigenous people proves no better as he comes into a few conflicts during a rebellion started by Louis Riel and Chief Big Bear. The Sarcee called him Matoxy Sex Apee Quin meaning Bad Black White Man.

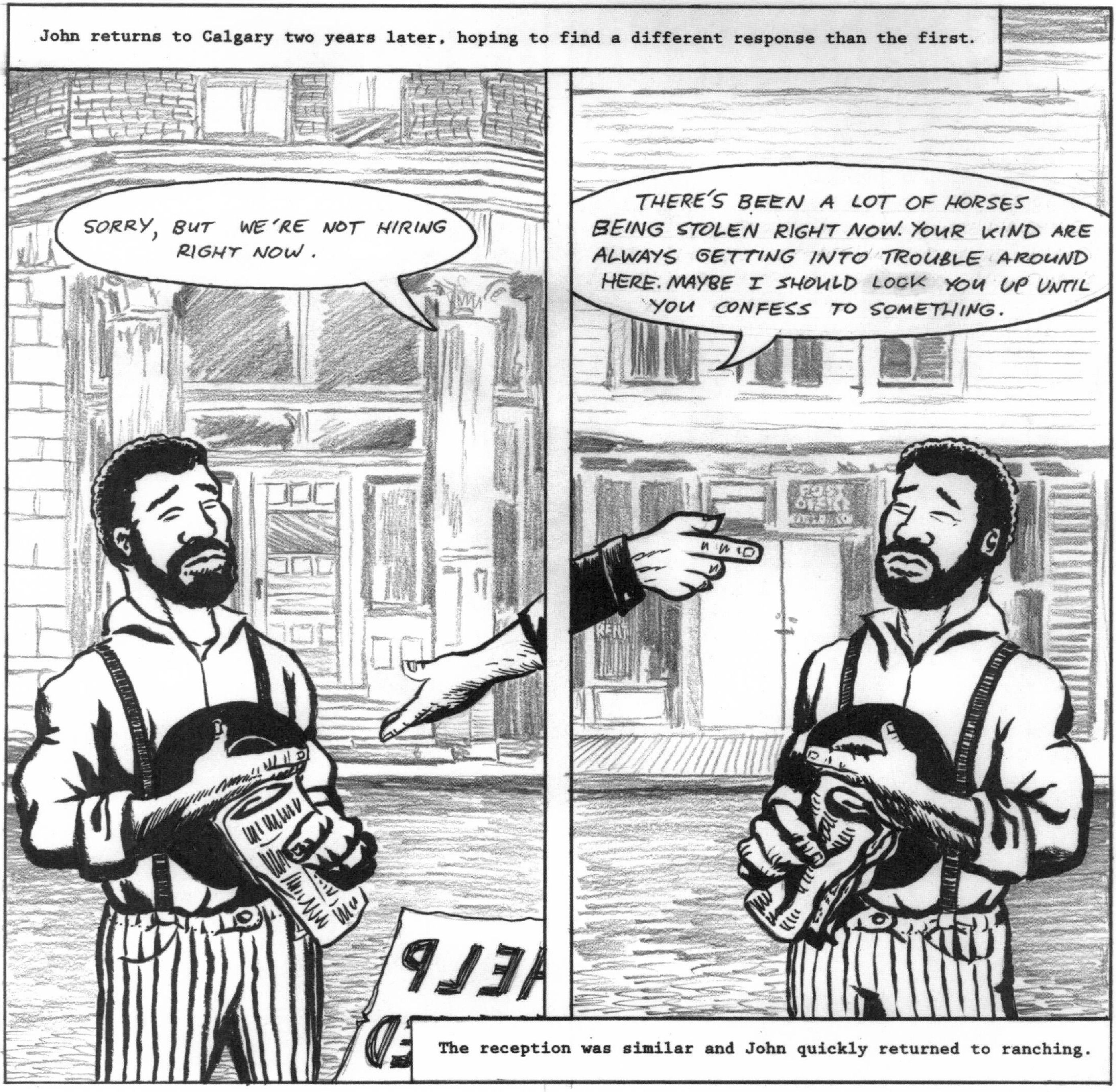
John returns to Calgary two years later, hoping to find a different response than the first.
SORRY, BUT WE'RE NOT HIRING RIGHT NOW.
THERE'S BEEN A LOT OF HORSES BEING STOLEN RIGHT NOW. YOUR KIND ARE ALWAYS GETTING INTO TROUBLE AROUND HERE. MAYBE I SHOULD LOCK YOU UP UNTIL YOU CONFESS TO SOMETHING.
The reception was similar and John quickly returned to ranching.

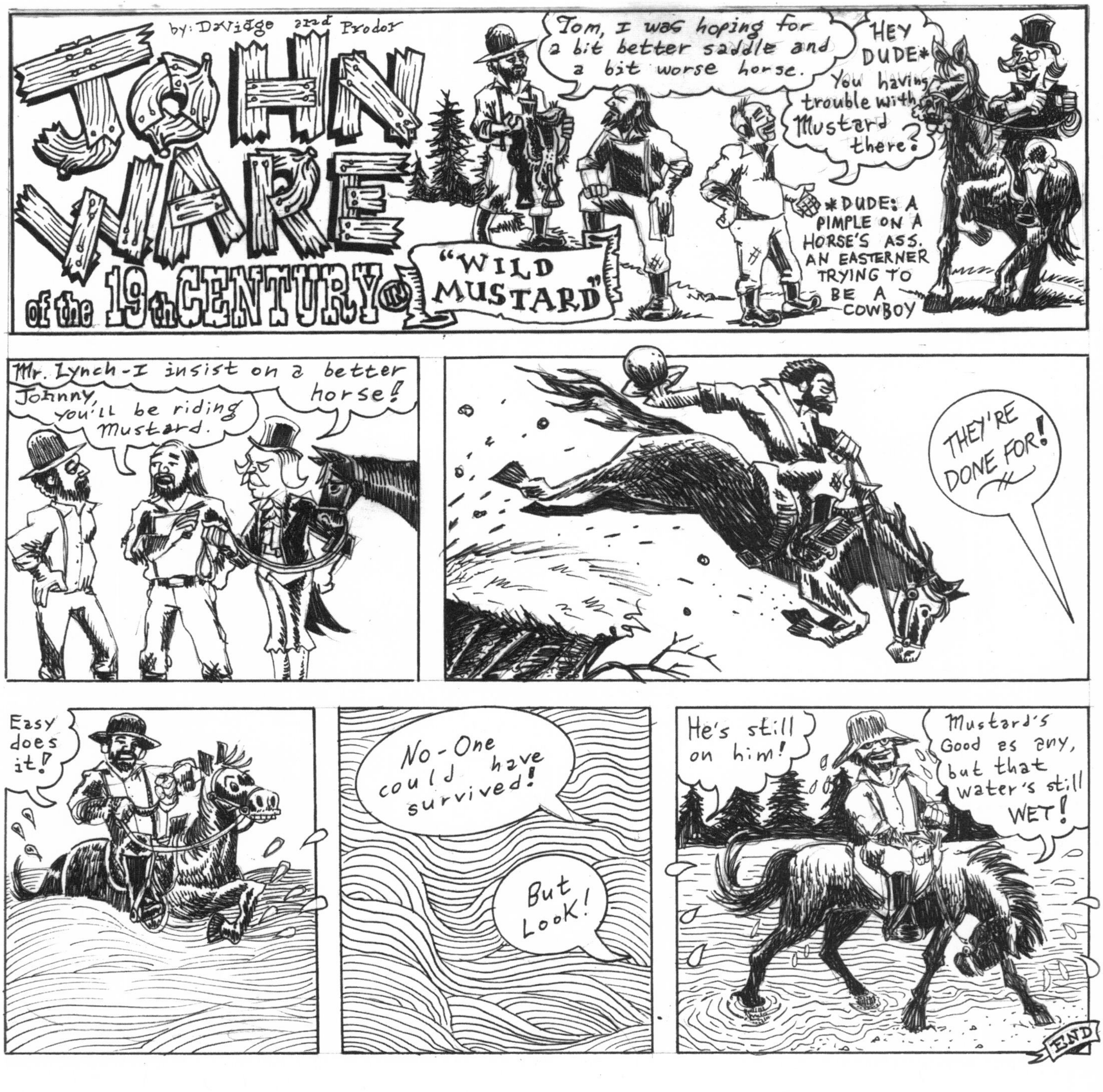
by: Davidge and Prodor
JOHN WARE of the 19th CENTURY in
"WILD MUSTARD"
Tom, I was hoping for a bit better saddle and a bit worse horse.
HEY DUDE* You having trouble with Mustard there?
*DUDE: A PIMPLE ON A HORSE'S ASS. AN EASTERNER TRYING TO BE A COWBOY
Mr. Lynch - I insist on a better horse!
Johnny, you'll be riding Mustard.
THEY'RE DONE FOR!
Easy does it!
No-One could have survived!
But Look!
He's still on him!
Mustard's Good as any, but that water's still WET!
END

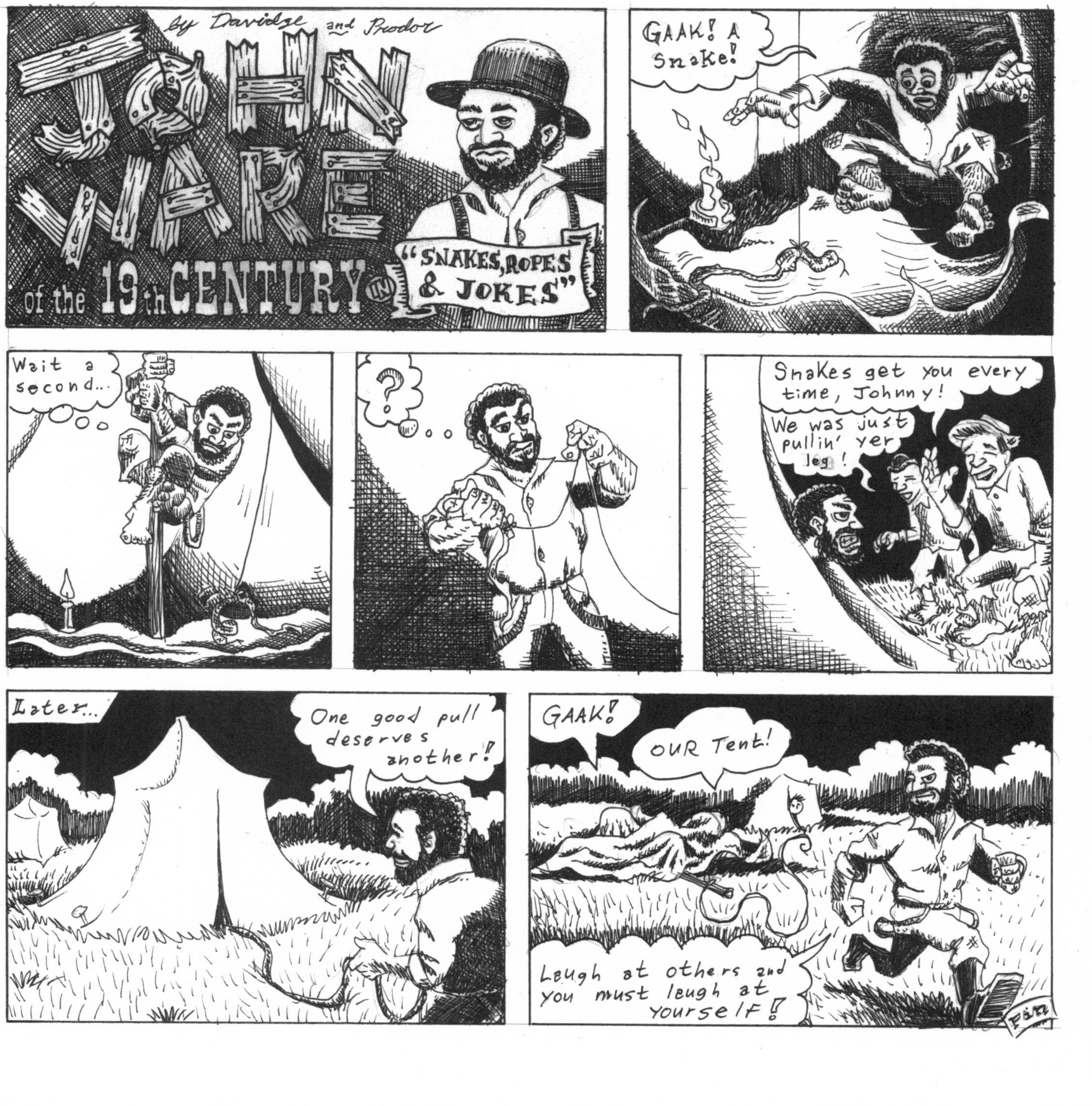
by Davidge and Prodor
JOHN WARE of the 19th CENTURY
IN
"SNAKES, ROPES & JOKES"
GAAK! A Snake!
Wait a second...
?
Snakes get you every time, Johnny!
We was just pullin' yer leg!
Later...
One good pull deserves another!
GAAK!
OUR Tent!
Laugh at others and you must laugh at yourself!
Fin

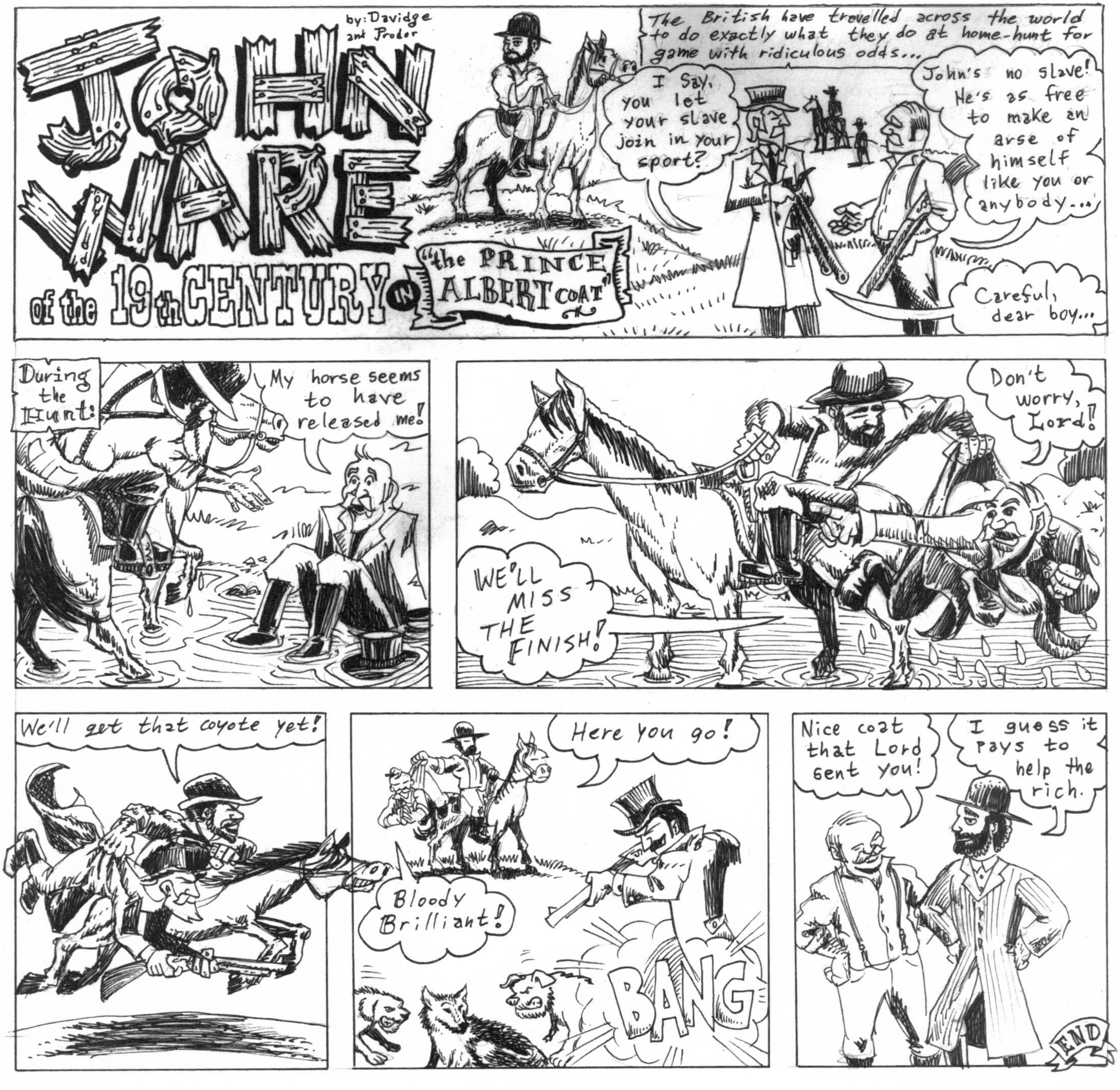
by: Davidge and Prodor
JOHN WARE of the 19th CENTURY in "the PRINCE ALBERT COAT"
The British have travelled across the world to do exactly what they do at home-hunt for game with ridiculous odds...
I say, you let your slave join in your sport?
John's no slave! He's as free to make an arse of himself like you or anybody...
Careful, dear boy...
During the Hunt!
My horse seems to have released me!
Don't worry, Lord!
WE'LL MISS THE FINISH!
We'll get that coyote yet!
Here you go!
Bloody Brilliant!
BANG
Nice coat that Lord sent you!
I guess it pays to help the rich.
END

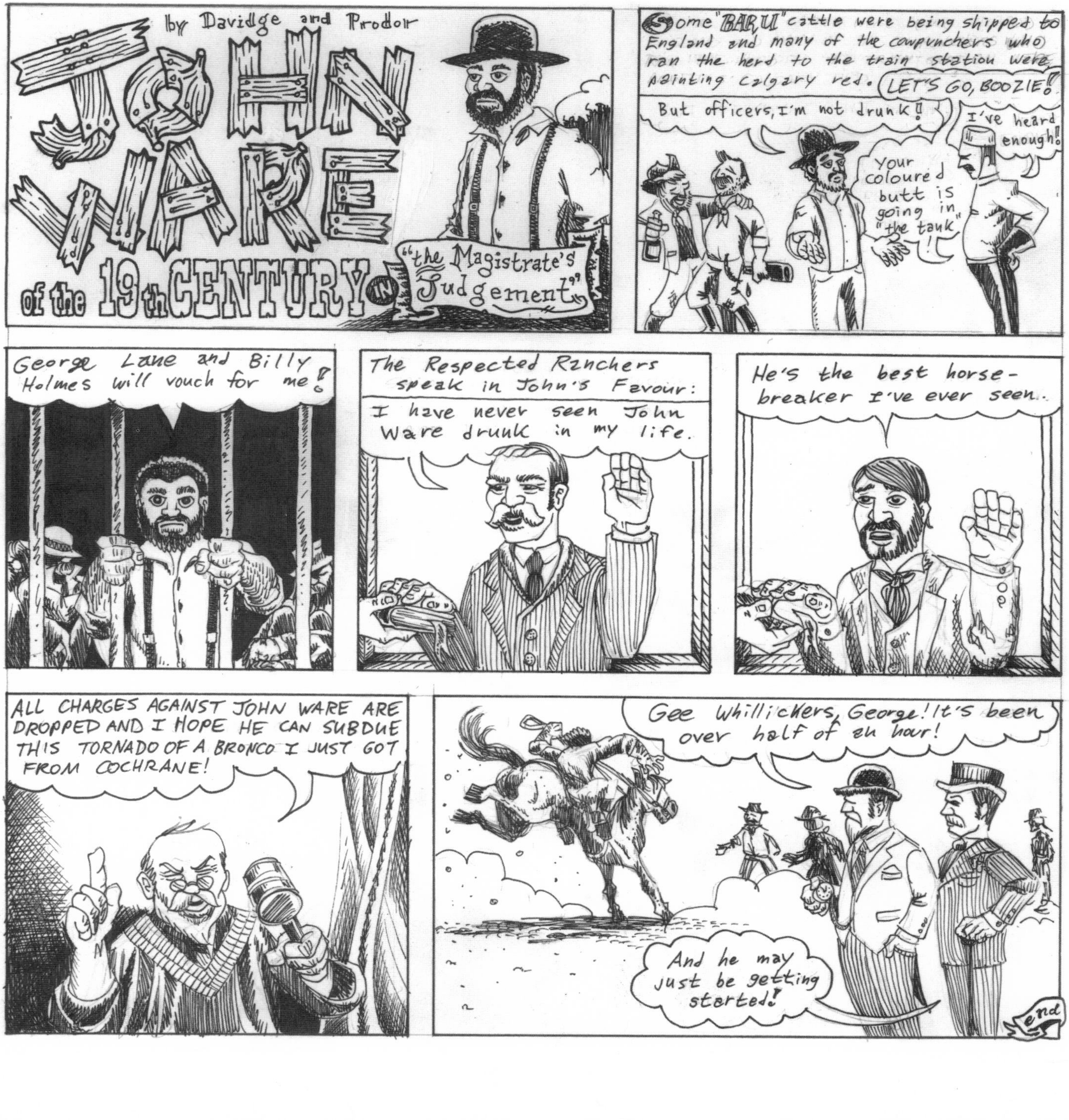
by Davidge and Prodor
JOHN WARE of the 19th CENTURY in "the Magistrate's Judgement"
Some "BAR U" cattle were being shipped to England and many of the cowpunchers who ran the herd to the train station were painting Calgary red.
LET'S GO, BOOZIE!
But officers, I'm not drunk!
I've heard enough!
Your coloured butt is going in "the tank"!
George Lane and Billy Holmes will vouch for me!
The Respected Ranchers speak in John's Favour:
I have never seen John Ware drunk in my life.
He's the best horse-breaker I've ever seen.
ALL CHARGES AGAINST JOHN WARE ARE DROPPED AND I HOPE HE CAN SUBDUE THIS TORNADO OF A BRONCO I JUST GOT FROM COCHRANE!
Gee Whillickers, George! It's been over half of an hour!
And he may just be getting started!
end

DAVIDGE PRODOR
JOHN WARE of the 19th CENTURY IN "the Better Letter"
Moses, I've got you, and my horses, and my cattle, but I don't really have a real family anywhere near me...
?
My heart's as bright as this match, but soon to burn out, as well, I'm afraid.
MOLLY, What stink water you gettin' into?
GET BACK MOLLY!
LOOK OUT, MOSES!
J.J, I found this fiery gunk down in Robert Turner's valley.
I'll send it off for testing John
You got two letters today, John, both from J.J. Barter.
What's in them?
One says that goop was oil.
Well, how do you like that?
...and the other says there's a black family that's moved to Shepard and they have a daughter of marrying age.
NOW THAT'S HOT STUFF!
End

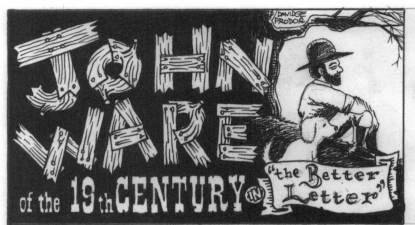

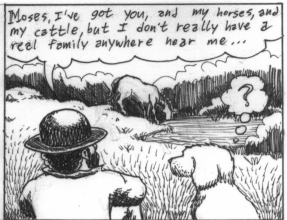

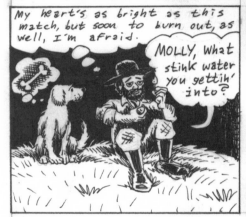

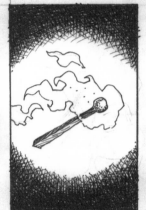

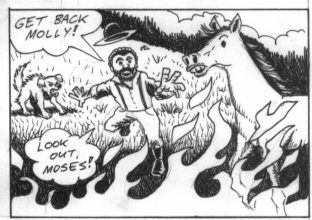

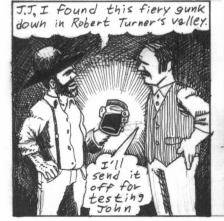

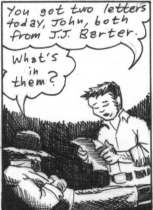

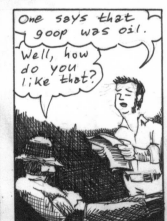

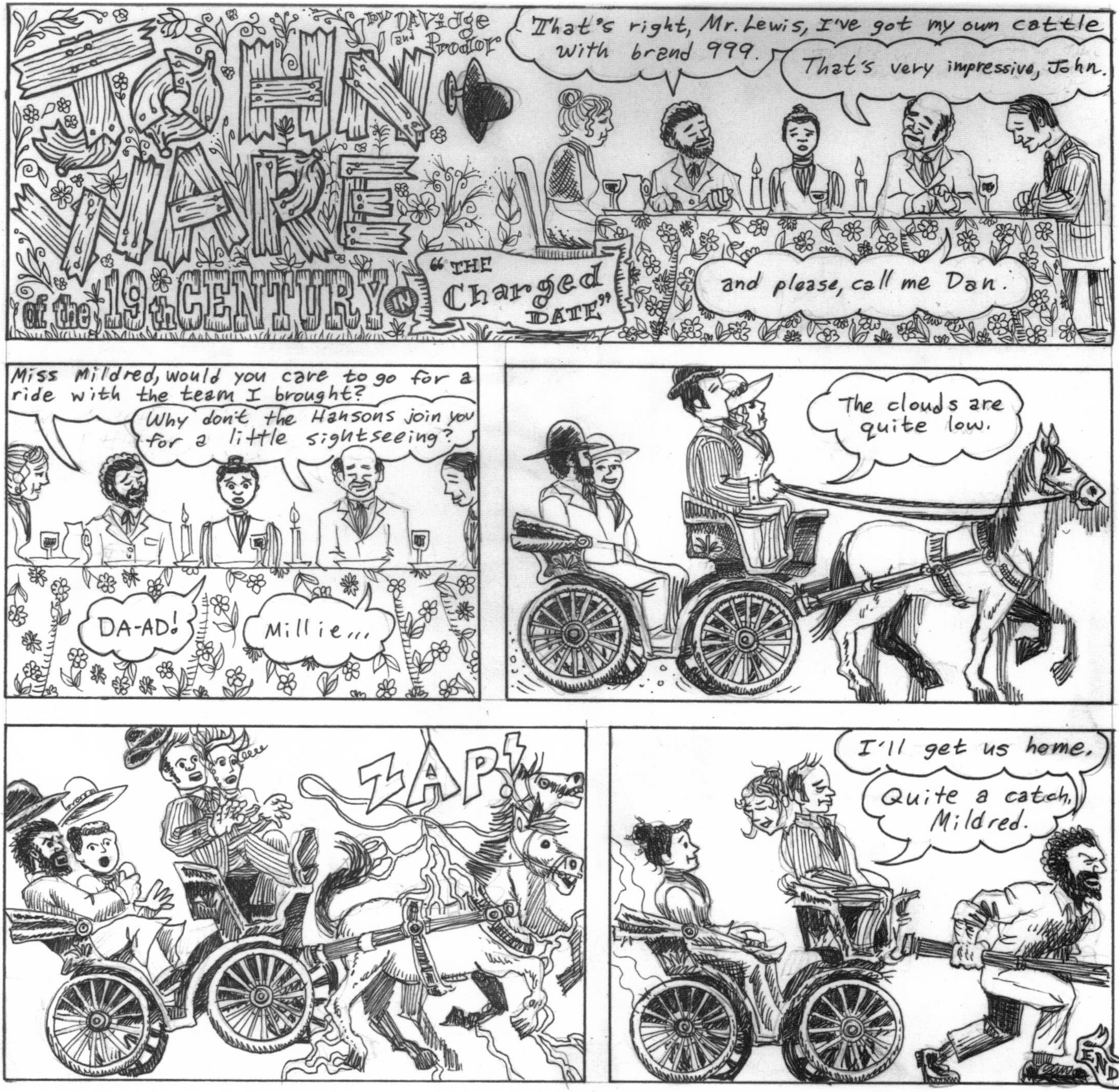
JOHN WARE of the 19th CENTURY
by Davidge and Proctor
in "THE Charged DATE"
That's right, Mr. Lewis, I've got my own cattle with brand 999.
That's very impressive, John.
and please, call me Dan.
Miss Mildred, would you care to go for a ride with the team I brought?
Why don't the Hansons join you for a little sightseeing?
DA-AD!
Millie...
The clouds are quite low.
ZAP!
I'll get us home.
Quite a catch, Mildred.
END

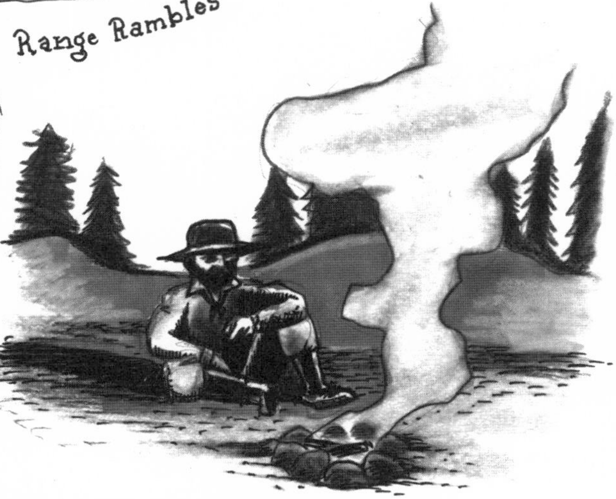

Rancher Nemeses

Sheep who eat the grass
Sodbusters who take the land
Fence poles that make their walls
Rustlers who steal the cattle
Foul weather that does the same
The state for taxes and laws
And the loneliness that walks
As freedom's partner

In Front of a Crowd

Twirl the lasso
Throw the loop
Catch half the legs
Jump off your horse
Don't break your spurs
Wrestle
Ignore the hoof to the chest
Wrap Wrap Wrap
Calf capture done

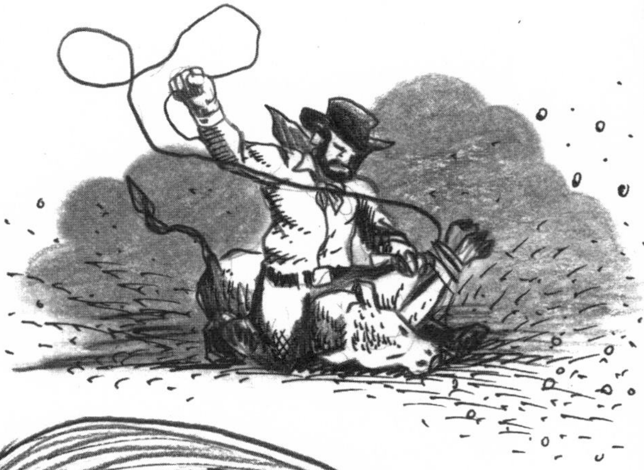

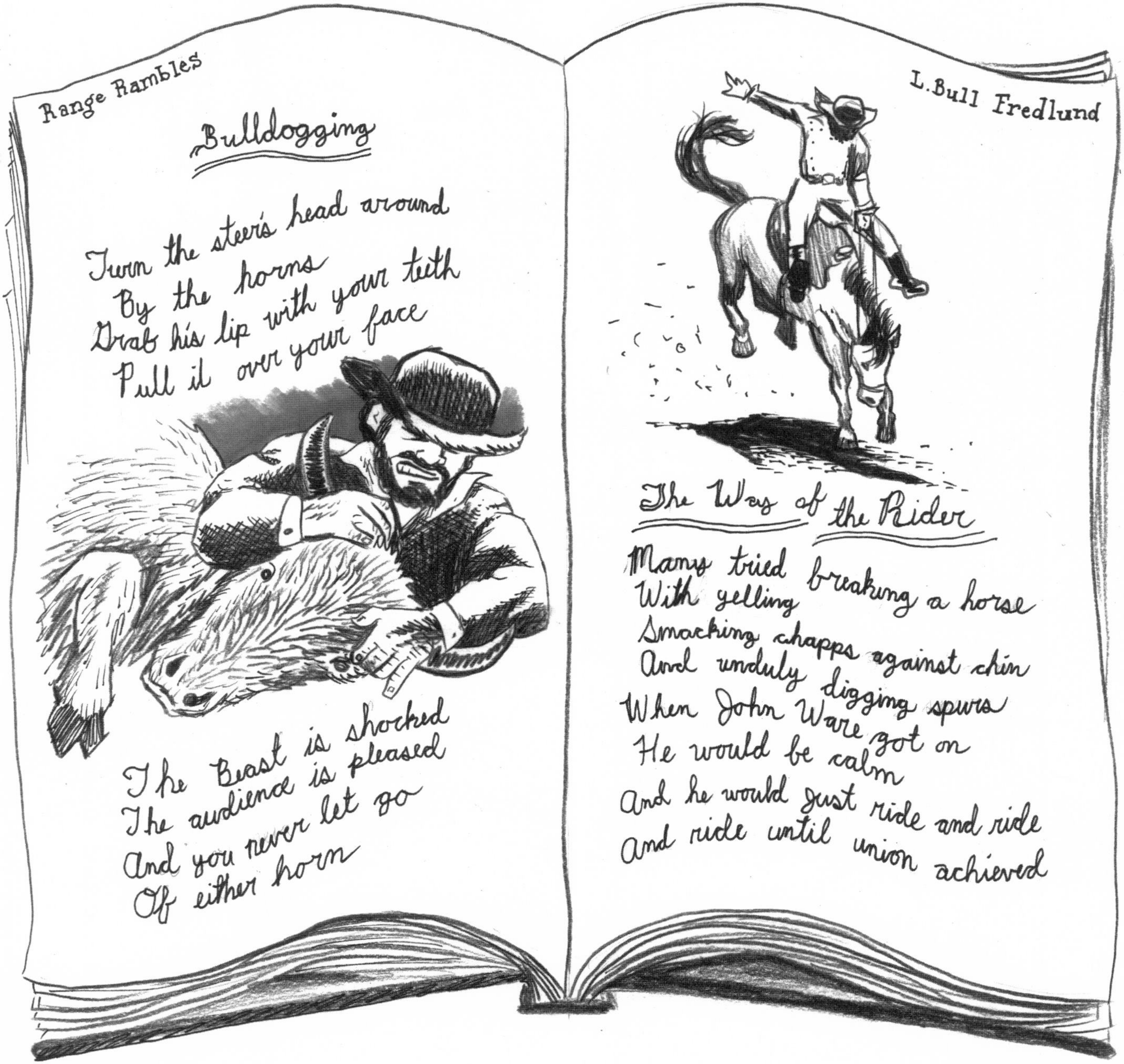
Range Rambles
L.Bull Fredlund
Bulldogging
Turn the steer's head around
By the horns
Grab his lip with your teeth
Pull it over your face
The Beast is shocked
The audience is pleased
And you never let go
Of either horn
The Way of the Rider
Manys tried breaking a horse
With yelling
Smacking chapps against chin
And unduly digging spurs
When John Ware got on
He would be calm
And he would just ride and ride
And ride until union achieved

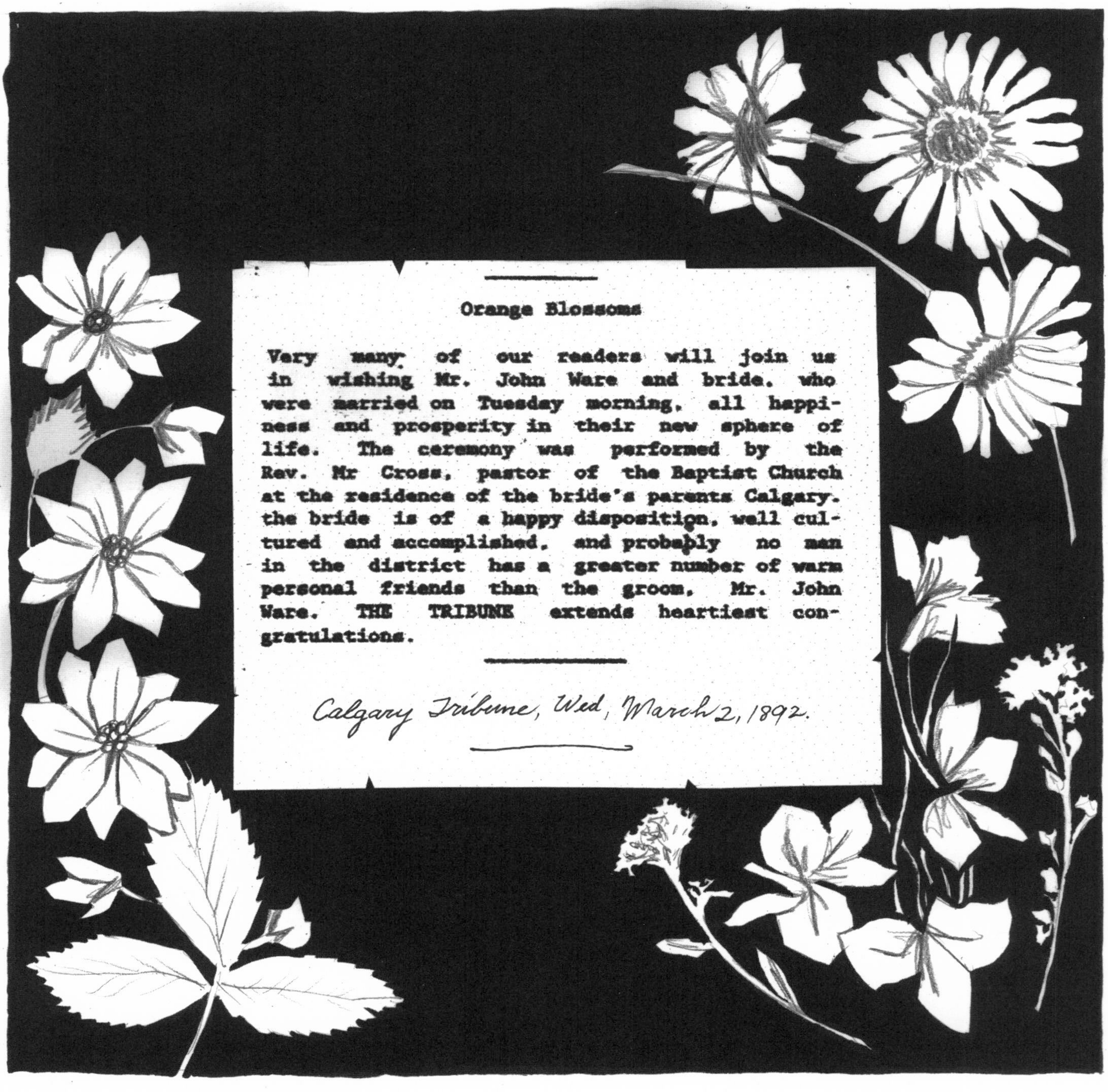

Orange Blossoms

Very many of our readers will join us in wishing Mr. John Ware and bride, who were married on Tuesday morning, all happiness and prosperity in their new sphere of life. The ceremony was performed by the Rev. Mr Cross, pastor of the Baptist Church at the residence of the bride's parents Calgary. the bride is of a happy disposition, well cultured and accomplished, and probably no man in the district has a greater number of warm personal friends than the groom, Mr. John Ware. THE TRIBUNE extends heartiest congratulations.

Calgary Tribune, Wed, March 2, 1892.

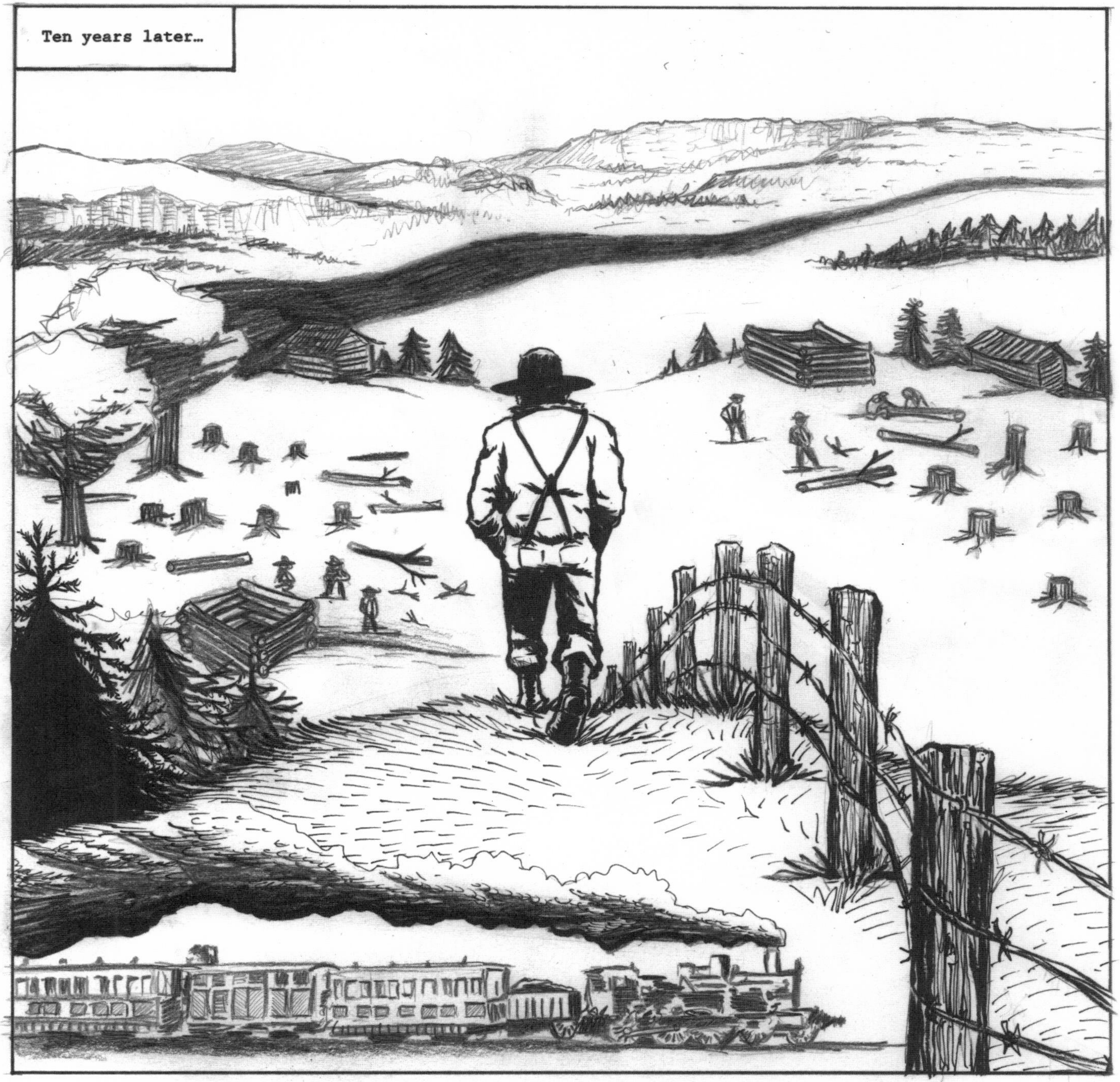
Ten years later…

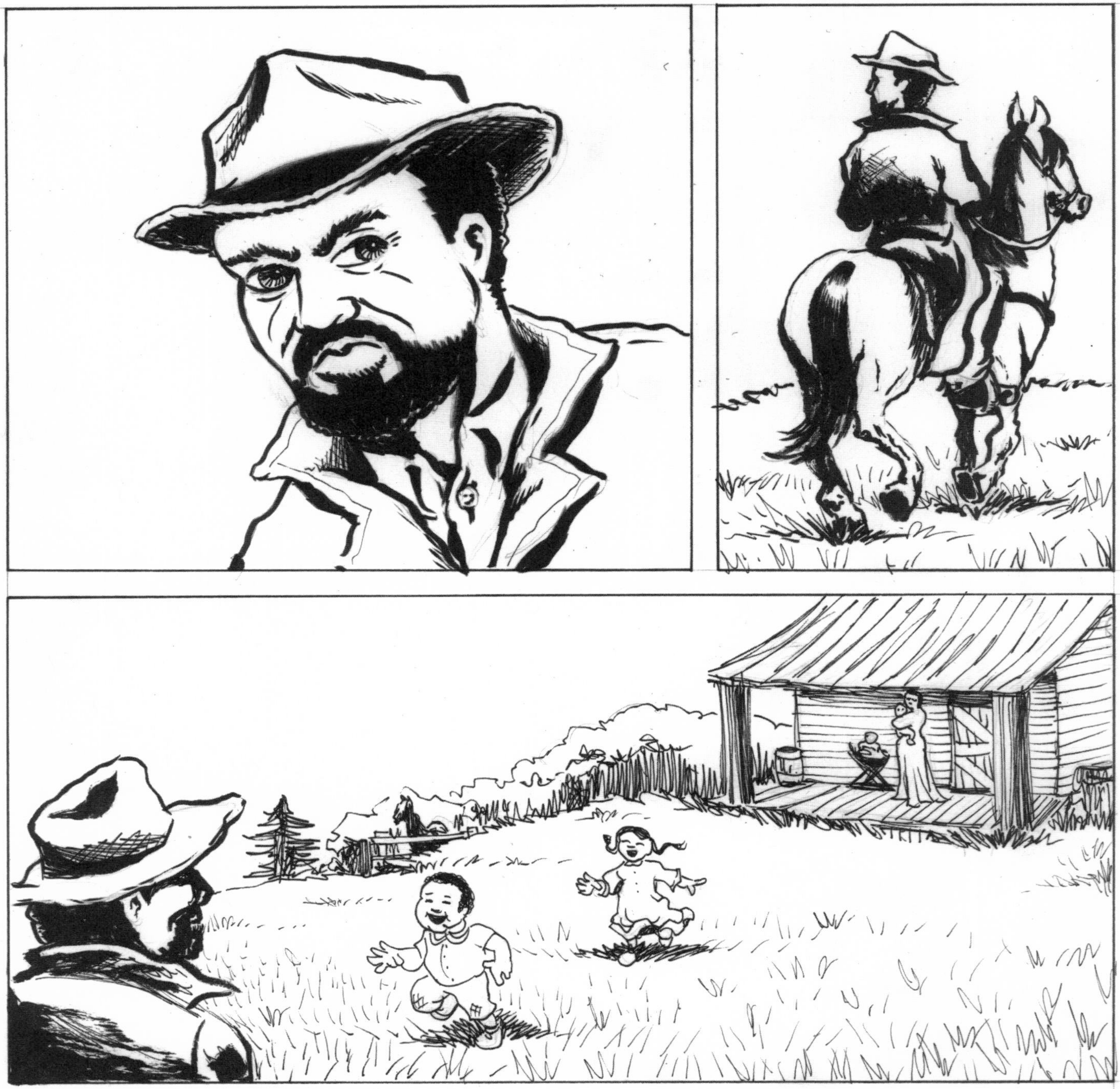

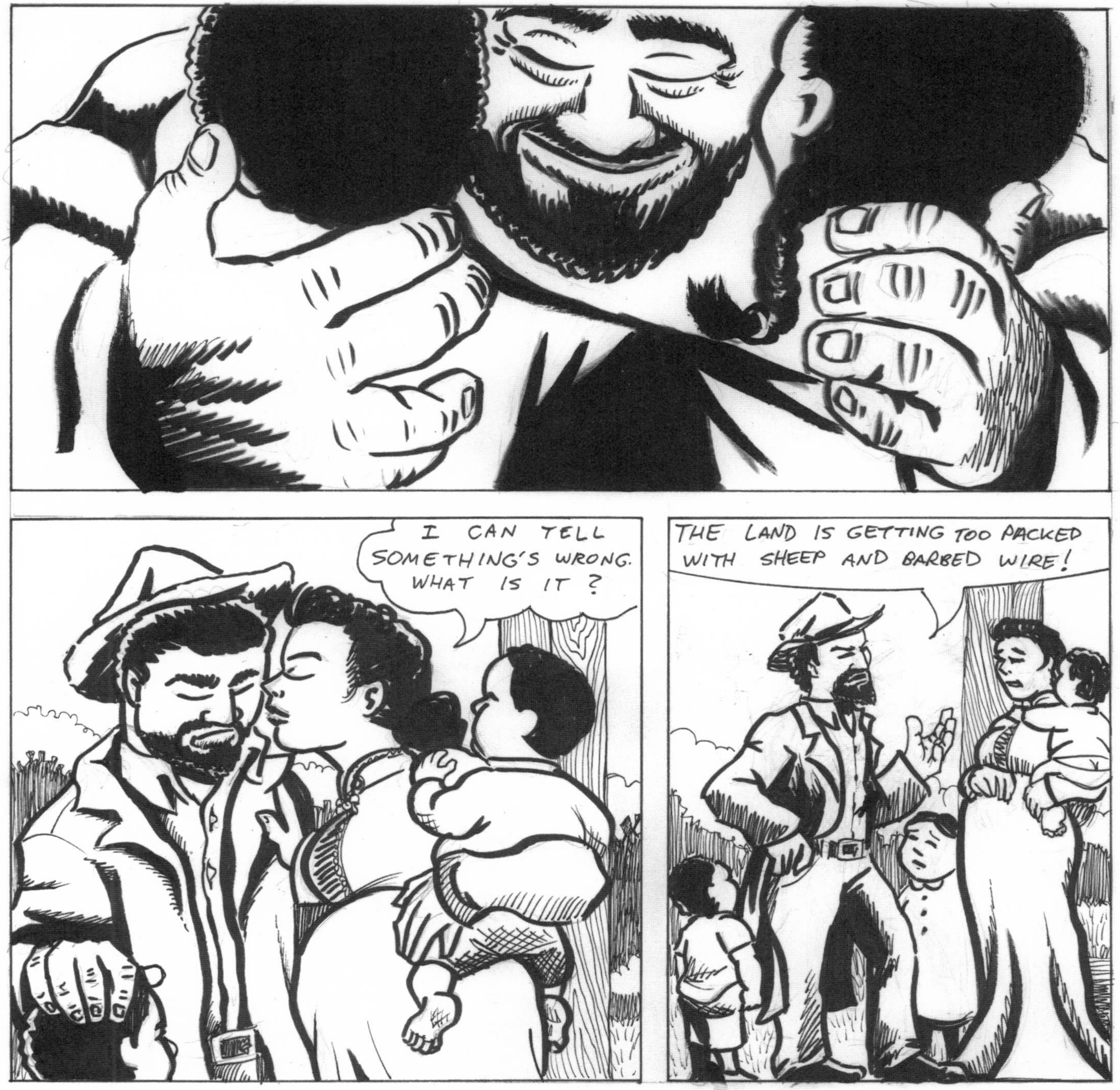
I CAN TELL SOMETHING'S WRONG. WHAT IS IT?
THE LAND IS GETTING TOO PACKED WITH SHEEP AND BARBED WIRE!

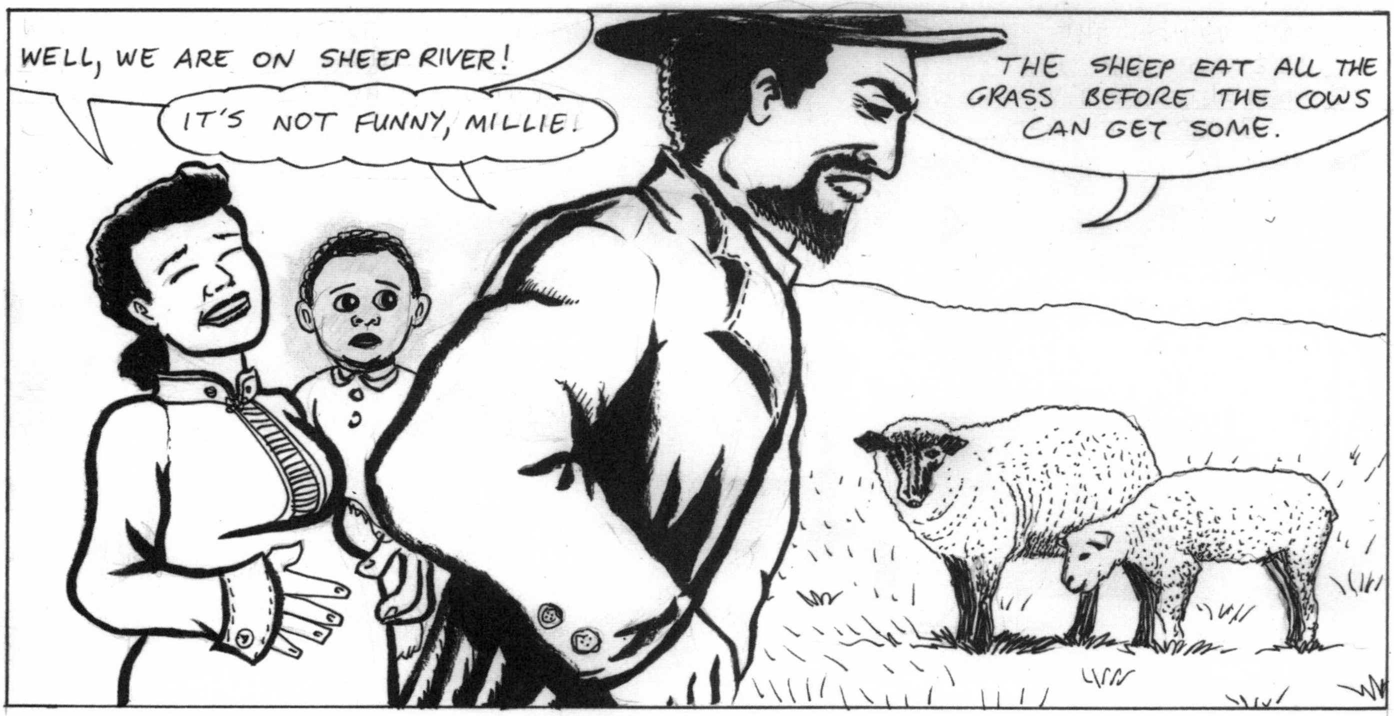
WELL, WE ARE ON SHEEP RIVER!
IT'S NOT FUNNY, MILLIE!
THE SHEEP EAT ALL THE GRASS BEFORE THE COWS CAN GET SOME.

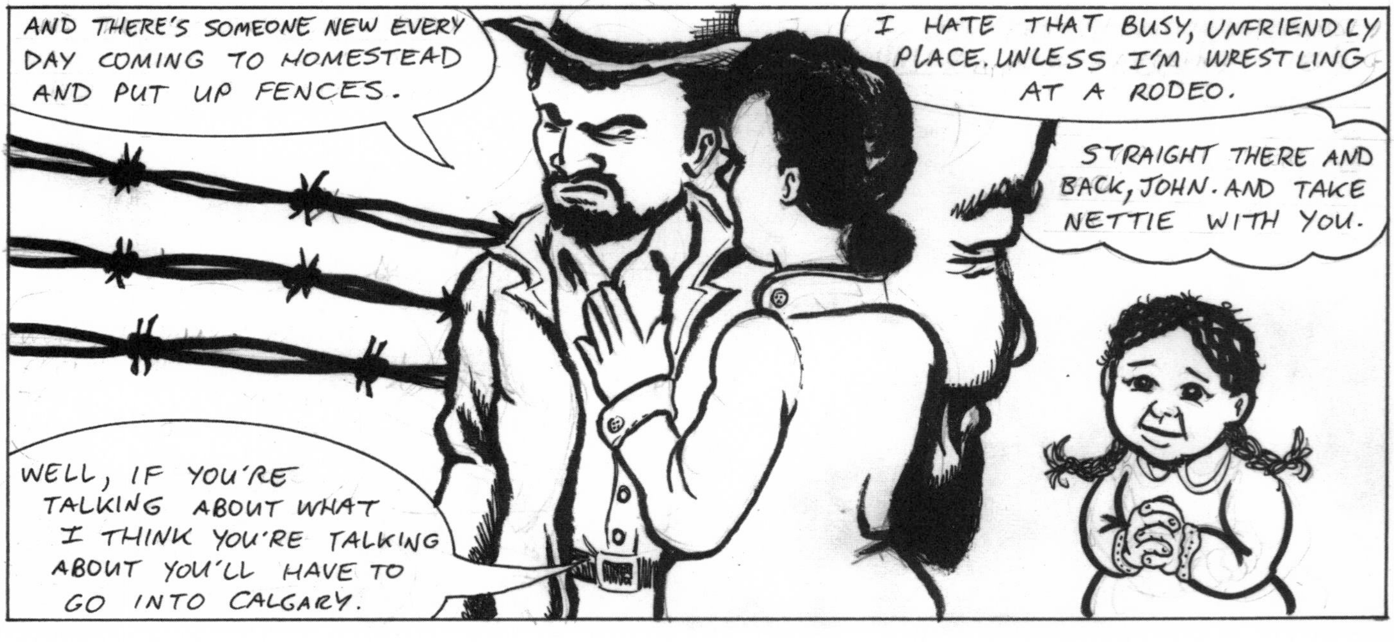
AND THERE'S SOMEONE NEW EVERY DAY COMING TO HOMESTEAD AND PUT UP FENCES.
WELL, IF YOU'RE TALKING ABOUT WHAT I THINK YOU'RE TALKING ABOUT YOU'LL HAVE TO GO INTO CALGARY.
I HATE THAT BUSY, UNFRIENDLY PLACE. UNLESS I'M WRESTLING AT A RODEO.
STRAIGHT THERE AND BACK, JOHN. AND TAKE NETTIE WITH YOU.

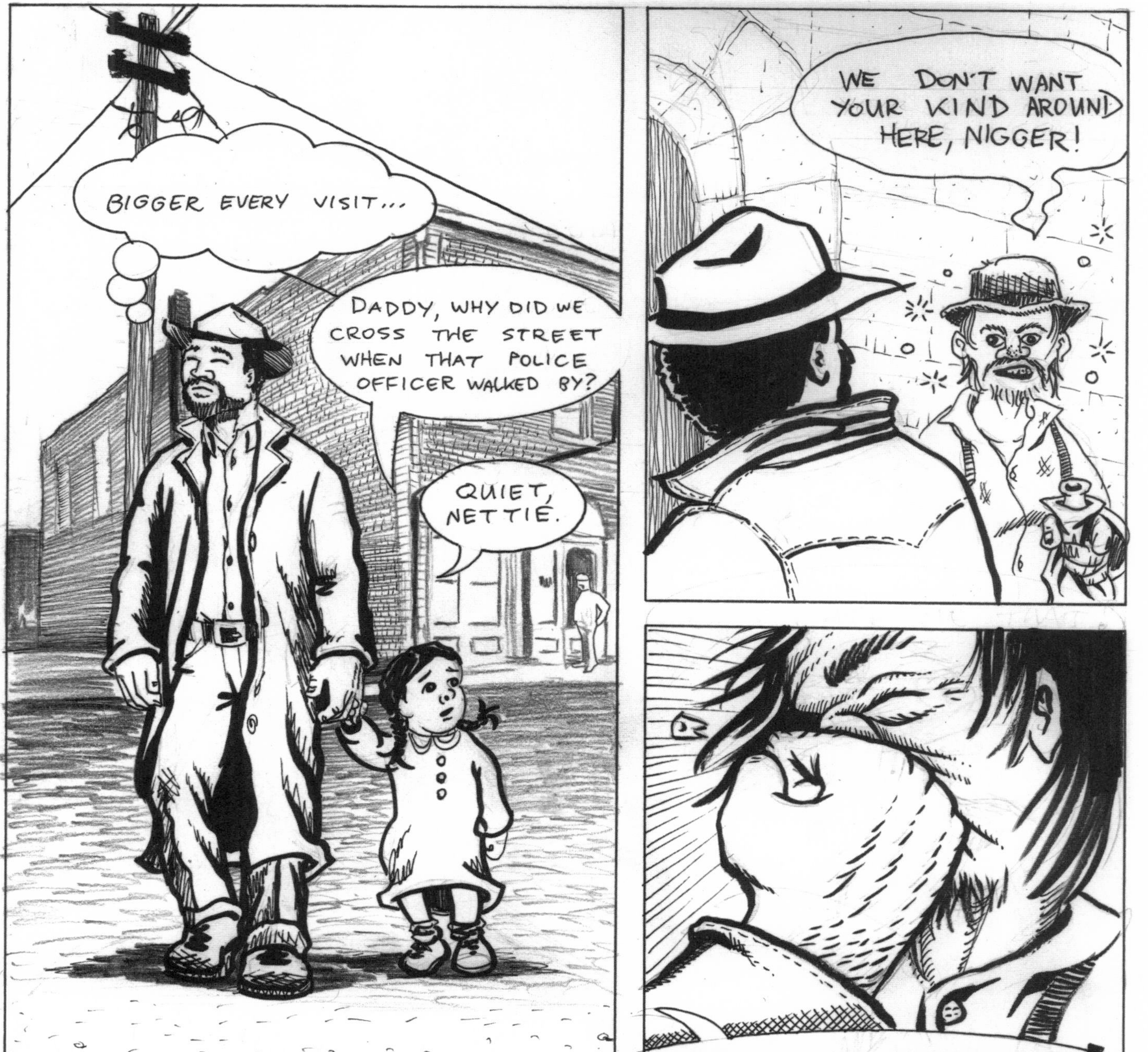
BIGGER EVERY VISIT...
DADDY, WHY DID WE CROSS THE STREET WHEN THAT POLICE OFFICER WALKED BY?
QUIET, NETTIE.
WE DON'T WANT YOUR KIND AROUND HERE, NIGGER!
DON'T CALL ME THAT!

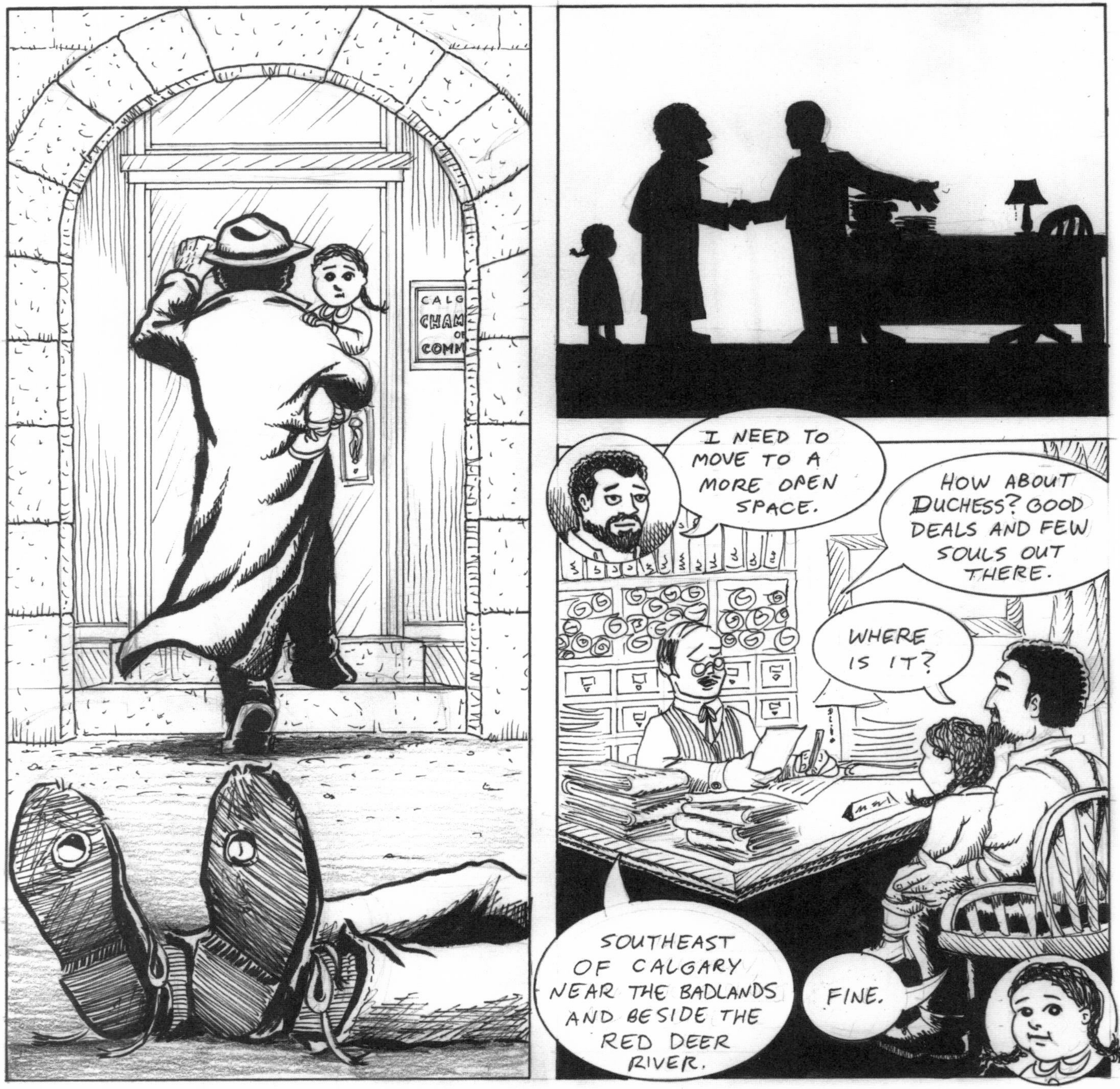
I NEED TO MOVE TO A MORE OPEN SPACE.
HOW ABOUT DUCHESS? GOOD DEALS AND FEW SOULS OUT THERE.
WHERE IS IT?
SOUTHEAST OF CALGARY NEAR THE BADLANDS AND BESIDE THE RED DEER RIVER.
FINE.

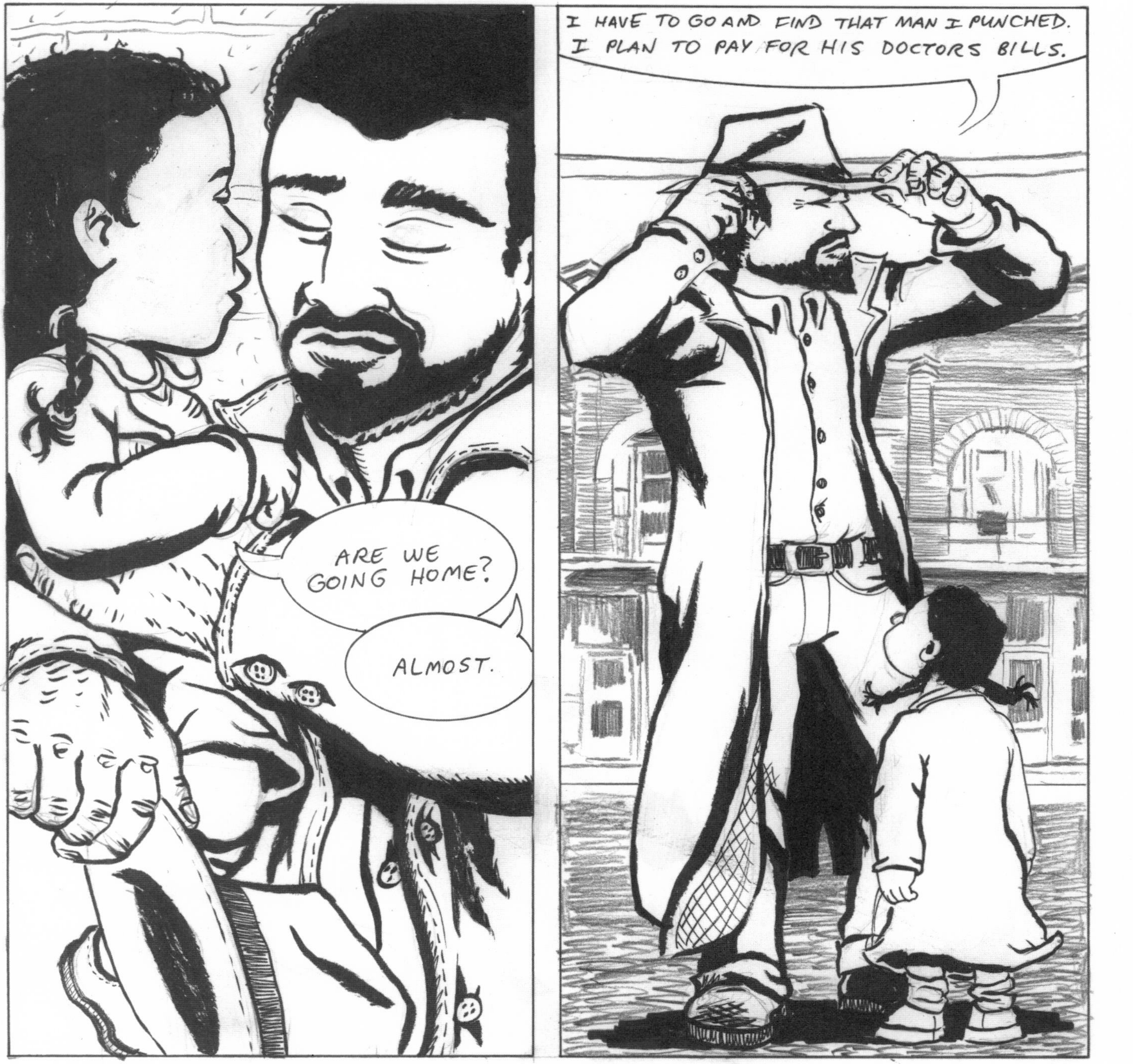
ARE WE GOING HOME?
ALMOST.
I HAVE TO GO AND FIND THAT MAN I PUNCHED. I PLAN TO PAY FOR HIS DOCTORS BILLS.

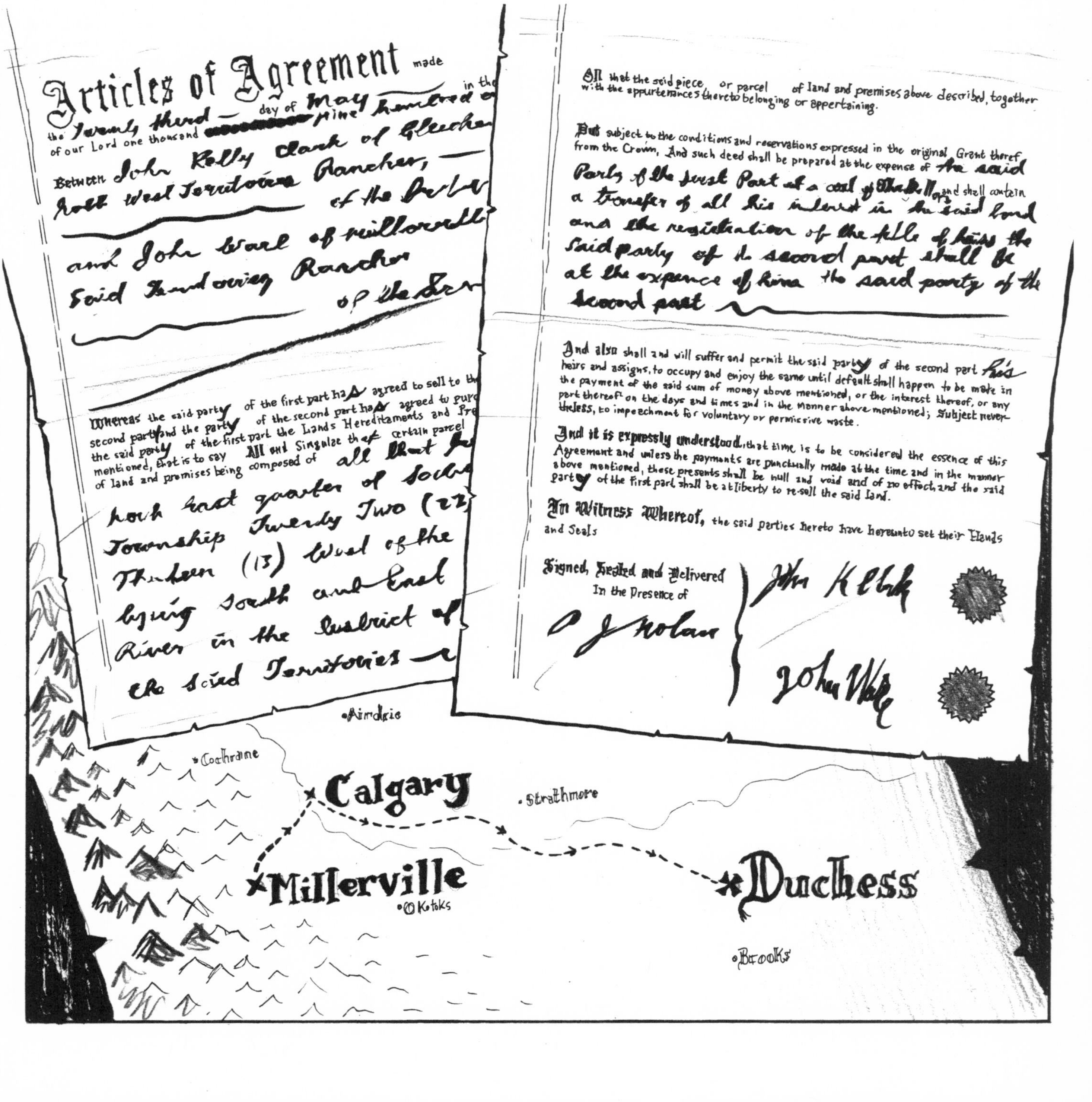

Articles of Agreement made
the day of May in the
of our Lord one thousand
Between John Kelly Clark of Gleichen
North West Territories Rancher,
of the first
and John Ward of Millarville
Said Territory Rancher
of the Second
Whereas the said party of the first part has agreed to sell to the
second part and the party of the second part has agreed to pur
the said party of the first part the Lands Hereditaments and Pre
mentioned, that is to say All and Singular that certain parcel
of land and premises being composed of all that
North East quarter of Section
Township Twenty Two (22)
Thirteen (13) West of the
lying South and East
River in the District of
the said Territories
All that the said piece or parcel of land and premises above described, together with the appurtenances thereto belonging or appertaining.
But subject to the conditions and reservations expressed in the original Grant thereof from the Crown, And such deed shall be prepared at the expence of the said Party of the first Part at a cost of and shall contain a transfer of all his interest in the said land and the registration of the title of him the said party of the second part shall be at the expence of him the said party of the second part
And also shall and will suffer and permit the said party of the second part his heirs and assigns, to occupy and enjoy the same until default shall happen to be made in the payment of the said sum of money above mentioned, or the interest thereof, or any part thereof on the days and times and in the manner above mentioned; Subject nevertheless, to impeachment for voluntary or permissive waste.
And it is expressly understood, that time is to be considered the essence of this Agreement and unless the payments are punctually made at the time and in the manner above mentioned, these presents shall be null and void and of no effect, and the said party of the first part shall be at liberty to re-sell the said land.
In Witness Whereof, the said parties hereto have hereunto set their Hands and Seals
Signed, Sealed and Delivered
In the Presence of
P J Nolan
John Kelly Clark
John Ward
Airdrie
Cochrane
Calgary
Strathmore
Millerville
Okotoks
Duchess
Brooks

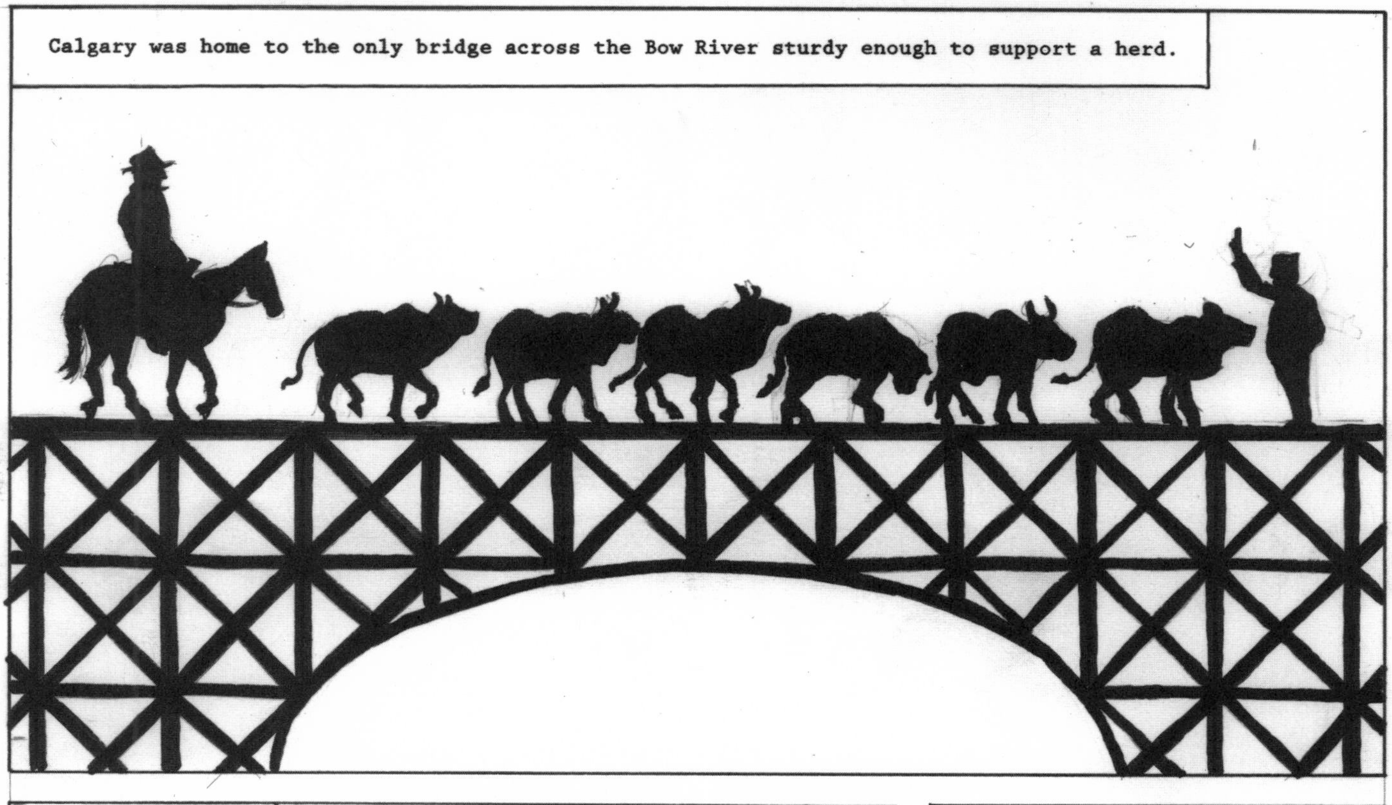
Calgary was home to the only bridge across the Bow River sturdy enough to support a herd.
NO CATTLE CROSSING ON THE BRIDGE.
BUT I ONLY NEED TO DO THIS ONCE.
YOU DON'T WANT TO GO TO PRISON OVER THIS, DO YOU, WARE?

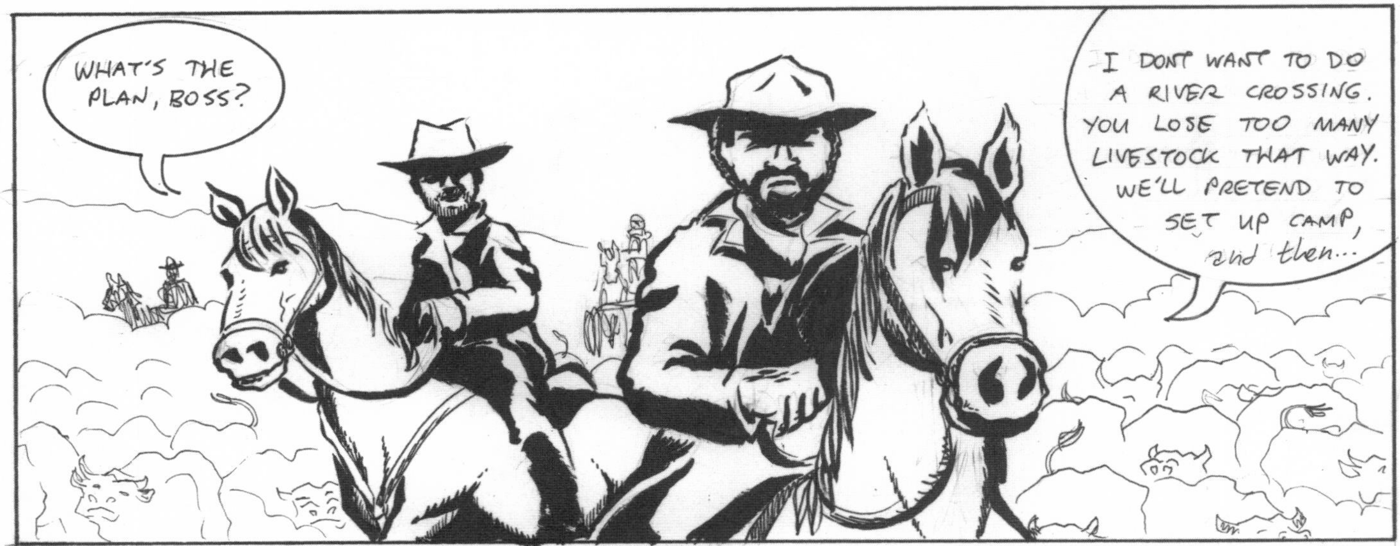
WHAT'S THE PLAN, BOSS?
I DONT WANT TO DO A RIVER CROSSING. YOU LOSE TOO MANY LIVESTOCK THAT WAY. WE'LL PRETEND TO SET UP CAMP, and then...

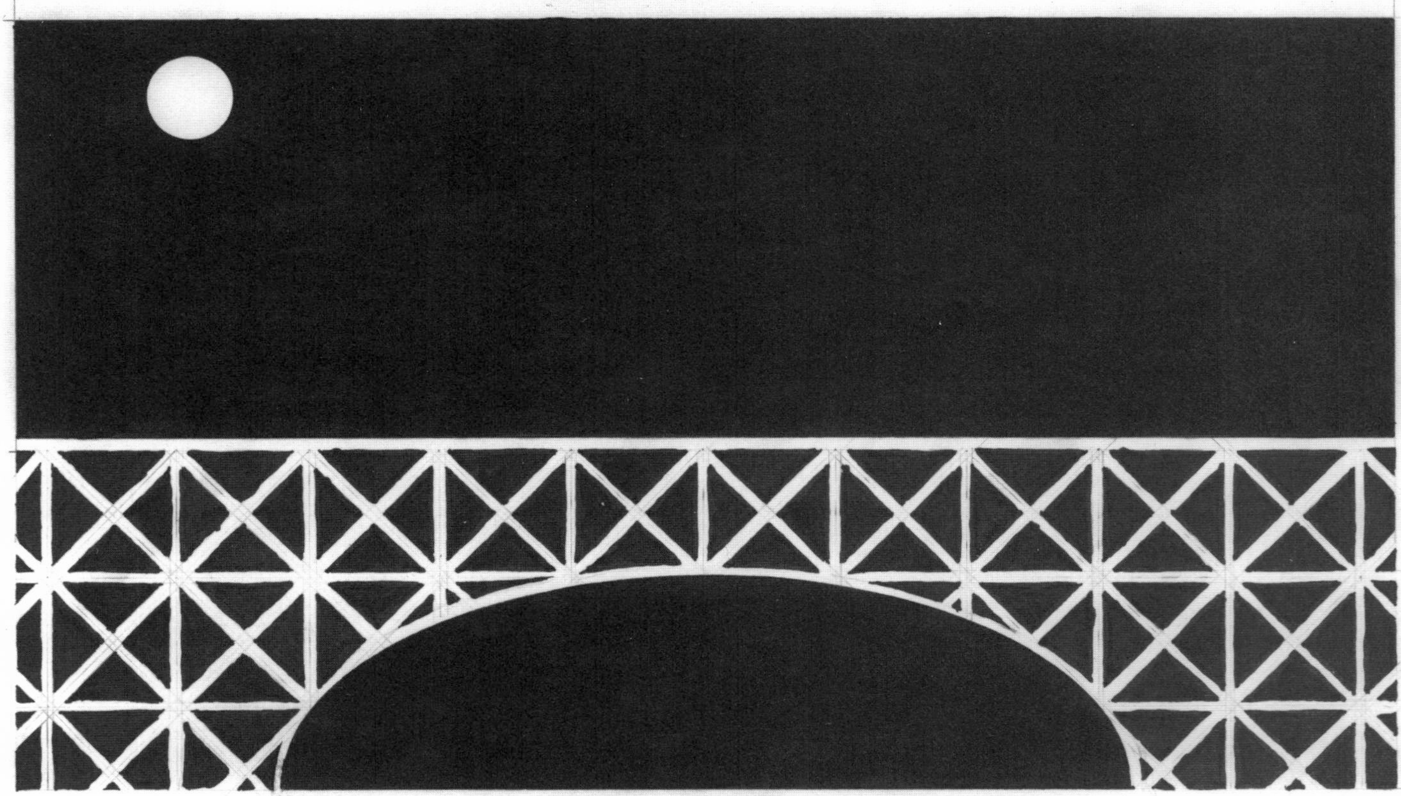

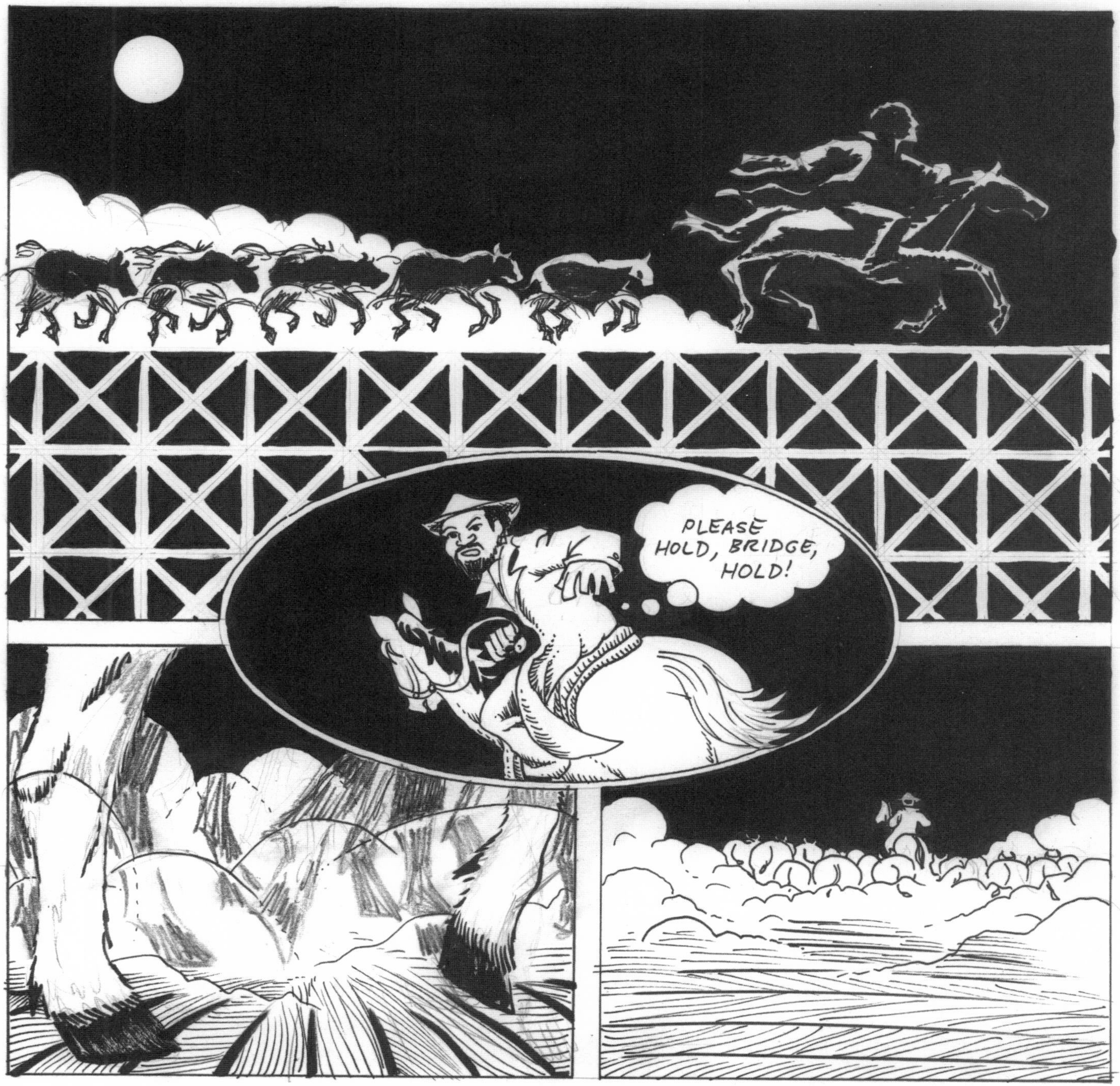
PLEASE
HOLD, BRIDGE,
HOLD!

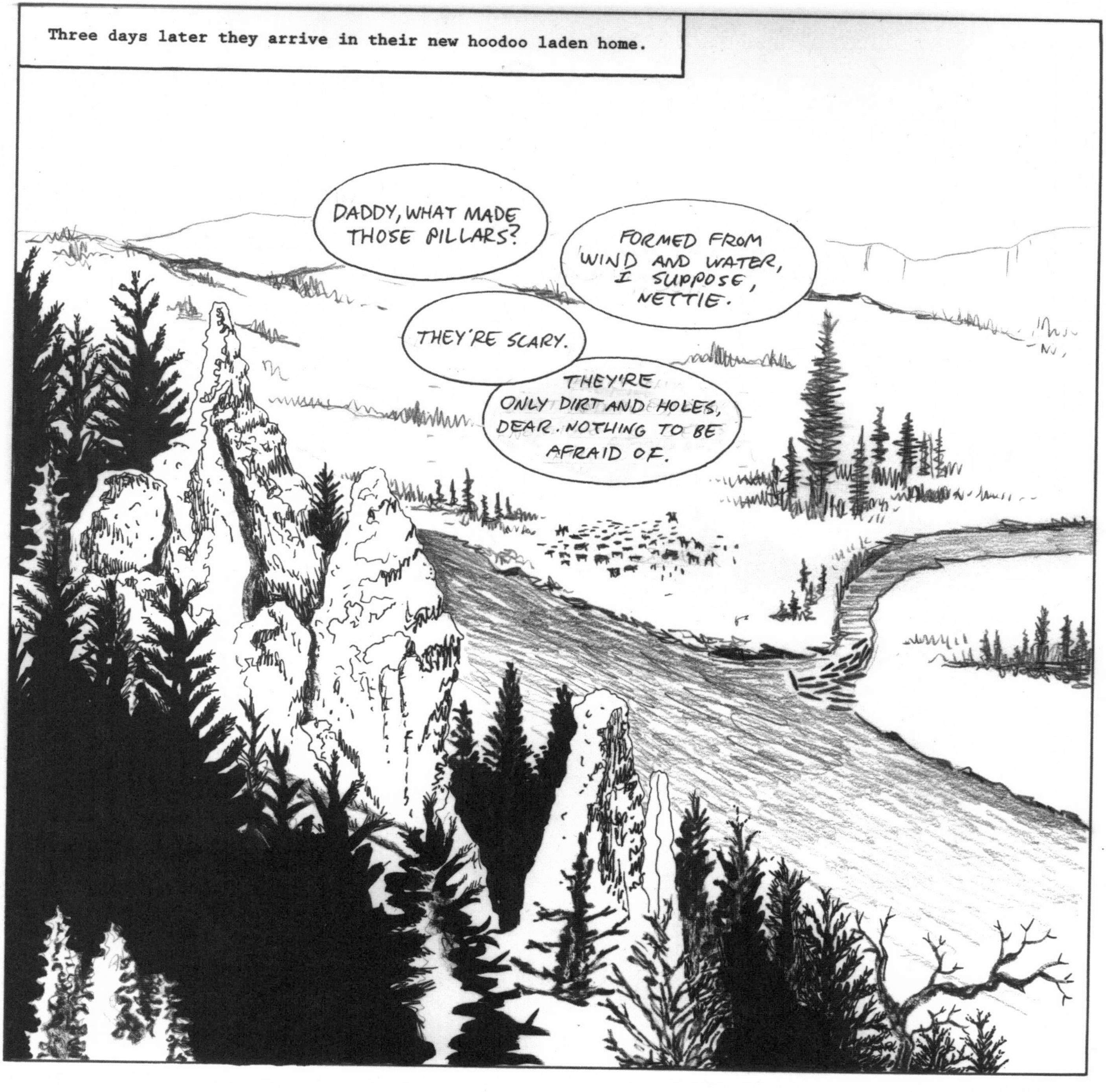
Three days later they arrive in their new hoodoo laden home.
DADDY, WHAT MADE THOSE PILLARS?
FORMED FROM WIND AND WATER, I SUPPOSE, NETTIE.
THEY'RE SCARY.
THEY'RE ONLY DIRT AND HOLES, DEAR. NOTHING TO BE AFRAID OF.

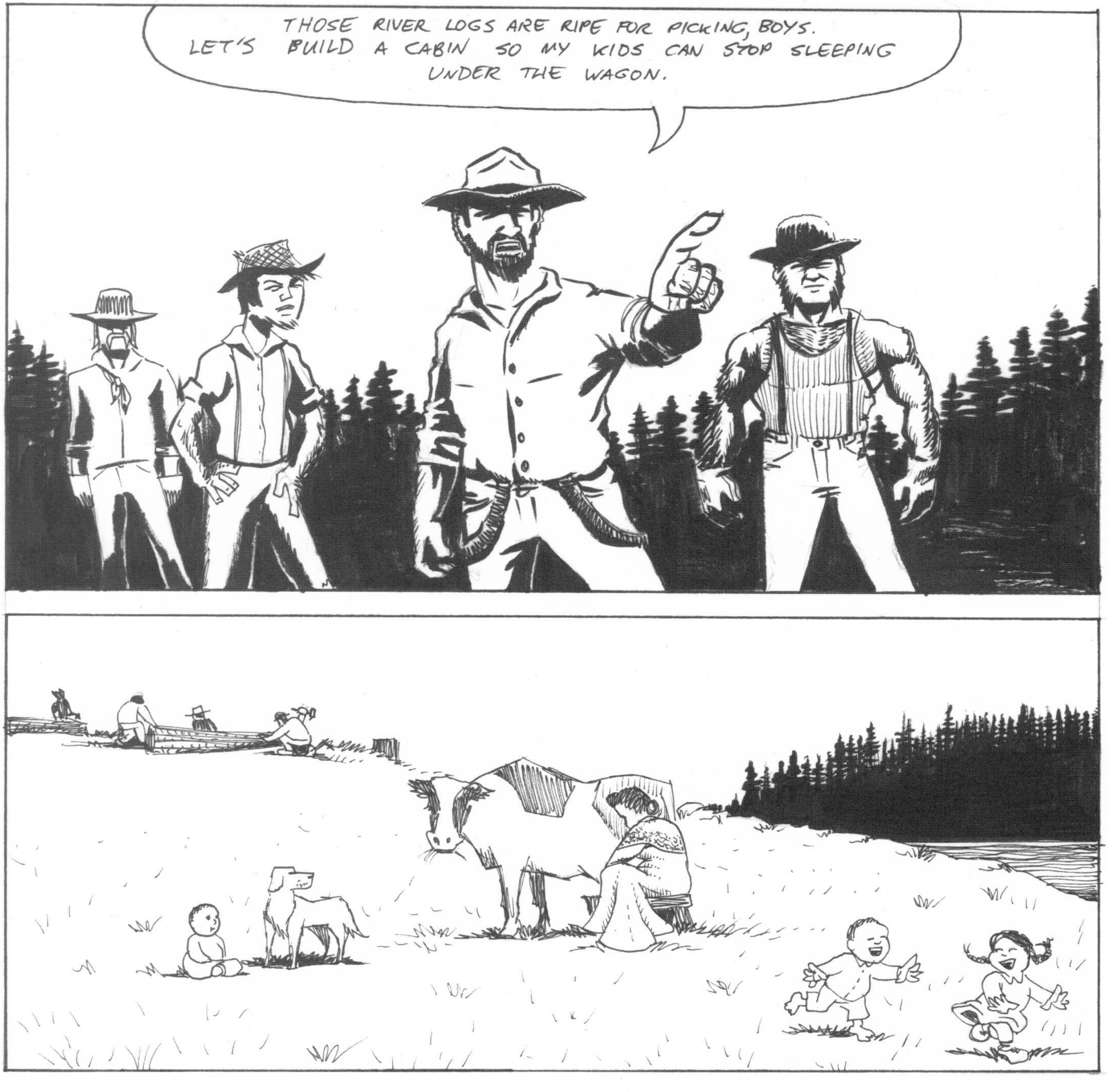
THOSE RIVER LOGS ARE RIPE FOR PICKING, BOYS. LET'S BUILD A CABIN SO MY KIDS CAN STOP SLEEPING UNDER THE WAGON.

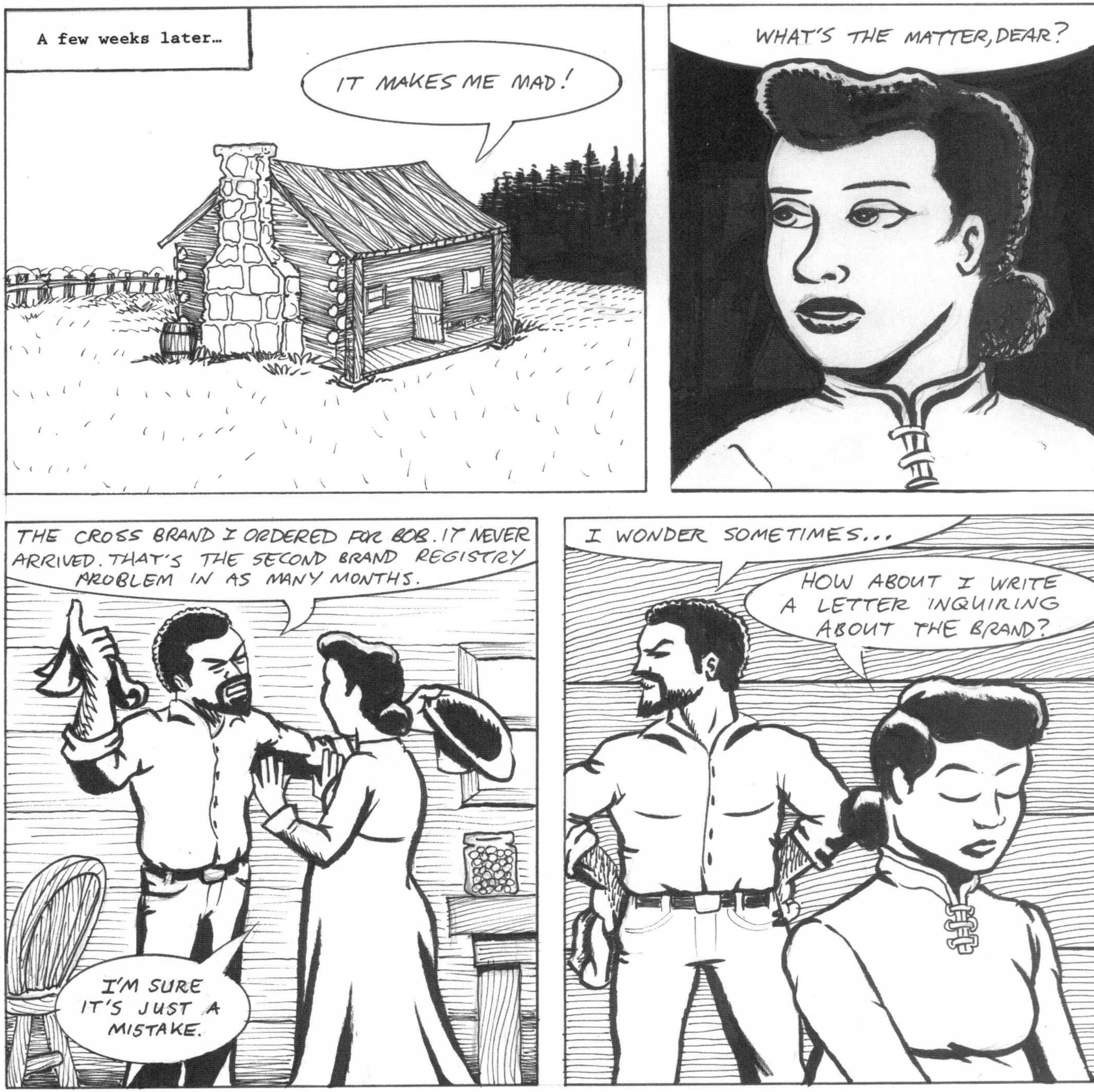
A few weeks later...
IT MAKES ME MAD!
WHAT'S THE MATTER, DEAR?
THE CROSS BRAND I ORDERED FOR BOB. IT NEVER ARRIVED. THAT'S THE SECOND BRAND REGISTRY PROBLEM IN AS MANY MONTHS.
I'M SURE IT'S JUST A MISTAKE.
I WONDER SOMETIMES...
HOW ABOUT I WRITE A LETTER INQUIRING ABOUT THE BRAND?

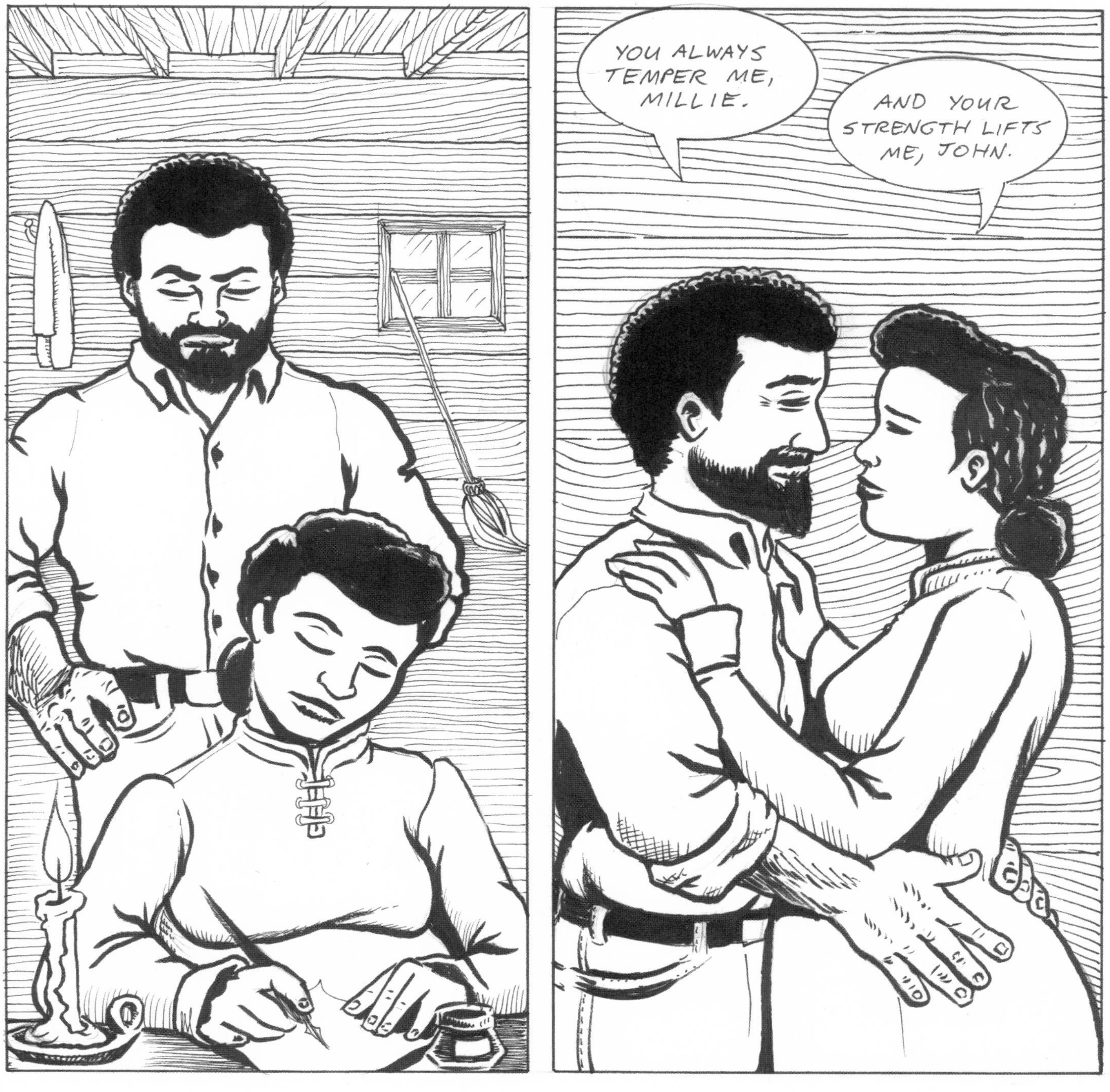
YOU ALWAYS TEMPER ME, MILLIE.
AND YOUR STRENGTH LIFTS ME, JOHN.

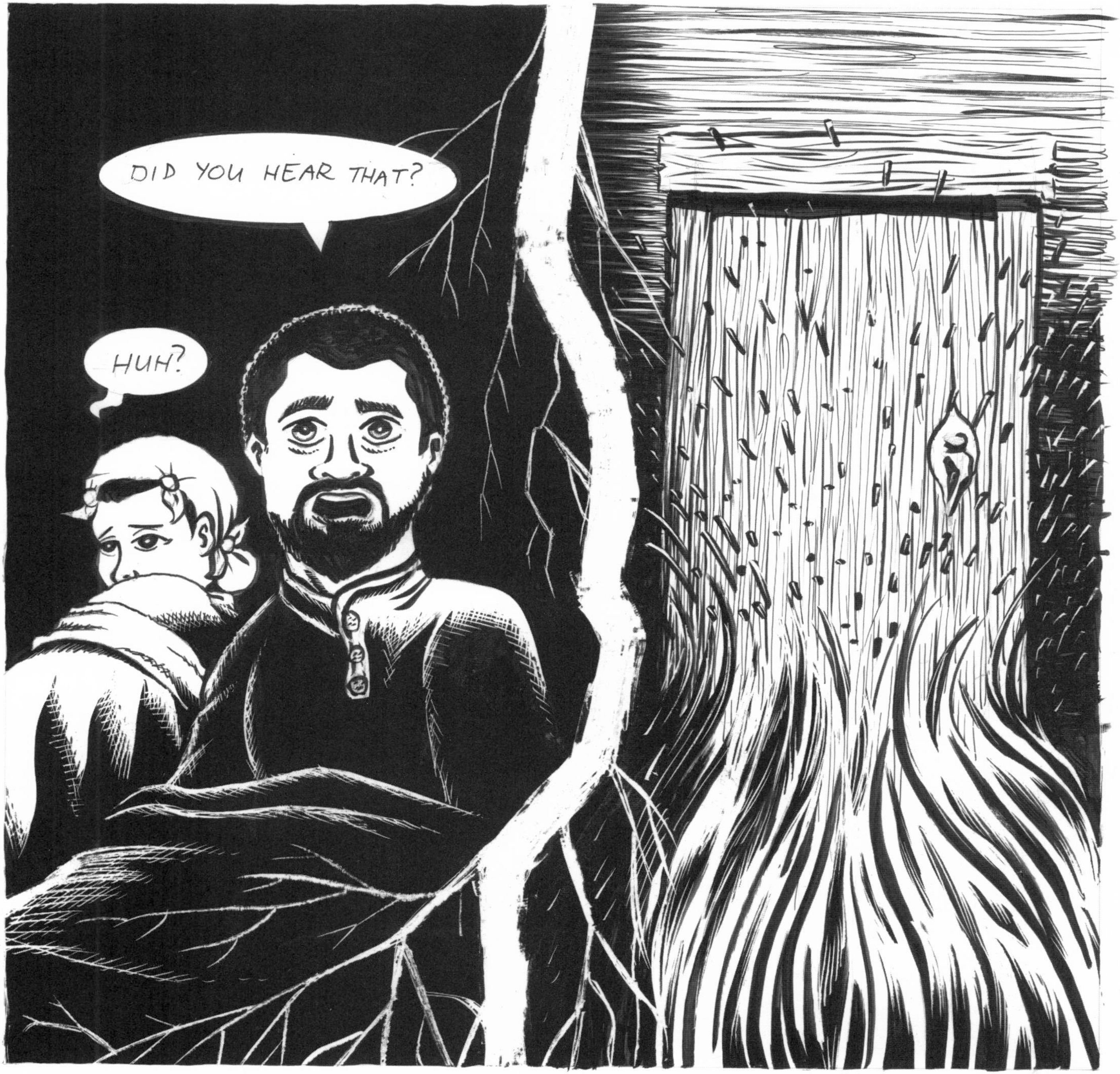
DID YOU HEAR THAT?
HUH?

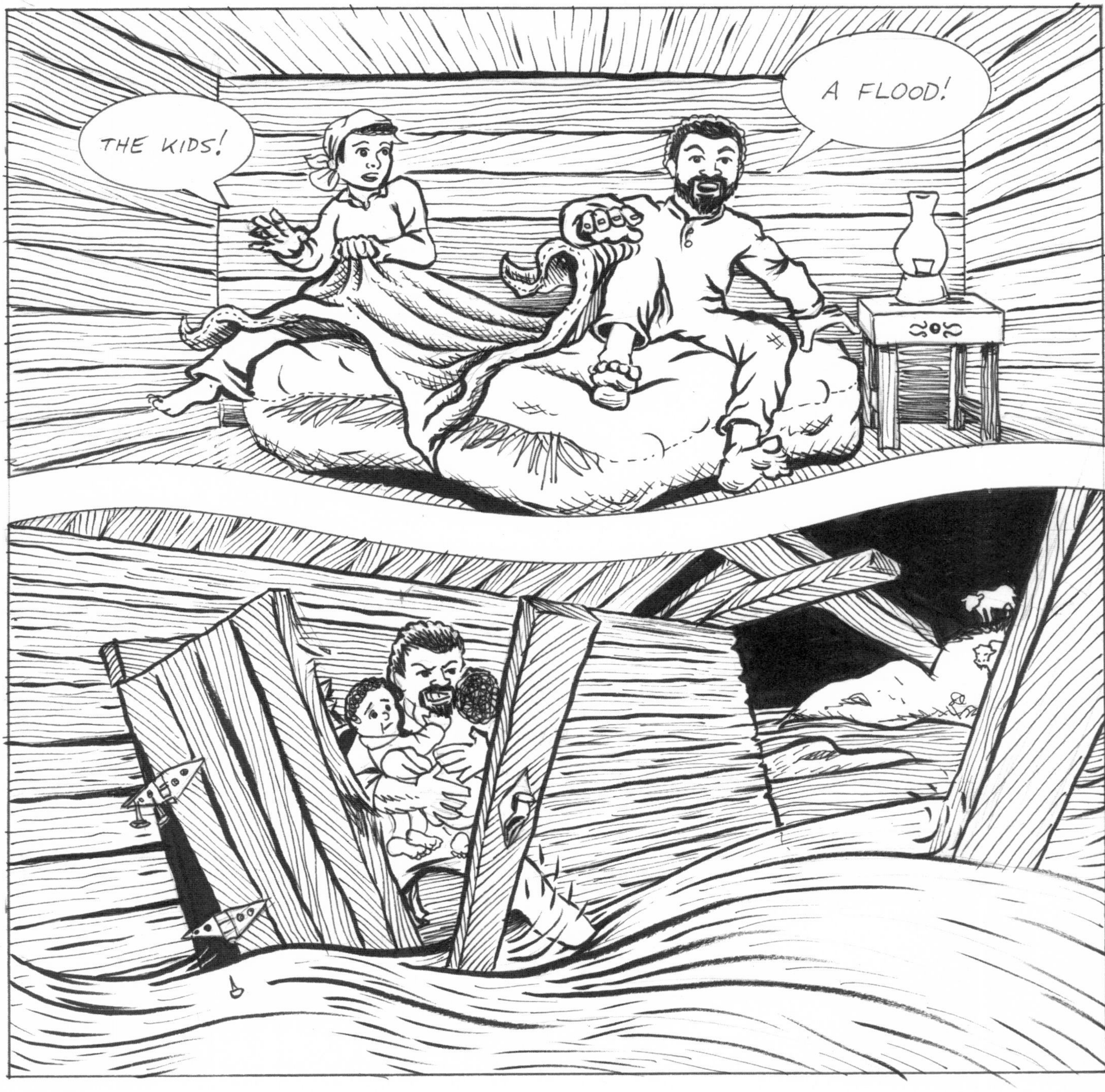
THE KIDS!
A FLOOD!

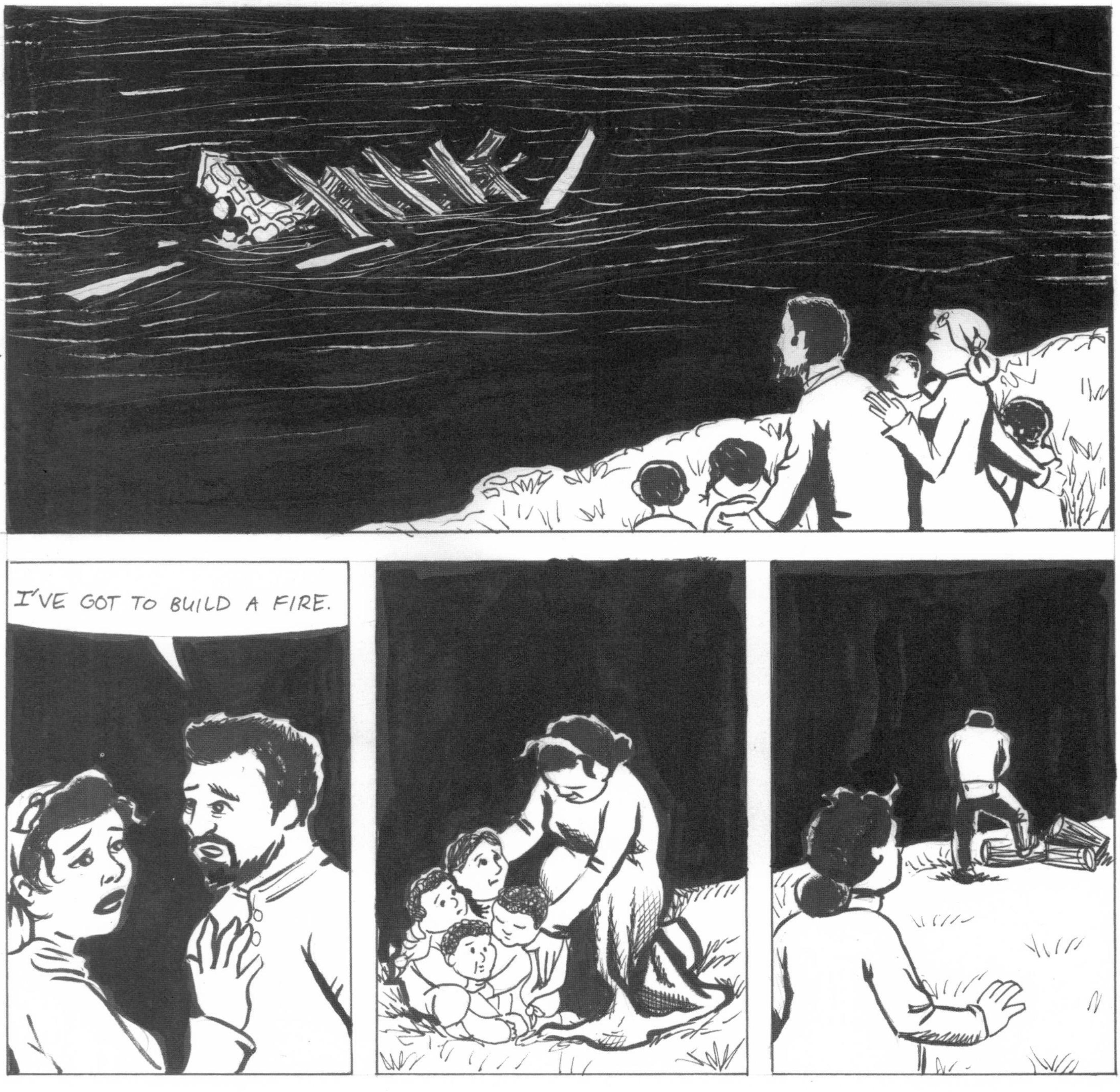
I'VE GOT TO BUILD A FIRE.

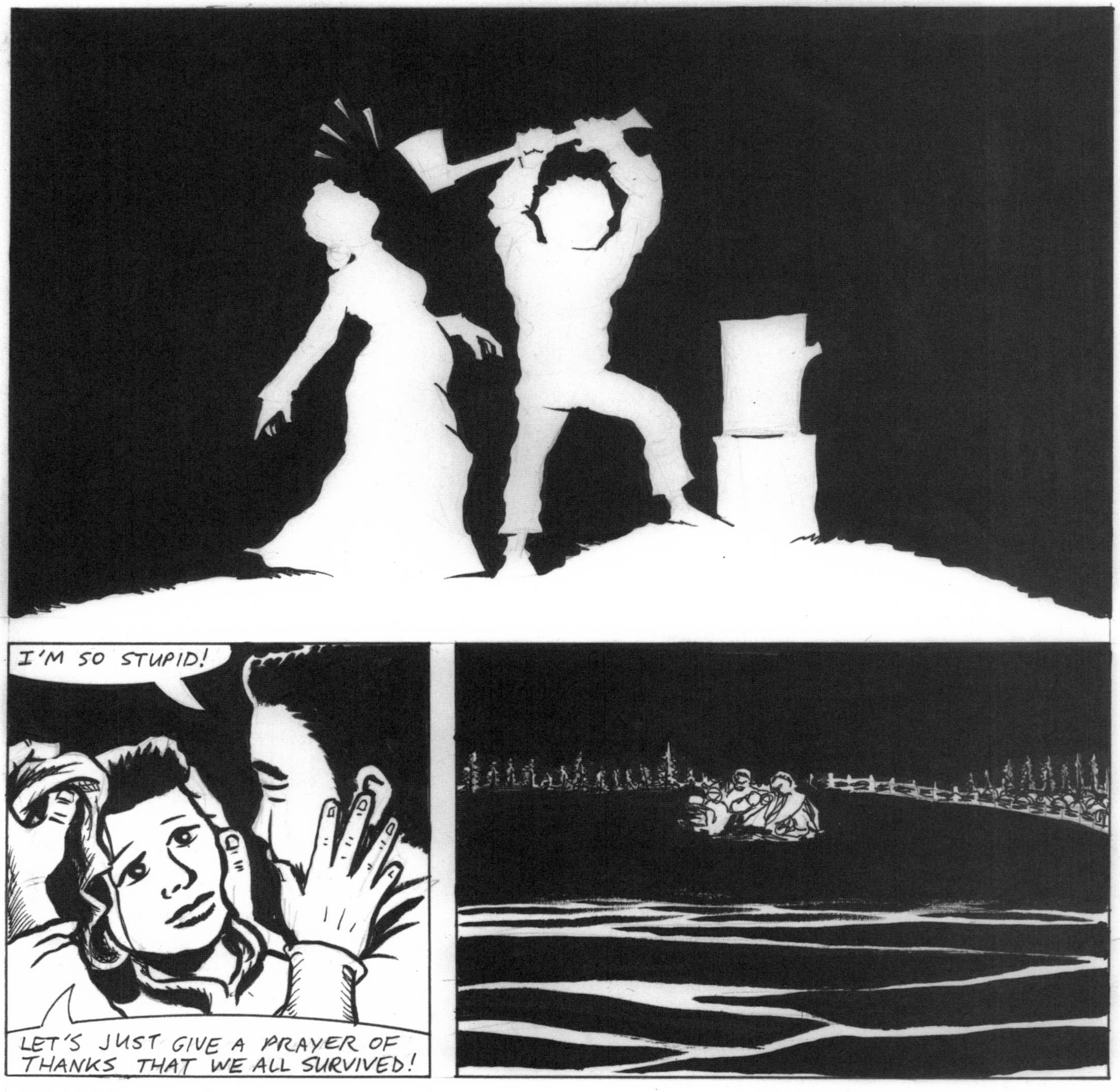
I'M SO STUPID!
LET'S JUST GIVE A PRAYER OF THANKS THAT WE ALL SURVIVED!

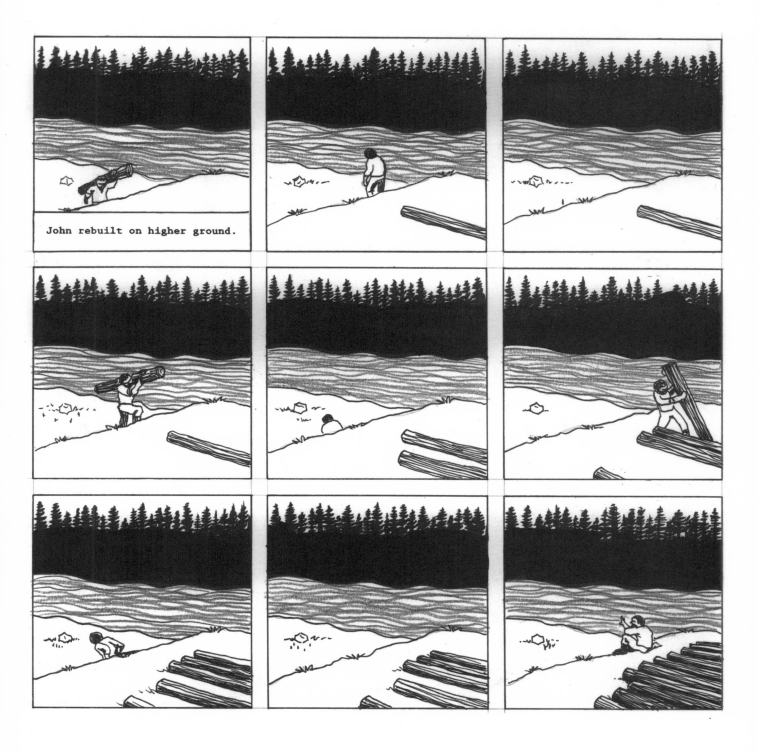

John rebuilt on higher ground.

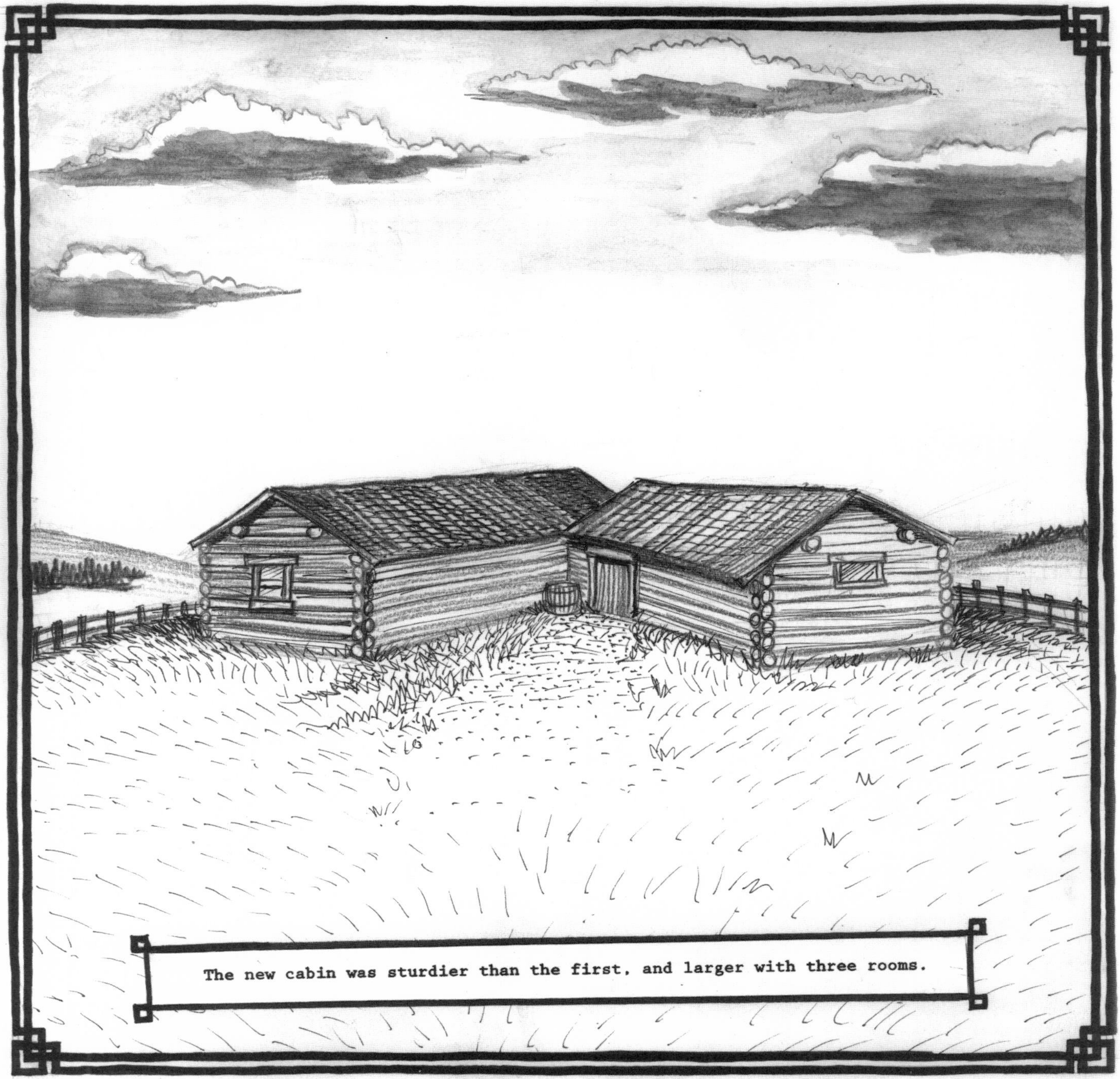
The new cabin was sturdier than the first, and larger with three rooms.

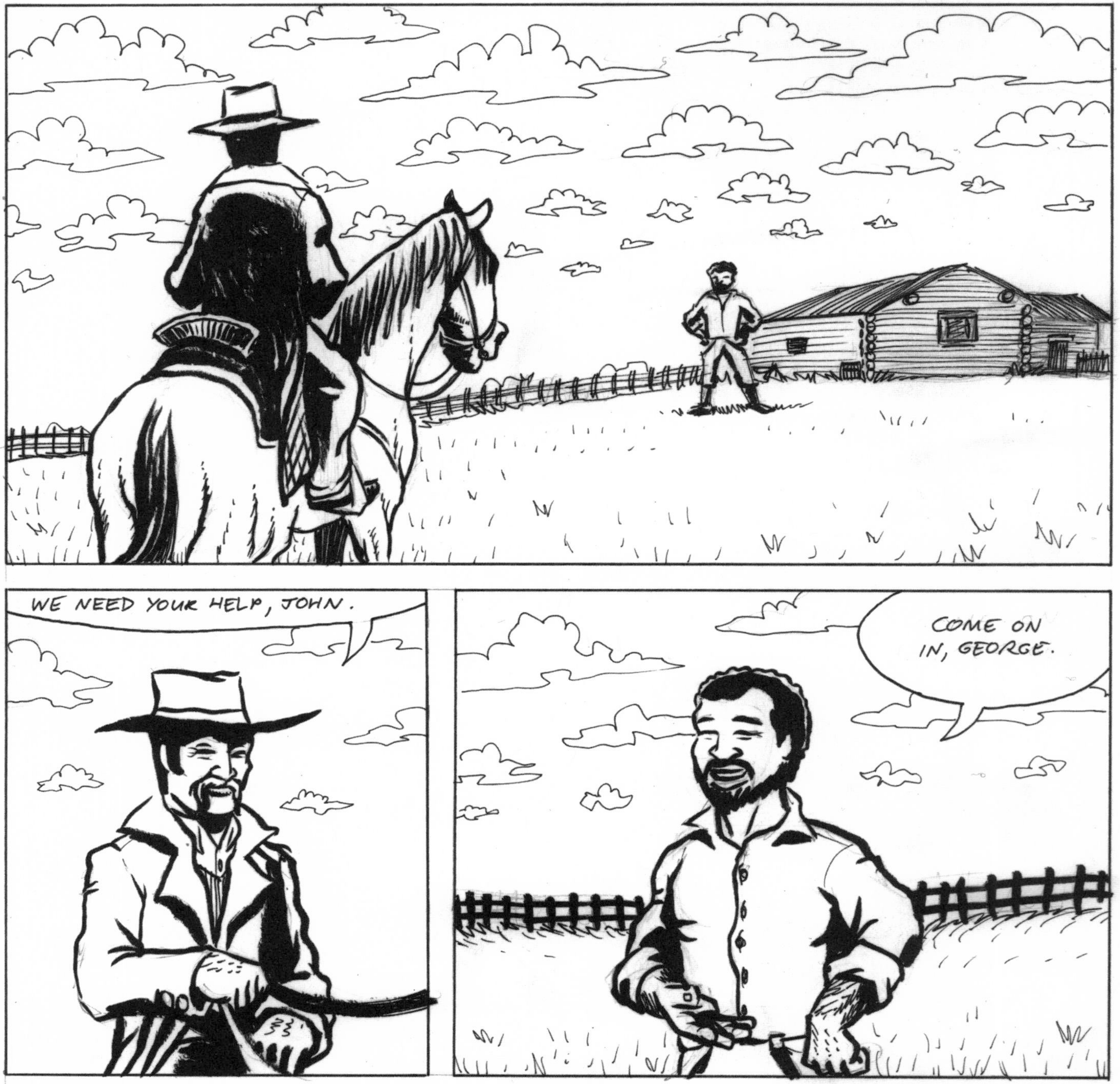
WE NEED YOUR HELP, JOHN.
COME ON IN, GEORGE.

THERE'S BEEN A NASTY OUTBREAK OF MANGE IN CATTLE THROUGHOUT THE LAND.
THE MOST EFFECTIVE WAY TO DEAL WITH IT IS THROUGH DIPPING. RUNNING THE CATTLE THROUGH A SOAPY VAT.
I KNOW. SOME OF MY COWS HAVE IT.
WE NEED SOMEONE RESPONSIBLE TO DONATE SOME LAND AND SUPERVISE THE PROCESS. MOST OF THE WRANGLERS OUT HERE ARE TOO GREEN.
THEY'RE AS CRAZY AS WE WERE TWENTY YEARS AGO.
I'D BE HONORED IF YOU USED MY PLACE.
THANKS, JOHN. YOU'RE A TRUE COMMUNITY GENTLEMAN.

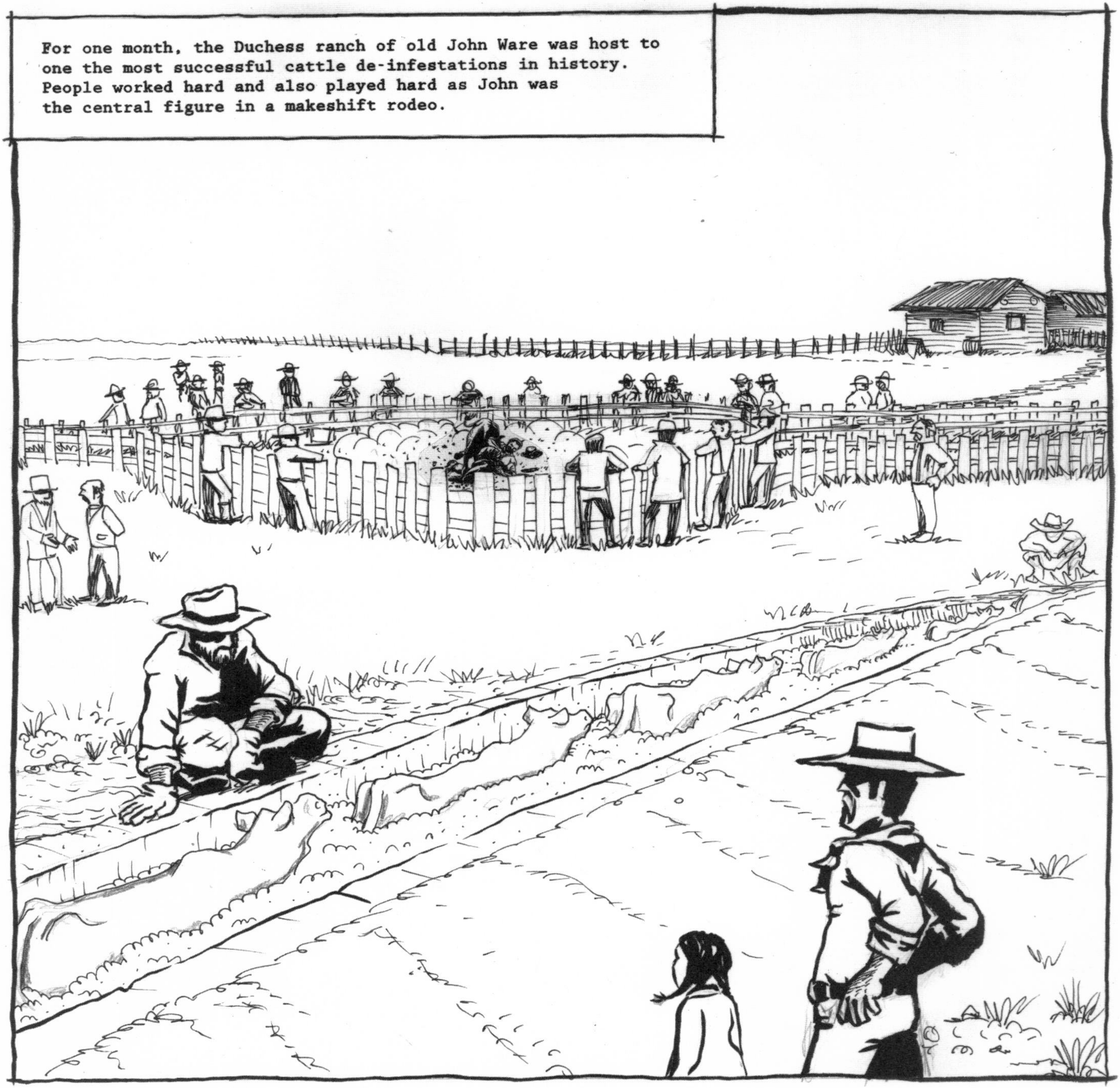
For one month, the Duchess ranch of old John Ware was host to one the most successful cattle de-infestations in history. People worked hard and also played hard as John was the central figure in a makeshift rodeo.

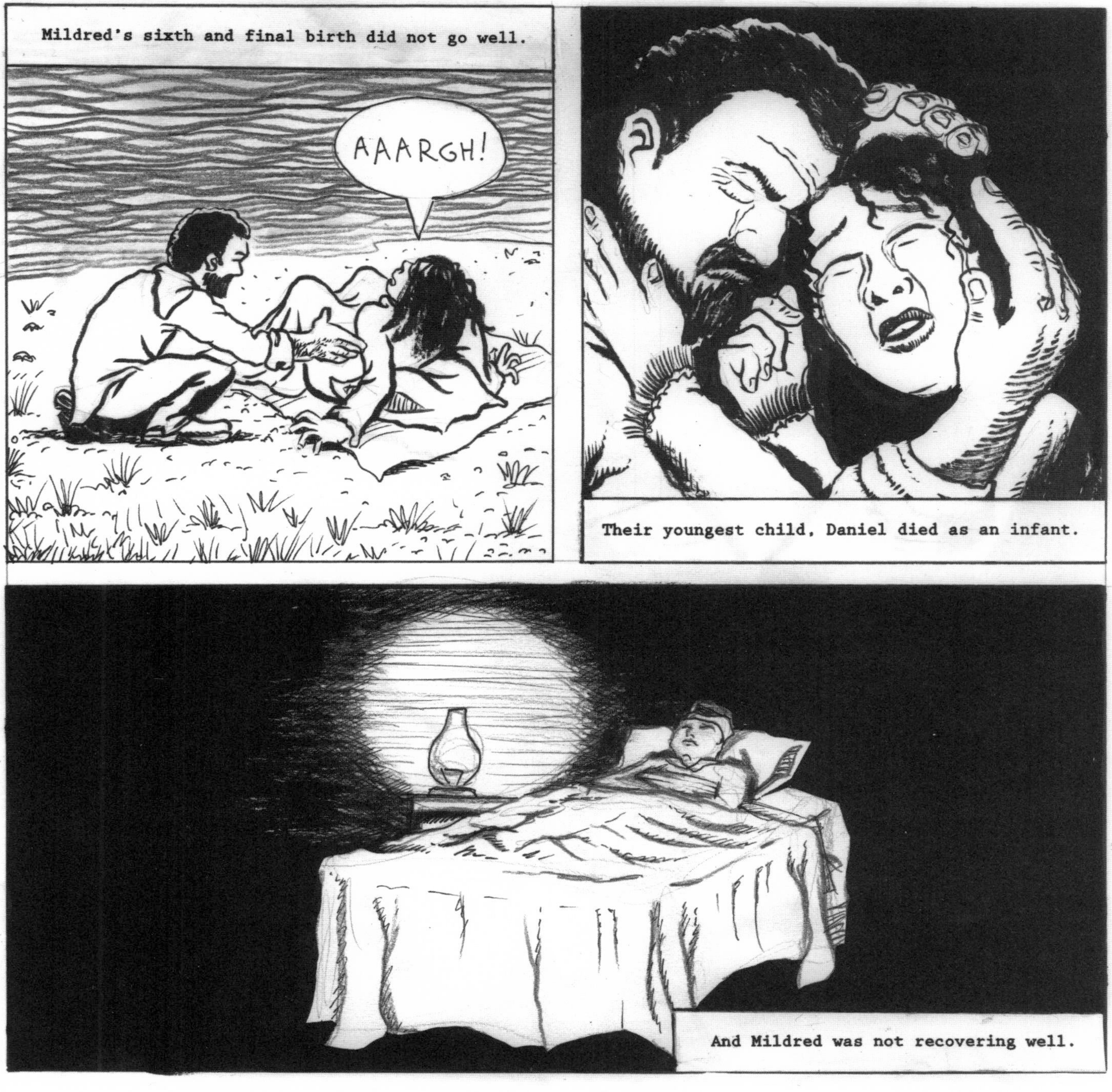
Mildred's sixth and final birth did not go well.
AAARGH!
Their youngest child, Daniel died as an infant.
And Mildred was not recovering well.

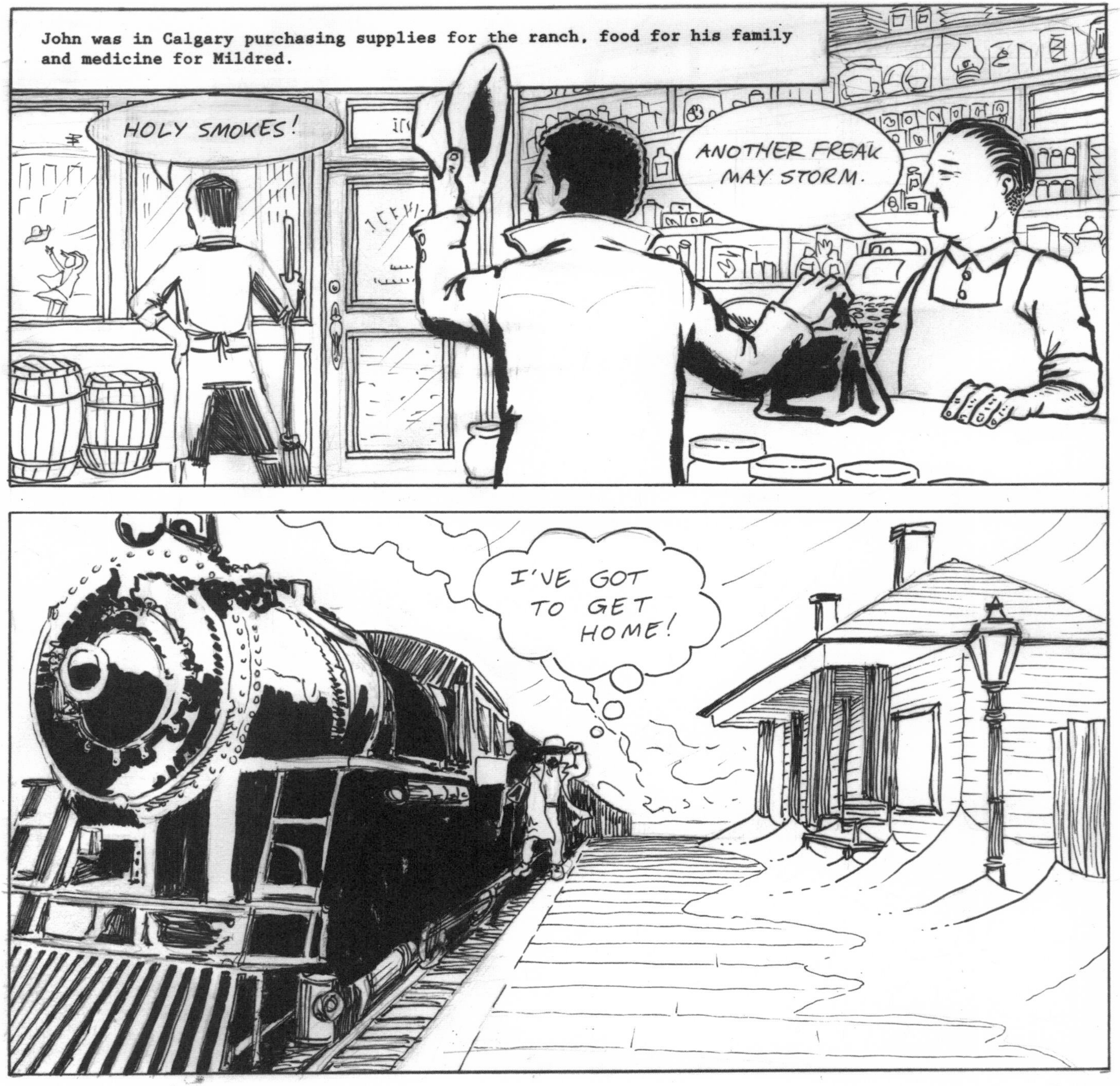
John was in Calgary purchasing supplies for the ranch, food for his family and medicine for Mildred.
HOLY SMOKES!
ANOTHER FREAK MAY STORM.
I'VE GOT TO GET HOME!

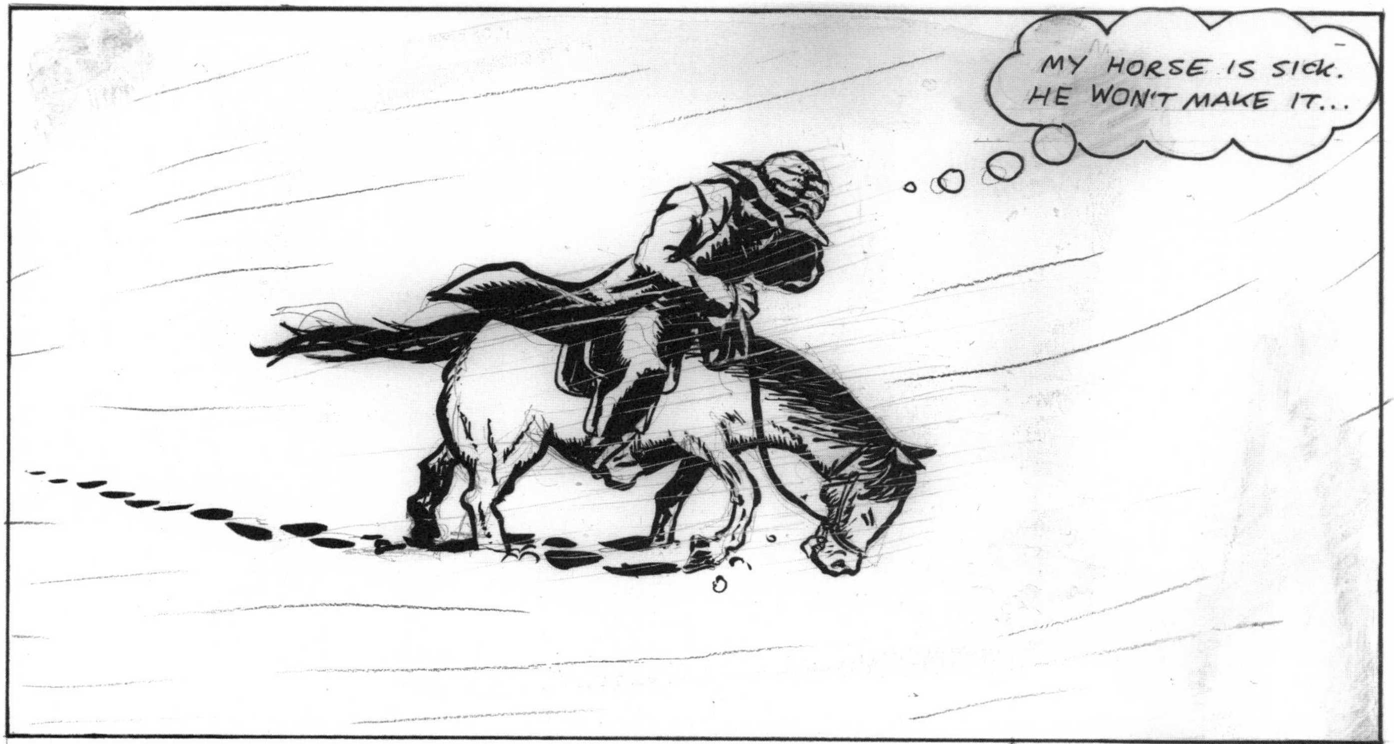
MY HORSE IS SICK. HE WON'T MAKE IT...

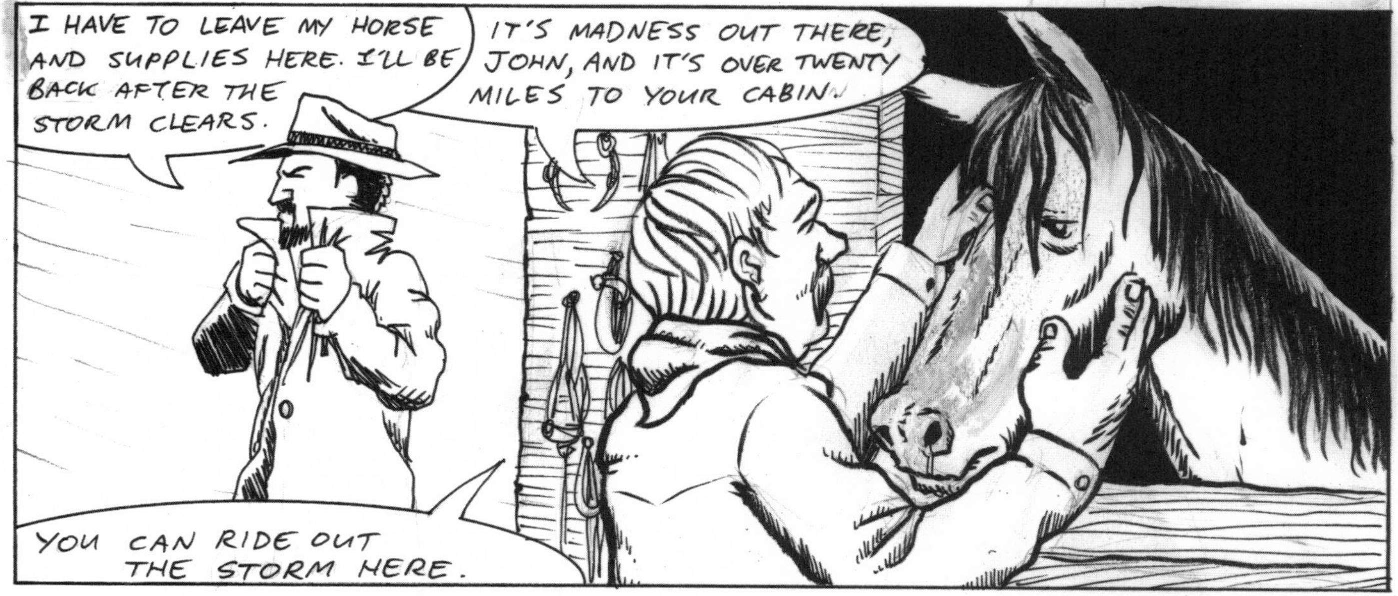
I HAVE TO LEAVE MY HORSE AND SUPPLIES HERE. I'LL BE BACK AFTER THE STORM CLEARS.
IT'S MADNESS OUT THERE, JOHN, AND IT'S OVER TWENTY MILES TO YOUR CABIN..
YOU CAN RIDE OUT THE STORM HERE.

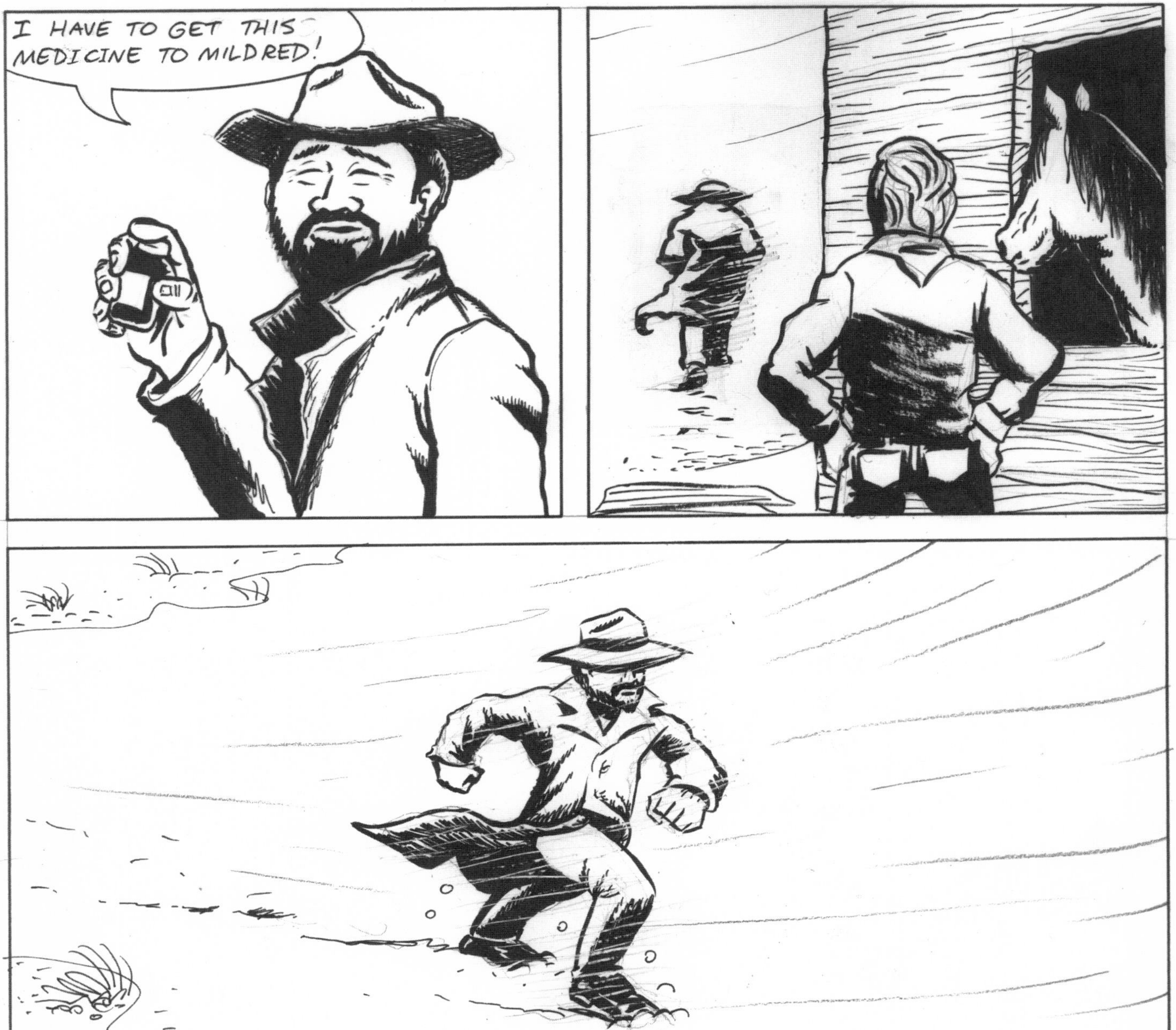
I HAVE TO GET THIS MEDICINE TO MILDRED!

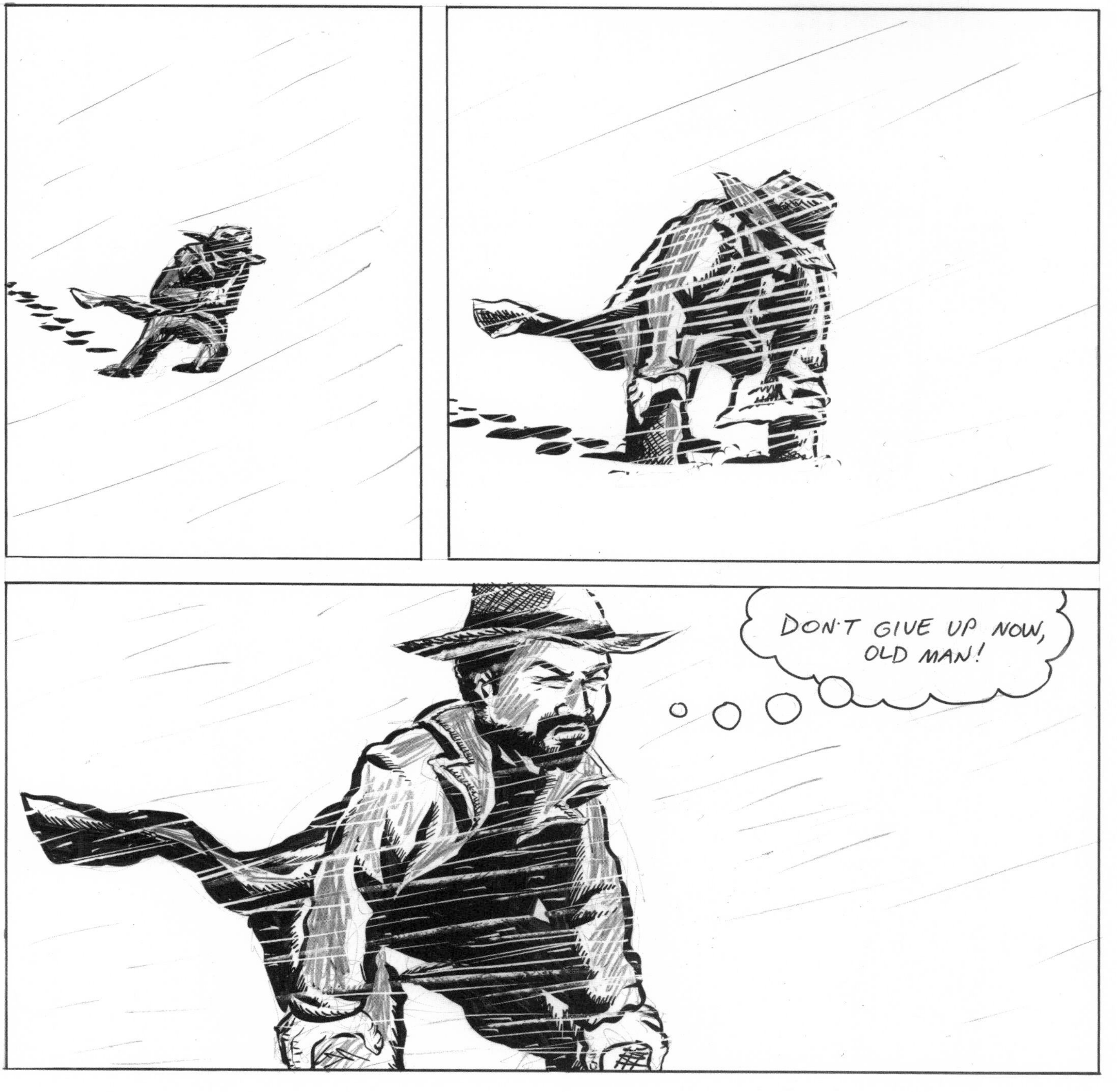
DON'T GIVE UP NOW, OLD MAN!

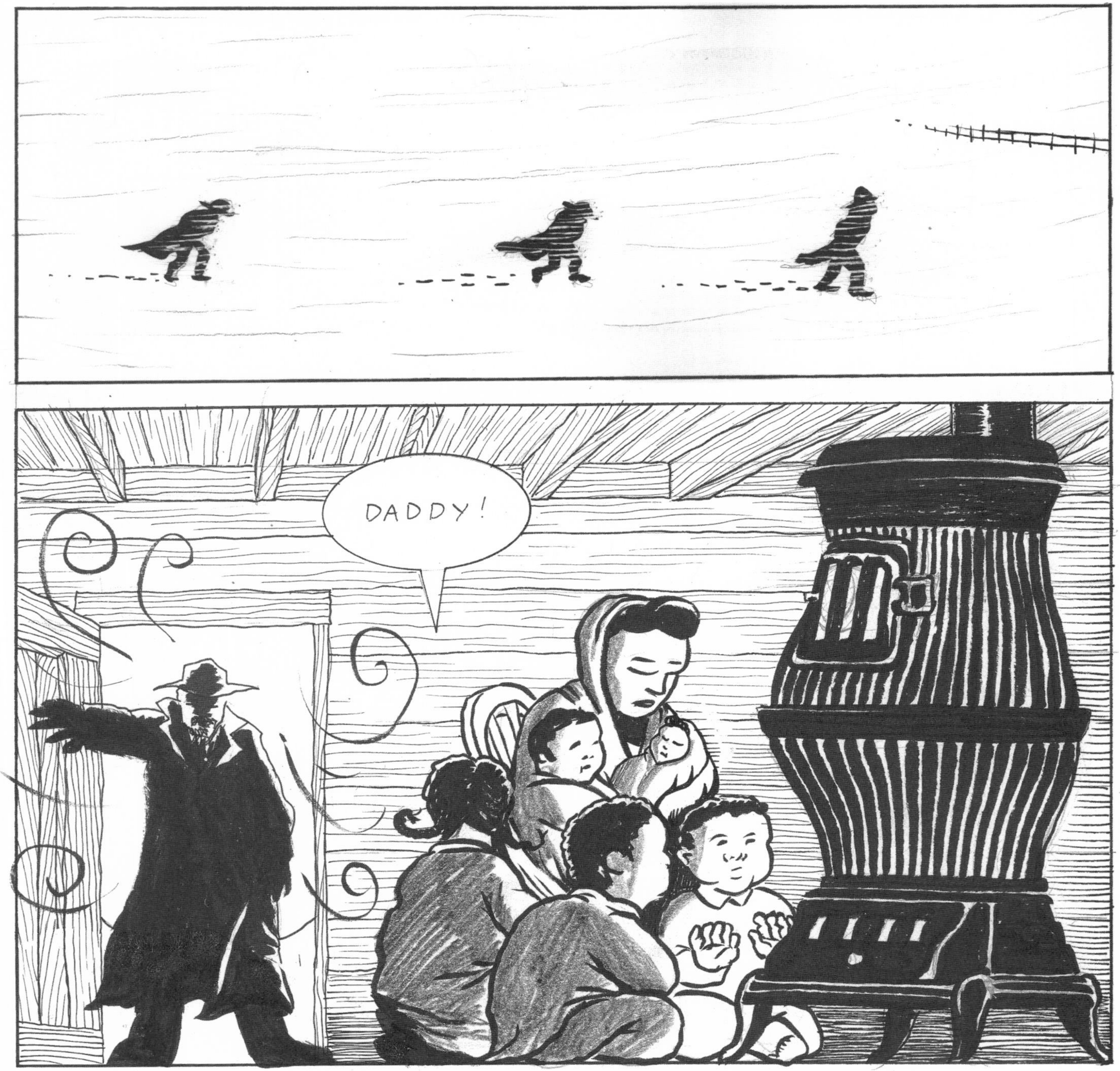
DADDY!

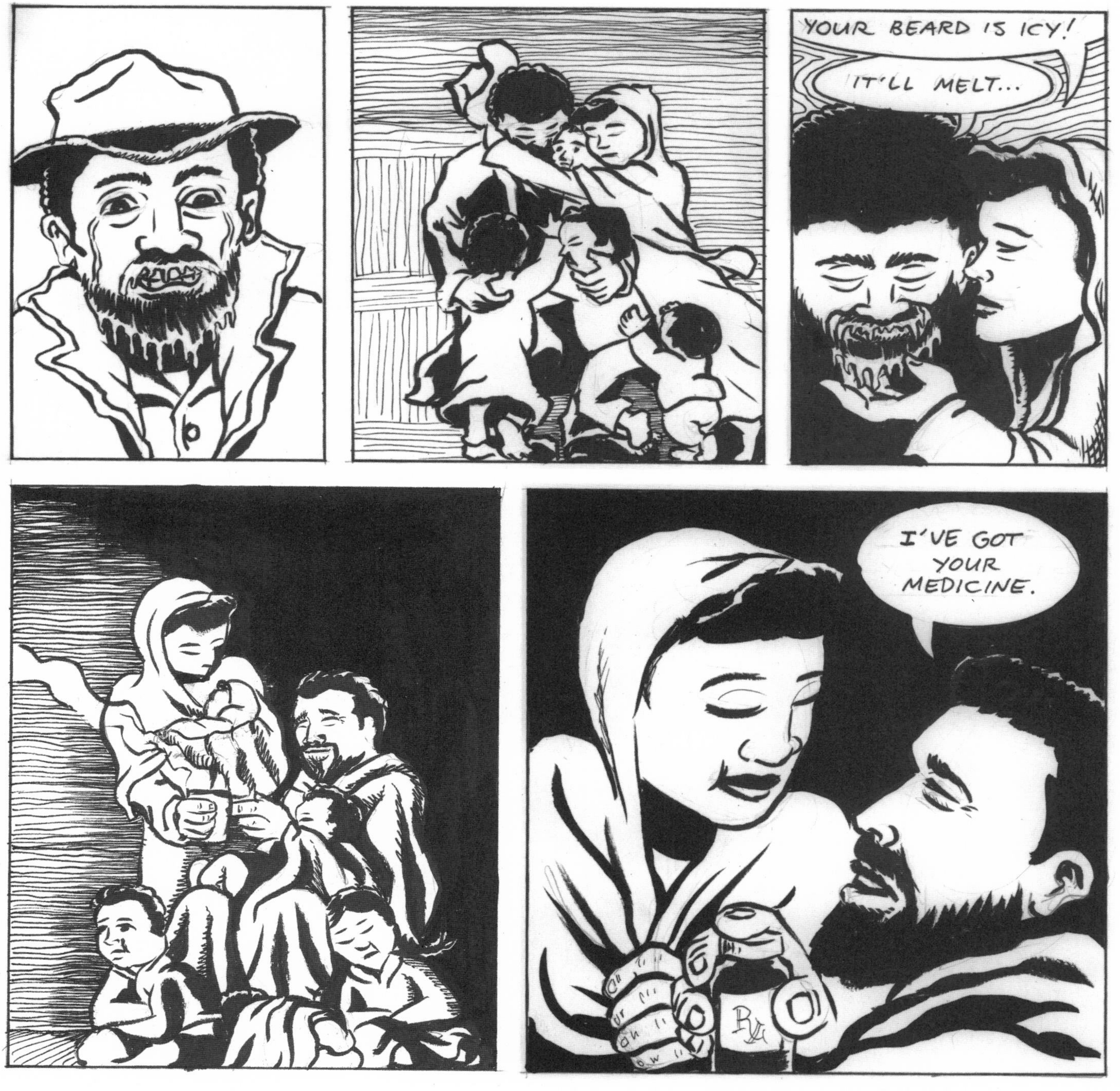
YOUR BEARD IS ICY!
IT'LL MELT...
I'VE GOT YOUR MEDICINE.

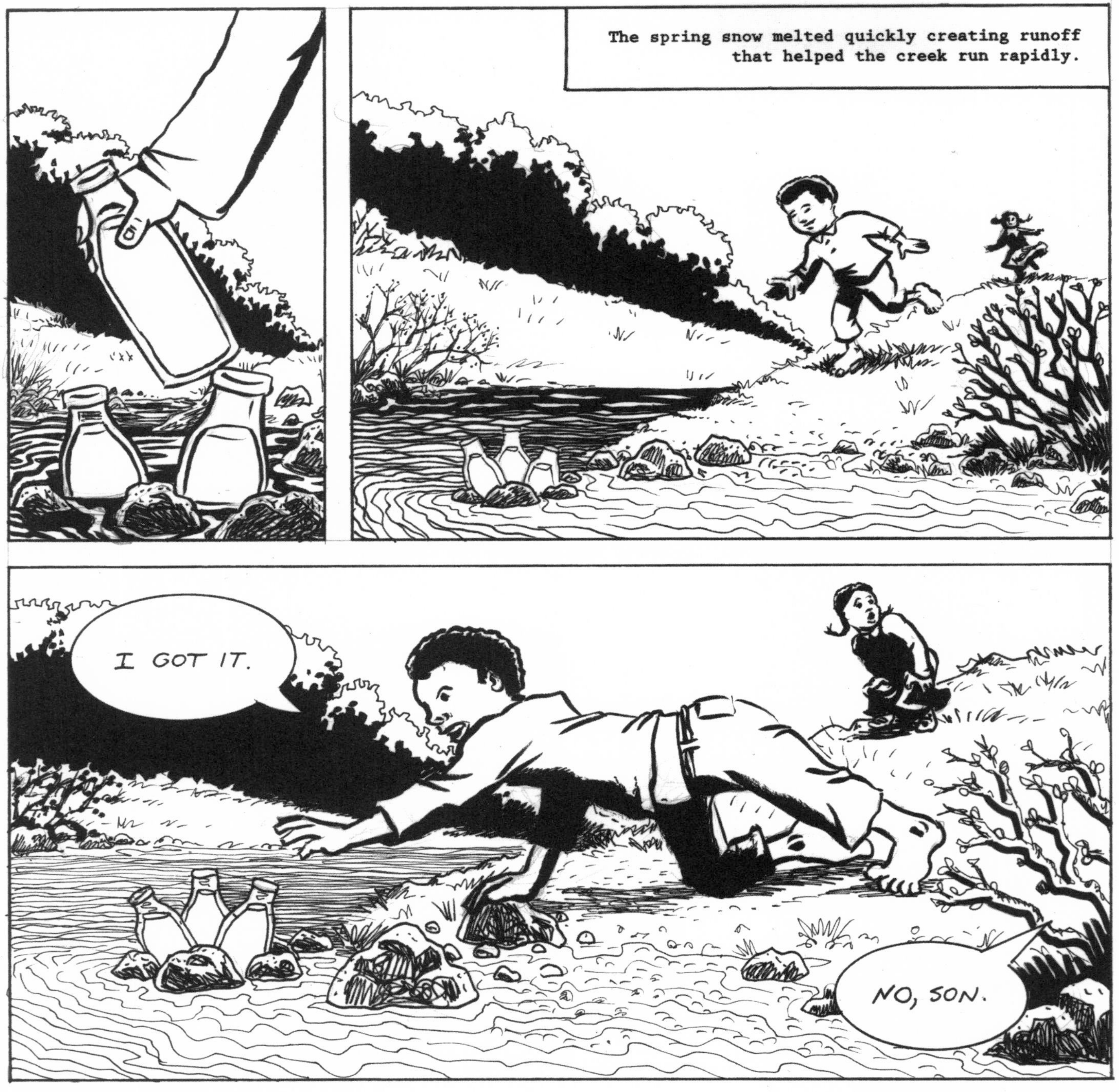
The spring snow melted quickly creating runoff that helped the creek run rapidly.
I GOT IT.
NO, SON.

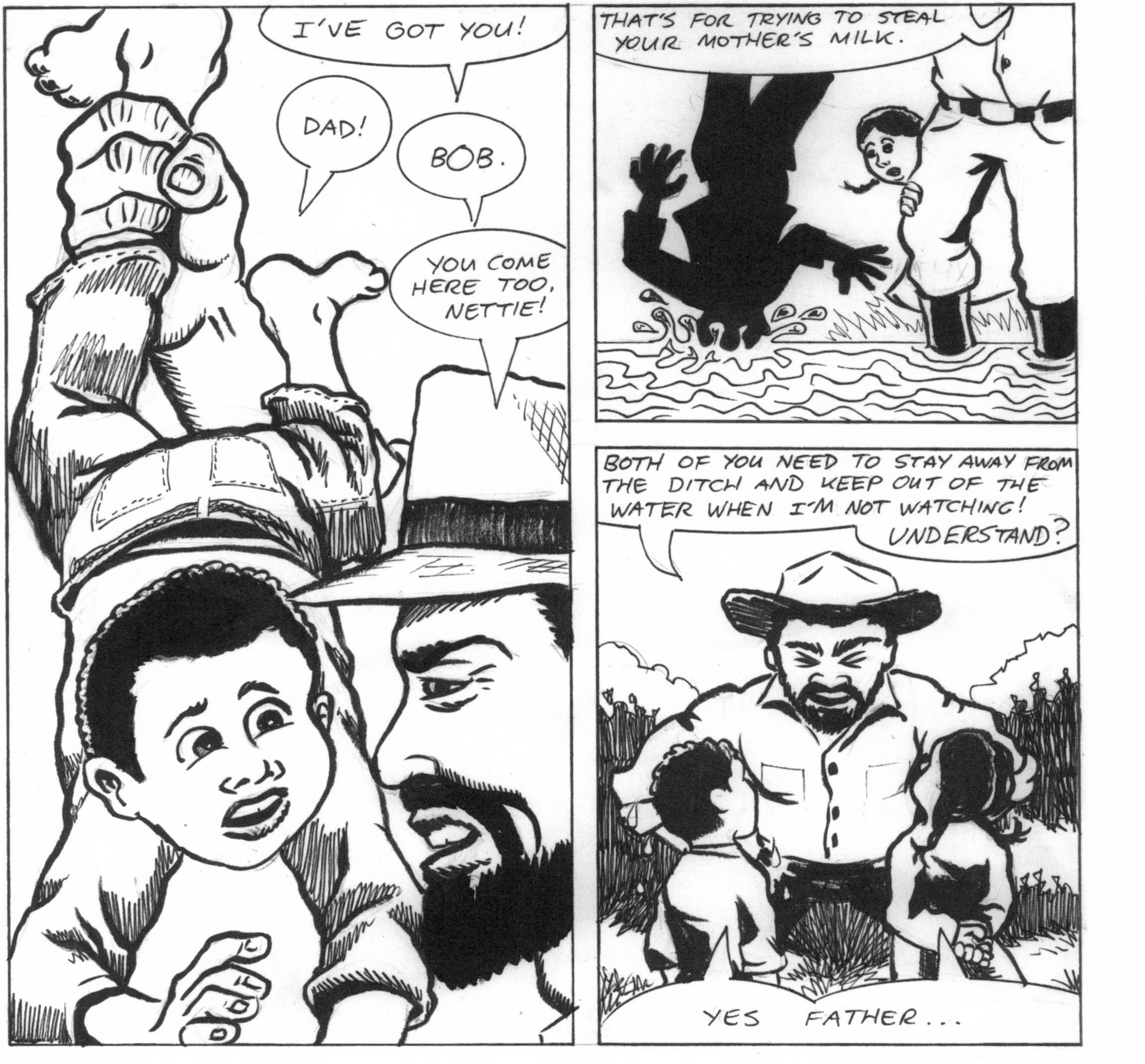
I'VE GOT YOU!
DAD!
BOB.
YOU COME HERE TOO, NETTIE!
THAT'S FOR TRYING TO STEAL YOUR MOTHER'S MILK.
BOTH OF YOU NEED TO STAY AWAY FROM THE DITCH AND KEEP OUT OF THE WATER WHEN I'M NOT WATCHING!
UNDERSTAND?
YES FATHER...

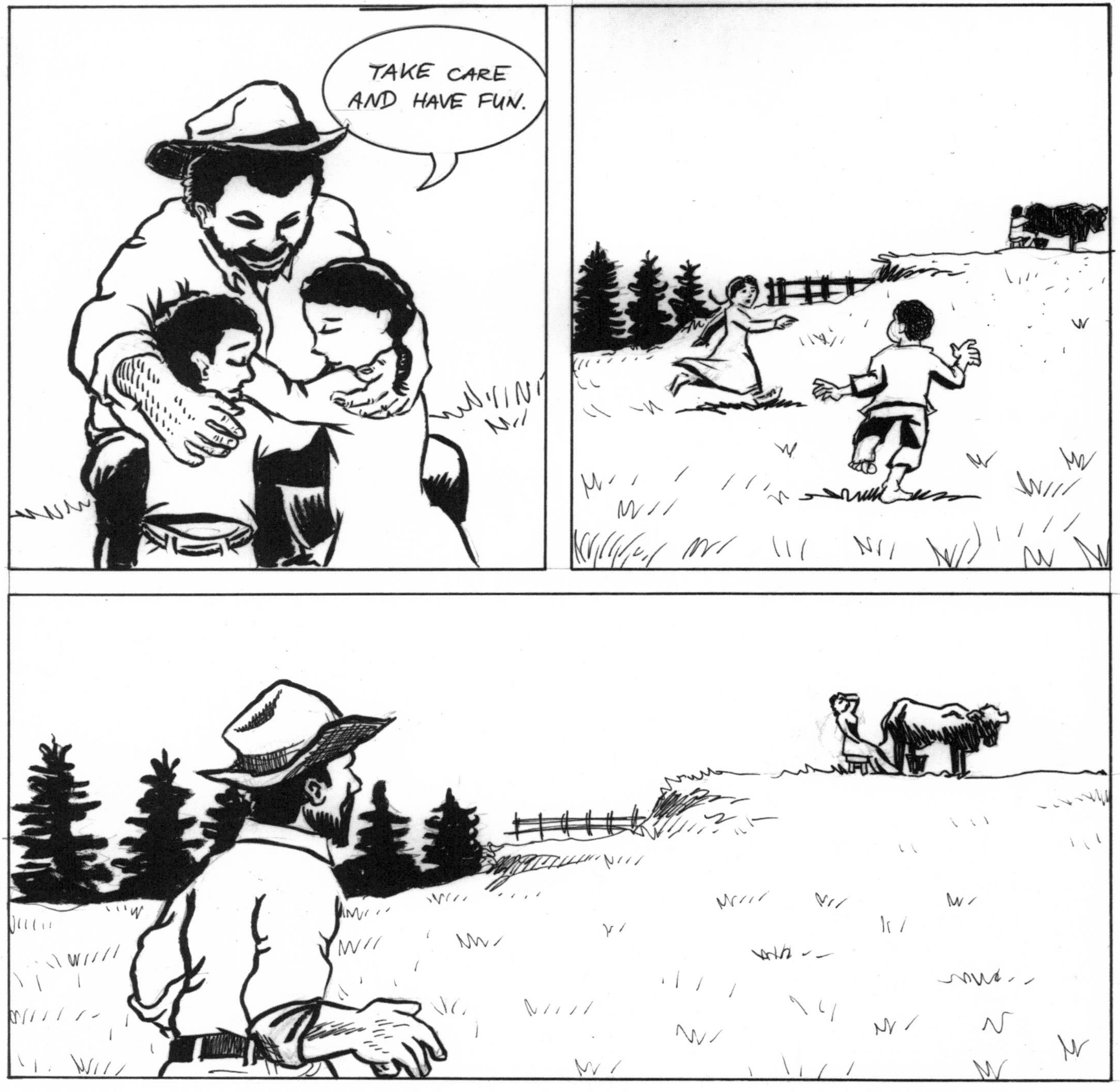
TAKE CARE AND HAVE FUN.

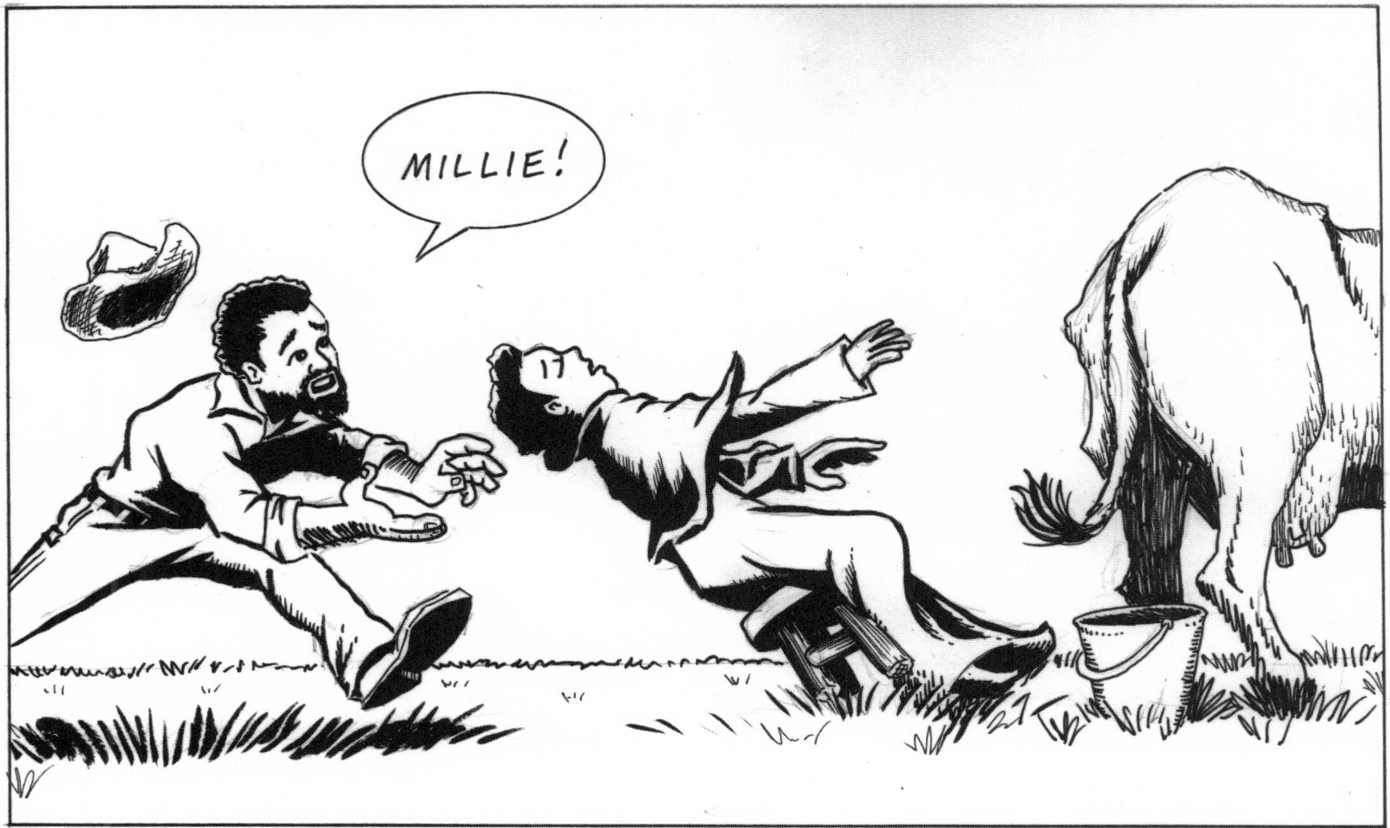
MILLIE!

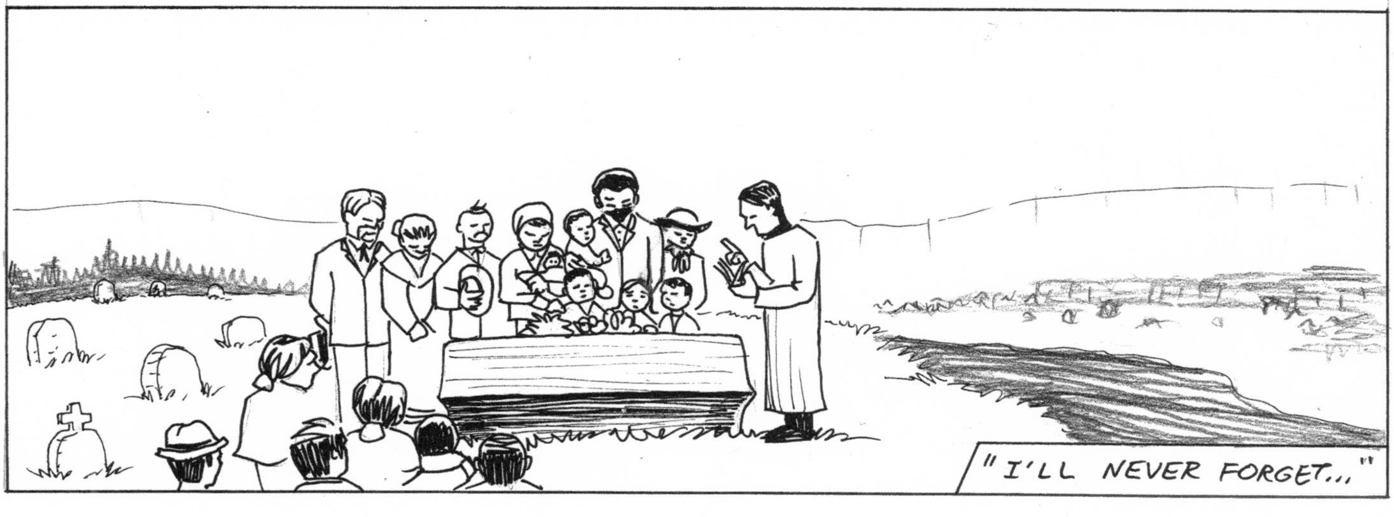
"I'LL NEVER FORGET..."

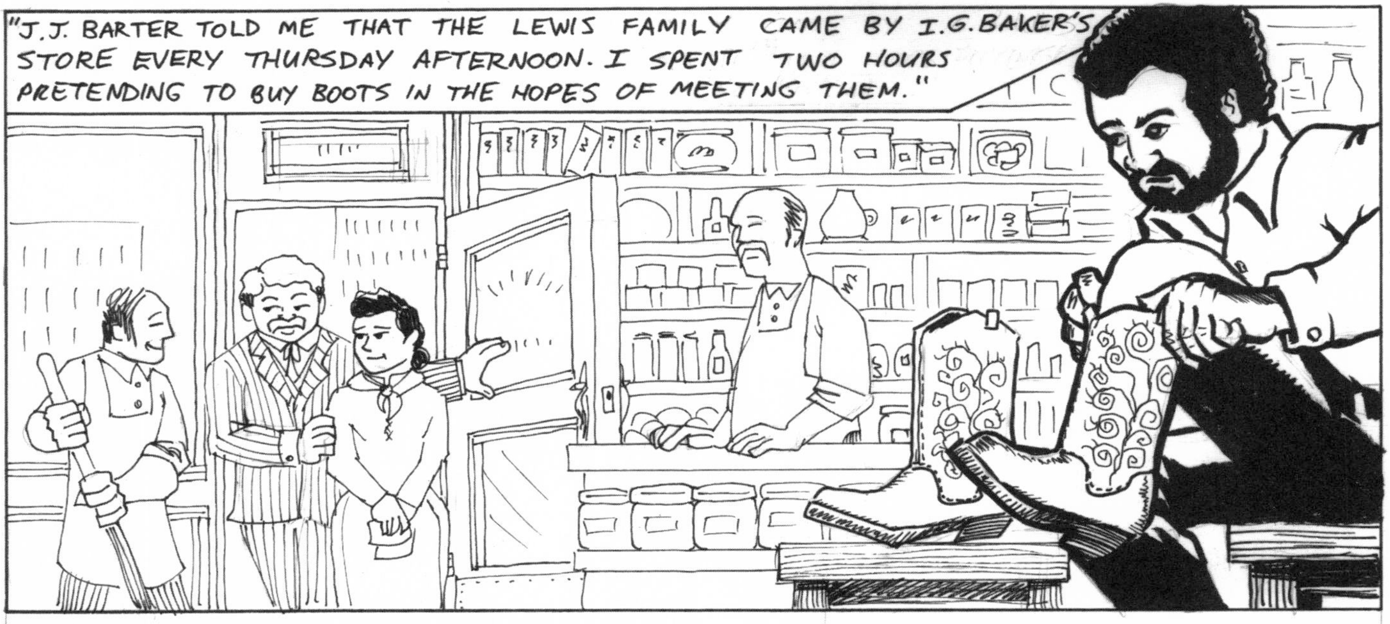
"J.J. BARTER TOLD ME THAT THE LEWIS FAMILY CAME BY I.G. BAKER'S STORE EVERY THURSDAY AFTERNOON. I SPENT TWO HOURS PRETENDING TO BUY BOOTS IN THE HOPES OF MEETING THEM."

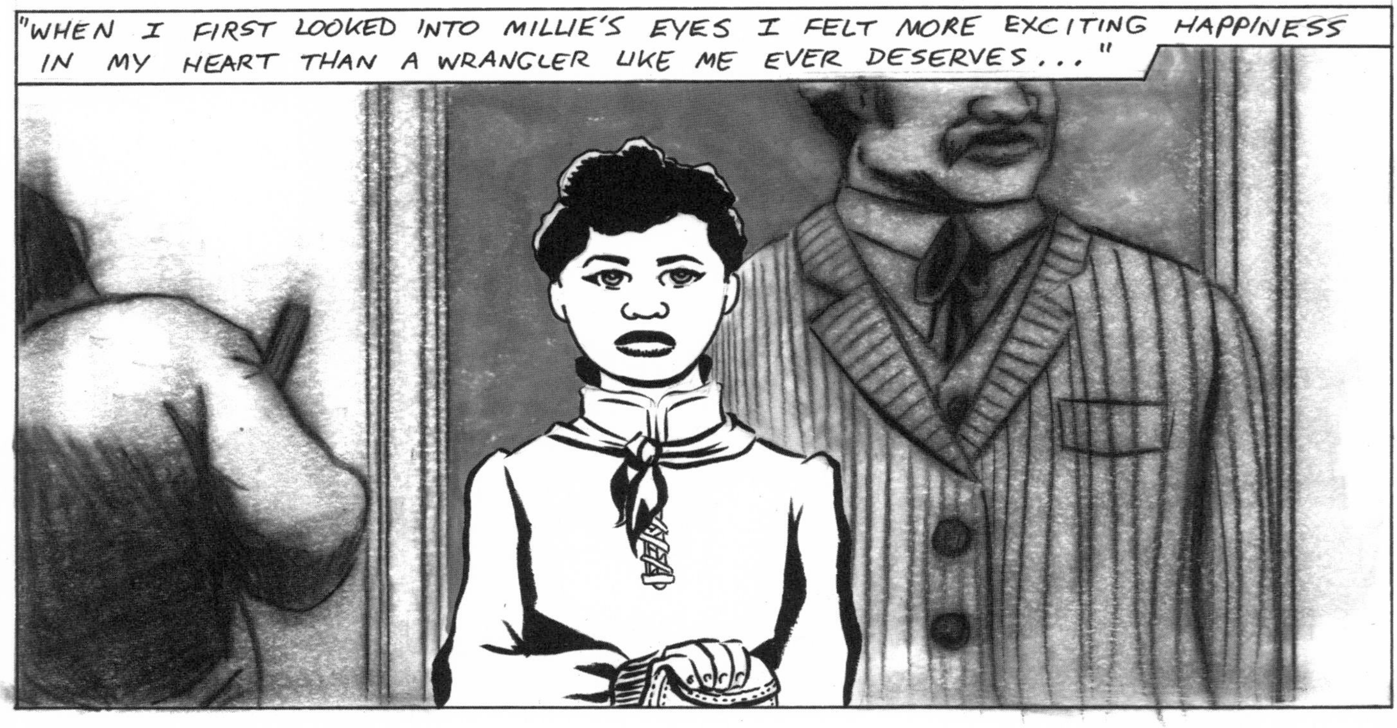
"WHEN I FIRST LOOKED INTO MILLIE'S EYES I FELT MORE EXCITING HAPPINESS IN MY HEART THAN A WRANGLER LIKE ME EVER DESERVES..."

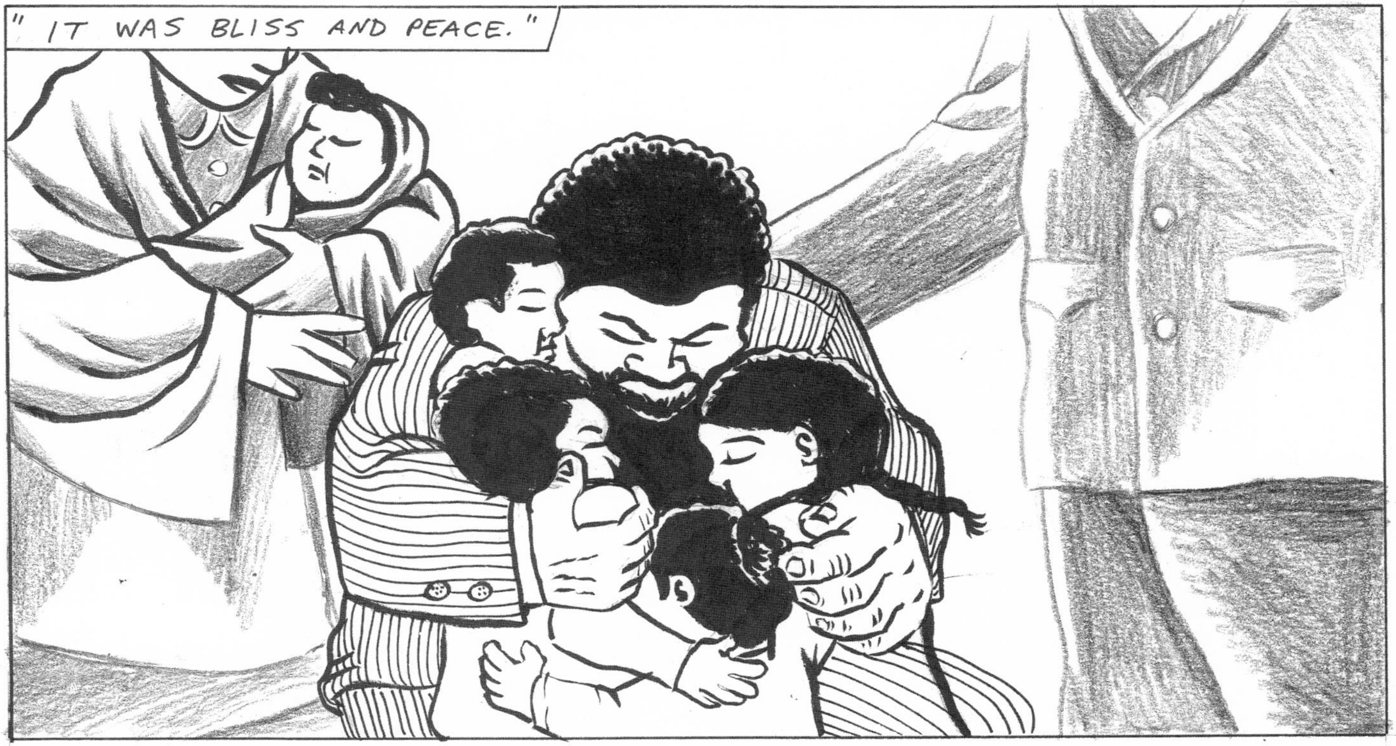
" IT WAS BLISS AND PEACE."

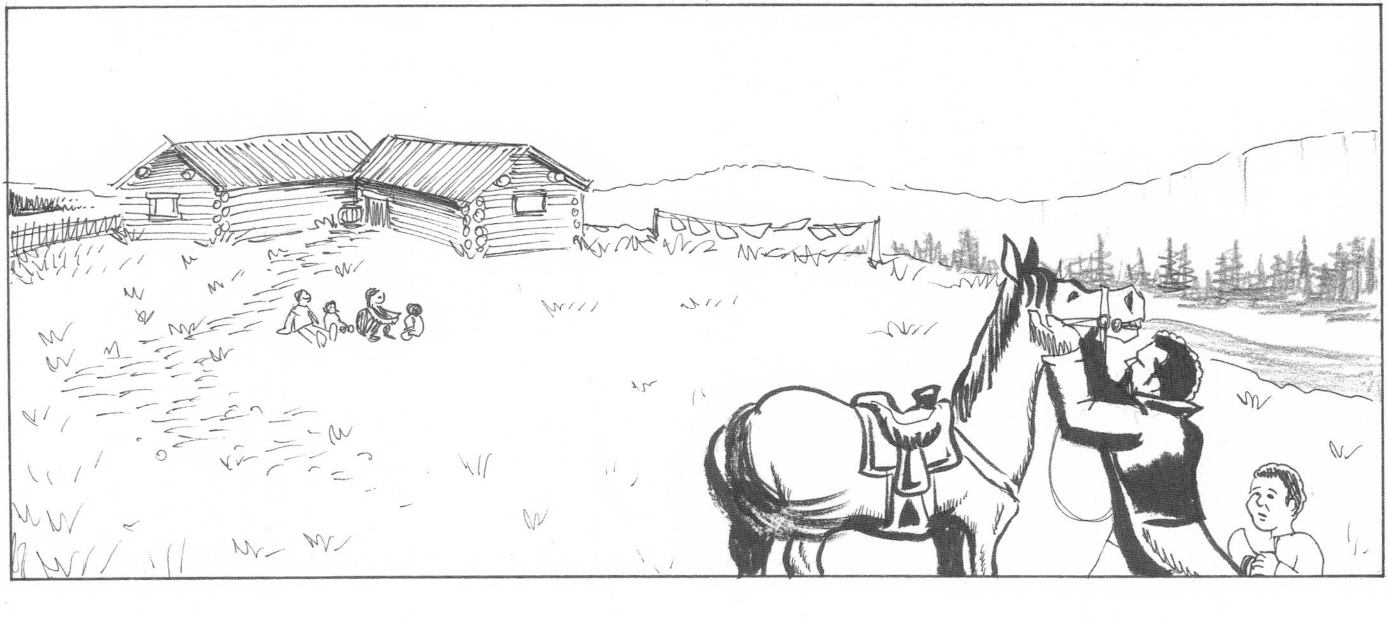

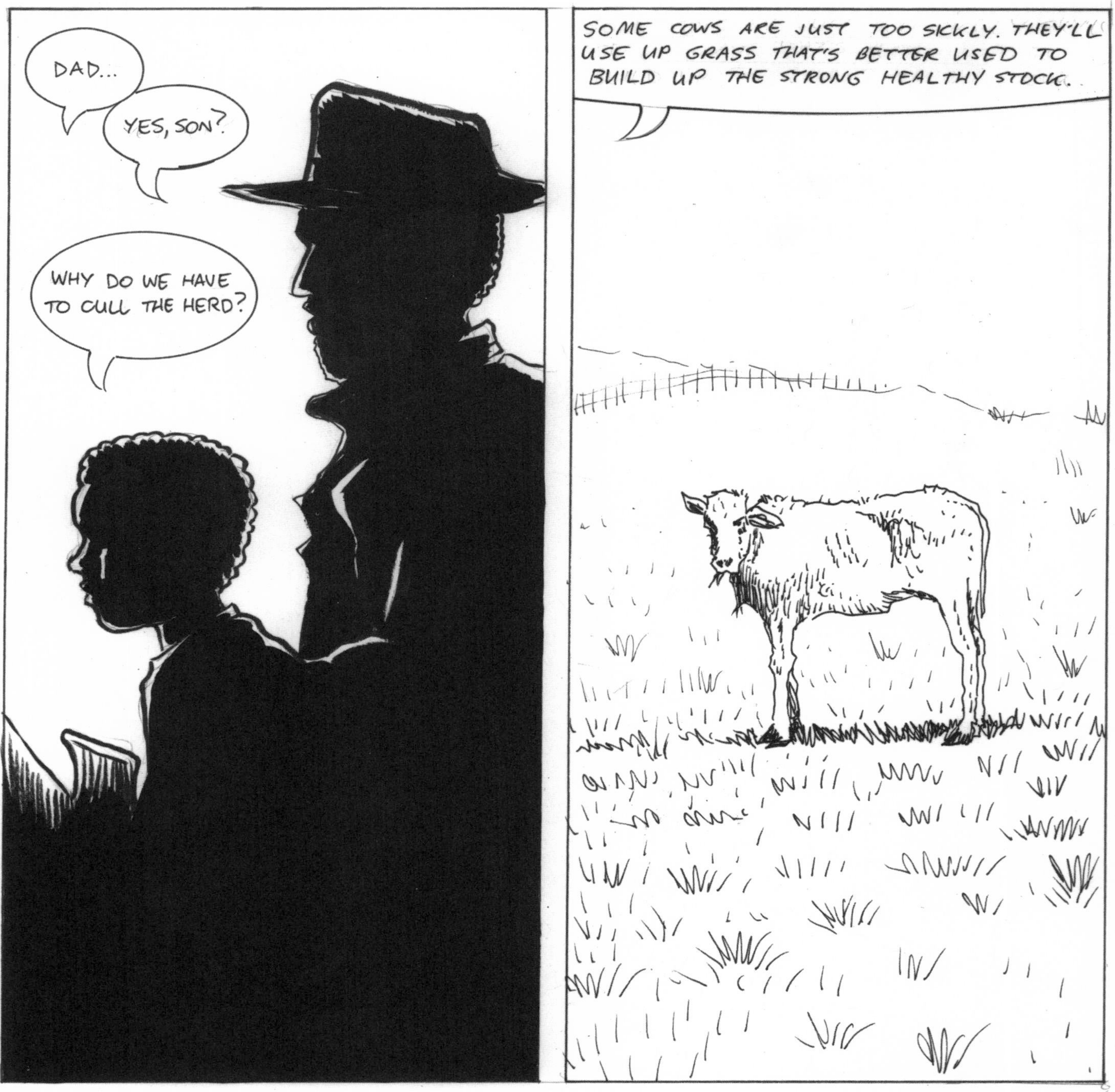
DAD...
YES, SON?
WHY DO WE HAVE TO CULL THE HERD?
SOME COWS ARE JUST TOO SICKLY. THEY'LL USE UP GRASS THAT'S BETTER USED TO BUILD UP THE STRONG HEALTHY STOCK.

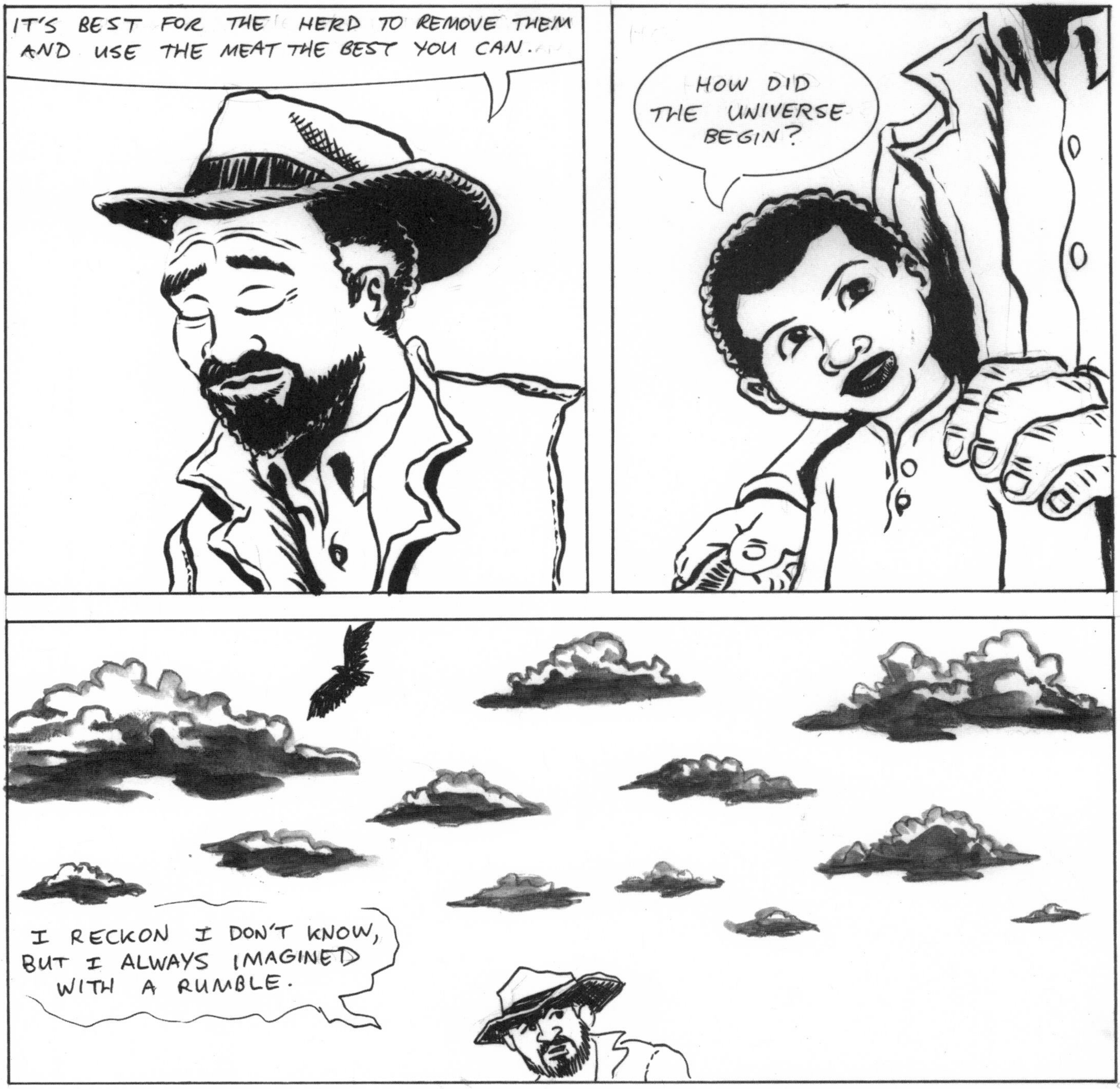
IT'S BEST FOR THE HERD TO REMOVE THEM AND USE THE MEAT THE BEST YOU CAN.
HOW DID THE UNIVERSE BEGIN?
I RECKON I DON'T KNOW, BUT I ALWAYS IMAGINED WITH A RUMBLE.

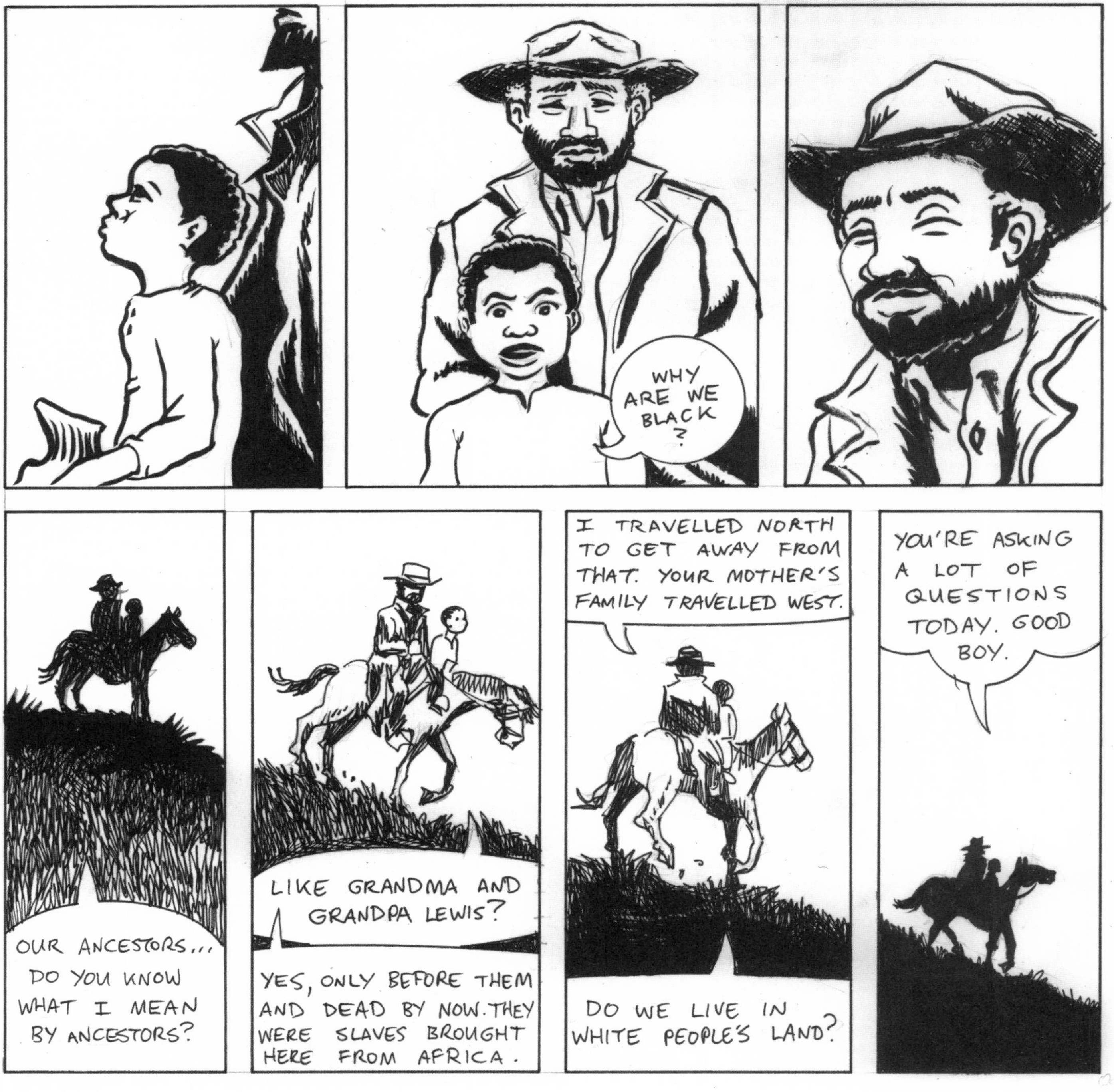
WHY ARE WE BLACK?
OUR ANCESTORS... DO YOU KNOW WHAT I MEAN BY ANCESTORS?
LIKE GRANDMA AND GRANDPA LEWIS?
YES, ONLY BEFORE THEM AND DEAD BY NOW. THEY WERE SLAVES BROUGHT HERE FROM AFRICA.
DO WE LIVE IN WHITE PEOPLE'S LAND?
I TRAVELLED NORTH TO GET AWAY FROM THAT. YOUR MOTHER'S FAMILY TRAVELLED WEST.
YOU'RE ASKING A LOT OF QUESTIONS TODAY. GOOD BOY.

A FEW HUNDRED YEARS AGO, THEY CAME FROM EUROPE AND BROUGHT US ALONG FOR THE RIDE. THE BLACKFOOT WERE THE FIRST PEOPLE TO WALK FREE IN THIS LAND. NOW, ANY PERSON CAN OWN LAND BUT THEY HAVE TO BUY IT.

ARE THE BLACKFOOT THE PEOPLE WHO LIVE IN THE FENCED UP TEEPEES THAT YOU SOMETIMES TRADE WITH?

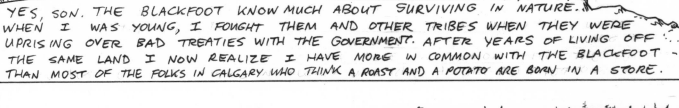

YES, SON. THE BLACKFOOT KNOW MUCH ABOUT SURVIVING IN NATURE. WHEN I WAS YOUNG, I FOUGHT THEM AND OTHER TRIBES WHEN THEY WERE UPRISING OVER BAD TREATIES WITH THE GOVERNMENT. AFTER YEARS OF LIVING OFF THE SAME LAND I NOW REALIZE I HAVE MORE IN COMMON WITH THE BLACKFOOT THAN MOST OF THE FOLKS IN CALGARY WHO THINK A ROAST AND A POTATO ARE BORN IN A STORE.

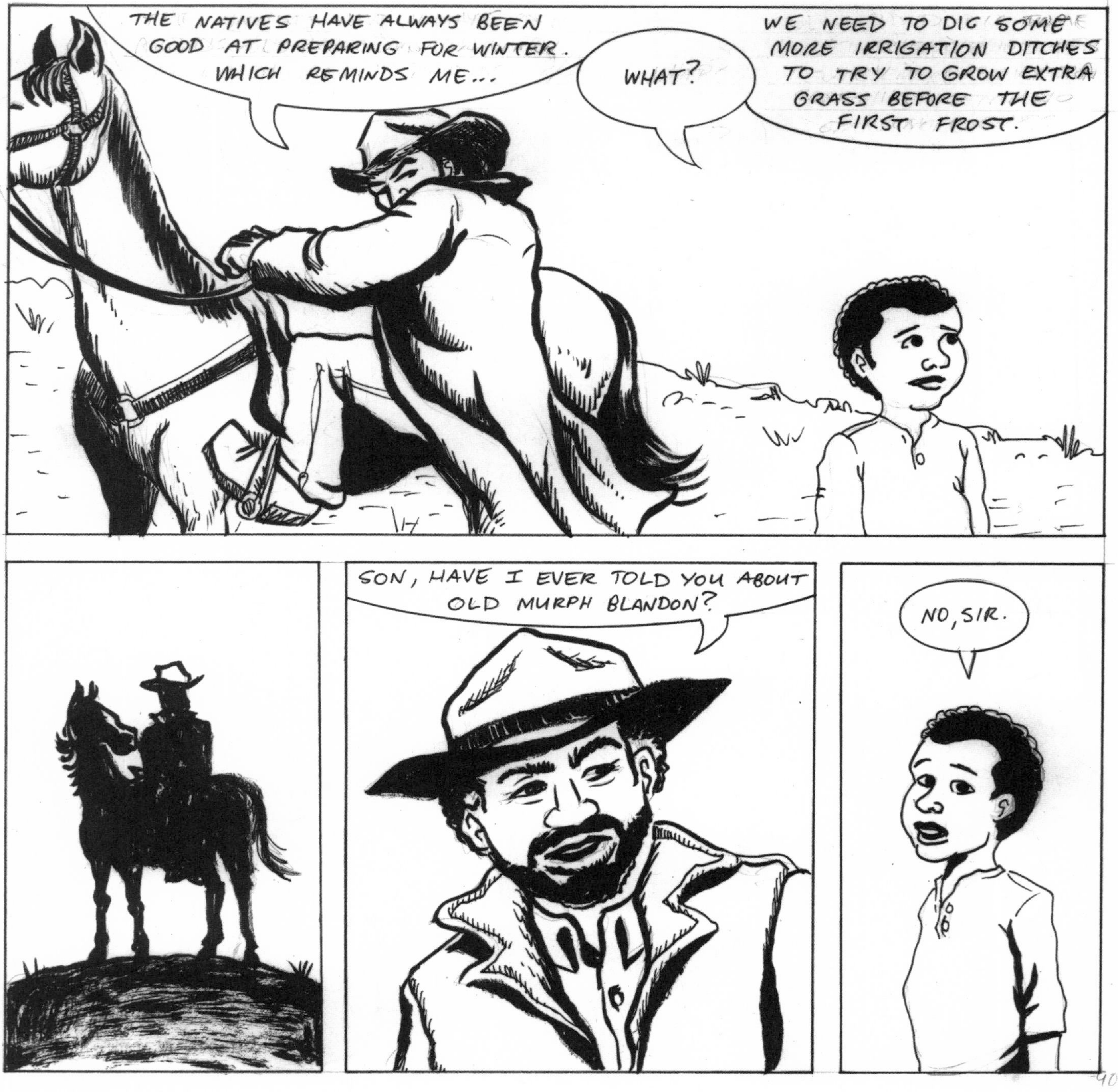
THE NATIVES HAVE ALWAYS BEEN GOOD AT PREPARING FOR WINTER. WHICH REMINDS ME...
WHAT?
WE NEED TO DIG SOME MORE IRRIGATION DITCHES TO TRY TO GROW EXTRA GRASS BEFORE THE FIRST FROST.
SON, HAVE I EVER TOLD YOU ABOUT OLD MURPH BLANDON?
NO, SIR.

"I WORKED FOR OLD MURPH FOR OVER TEN YEARS IN FORT WORTH, TEXAS. ASIDE FROM SLAVEMASTER CHAUNCEY, HE WAS THE LONGEST BOSS I EVER WORKED FOR. AND I CHOSE TO WORK FOR HIM.

HE WAS A GOOD MAN.

I LEARNT MANY THINGS FROM HIM IN THE DECADE BEFORE I STARTED ON MY FIRST DRIVE...

"AND AS I LEFT HE GAVE ME SOME IMPORTANT WORDS..."

THE FRONTIER IS HARD ON ANY MAN, JOHN. IF YOU FIND YOURSELF MISJUDGED, AND YOU WILL, YOU CAN'T GET ANGRY,

YOU'LL JUST HAVE TO PROVE THEM WRONG AND BE BETTER THAN MOST OF 'EM.

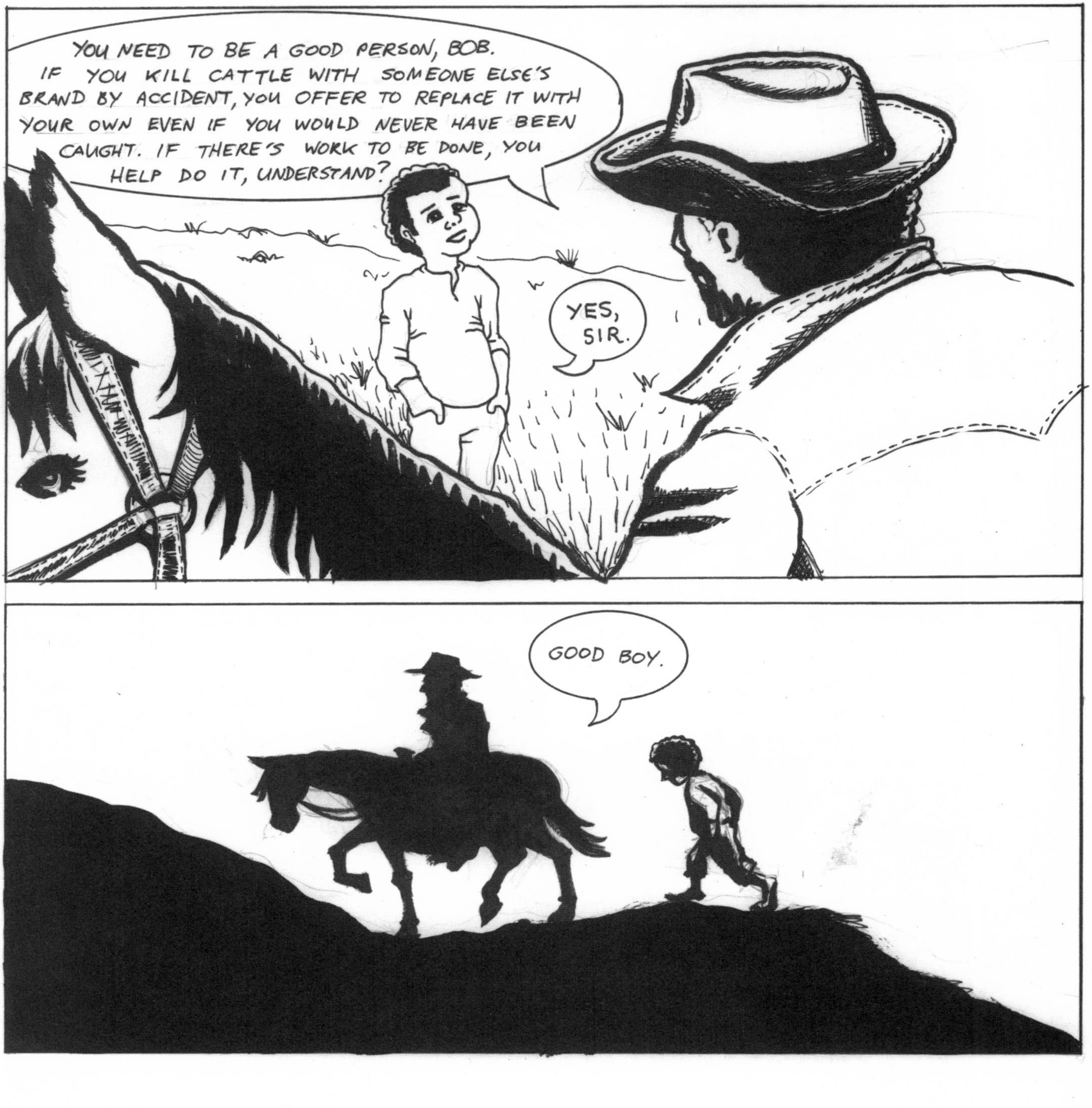
YOU NEED TO BE A GOOD PERSON, BOB. IF YOU KILL CATTLE WITH SOMEONE ELSE'S BRAND BY ACCIDENT, YOU OFFER TO REPLACE IT WITH YOUR OWN EVEN IF YOU WOULD NEVER HAVE BEEN CAUGHT. IF THERE'S WORK TO BE DONE, YOU HELP DO IT, UNDERSTAND?
YES, SIR.
GOOD BOY.

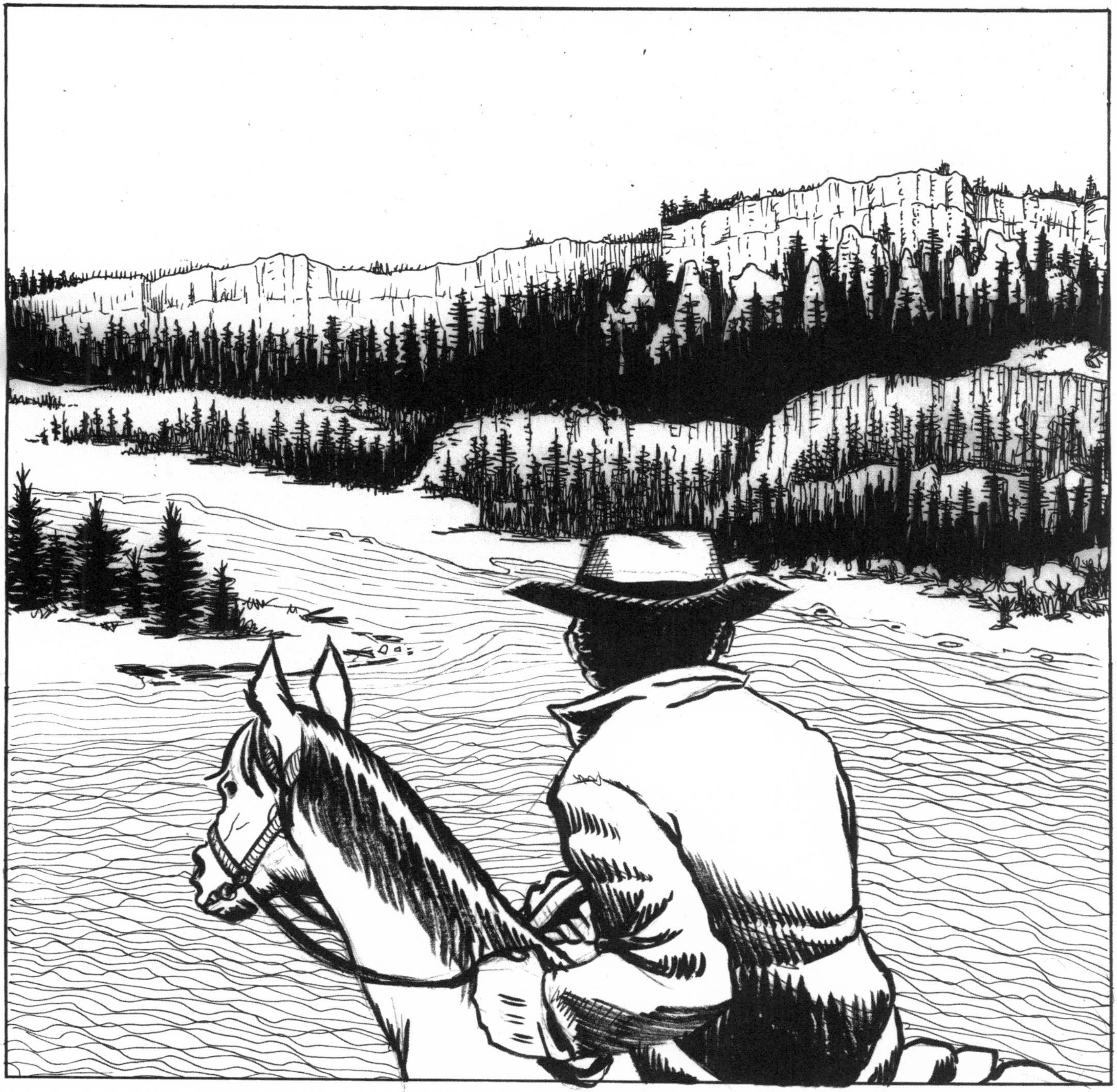

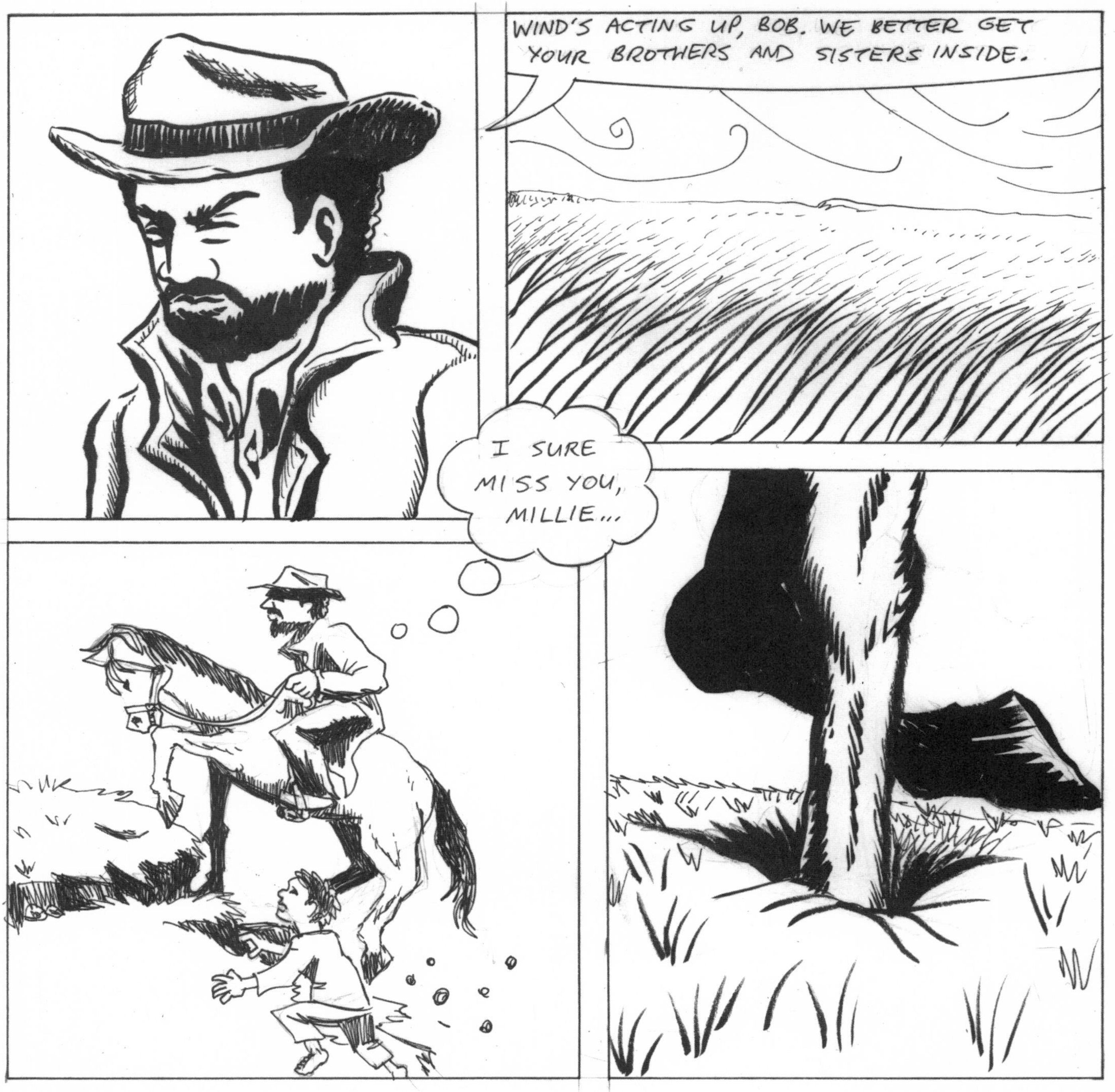

WIND'S ACTING UP, BOB. WE BETTER GET YOUR BROTHERS AND SISTERS INSIDE.
I SURE MISS YOU, MILLIE...

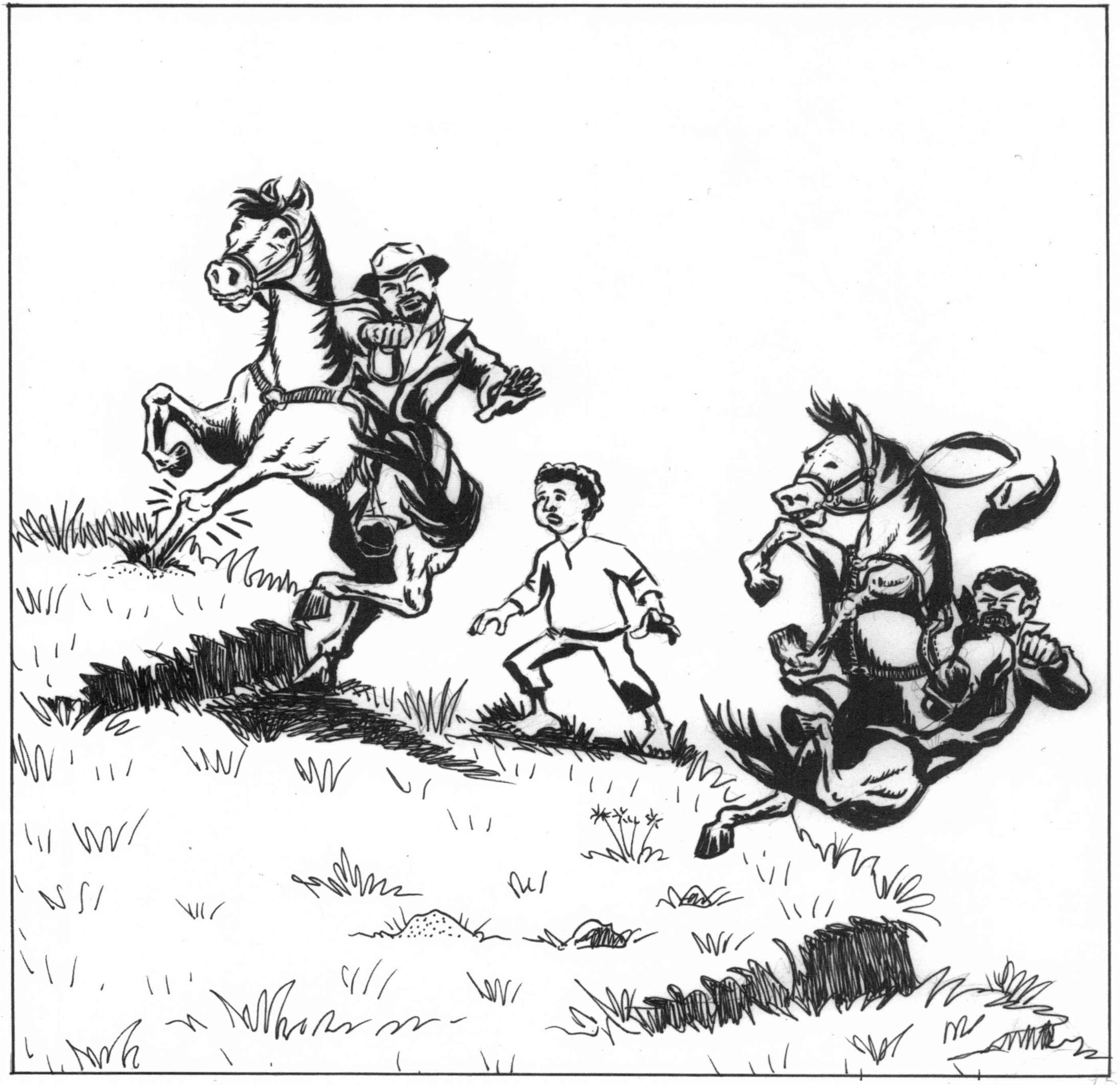

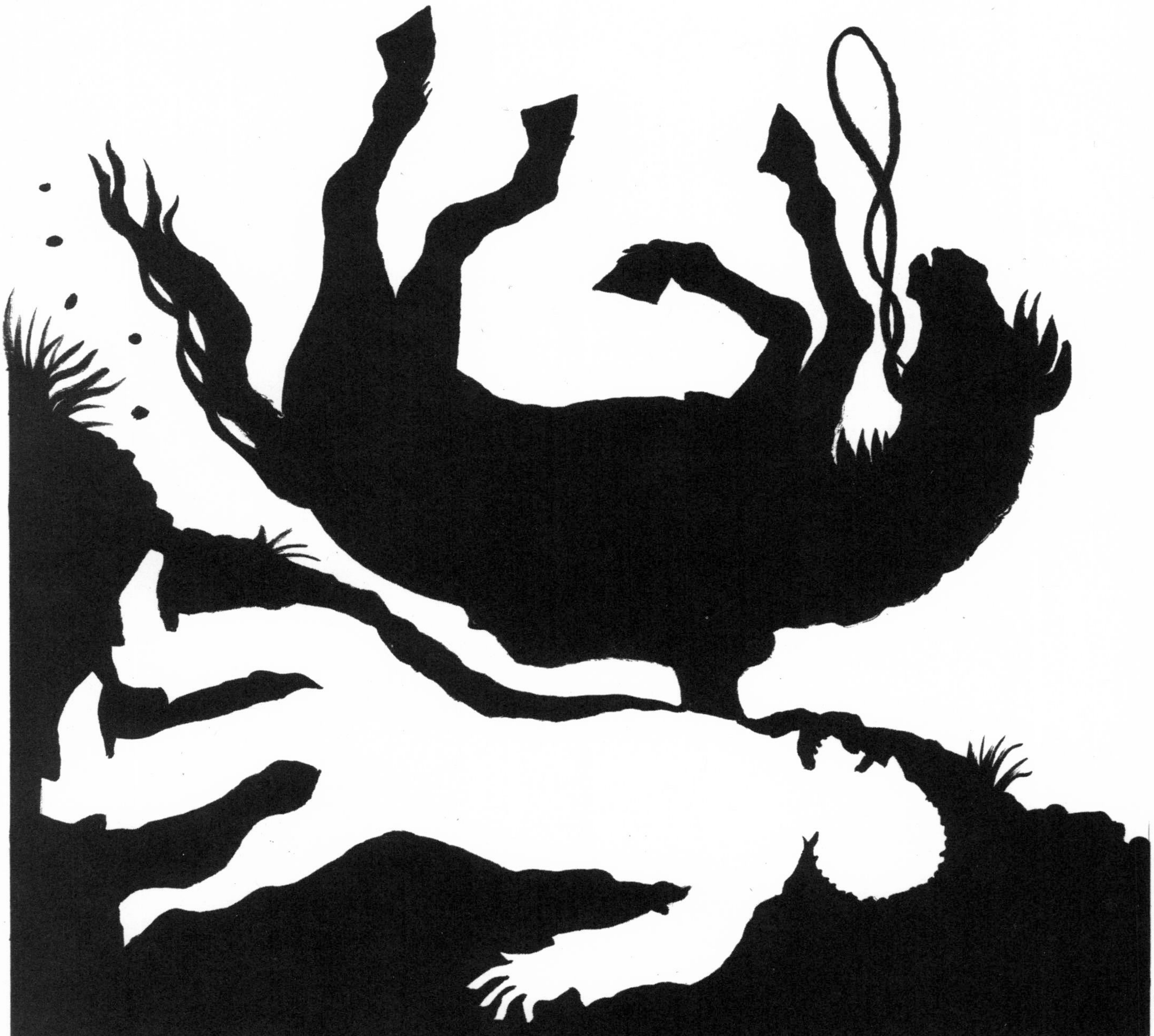

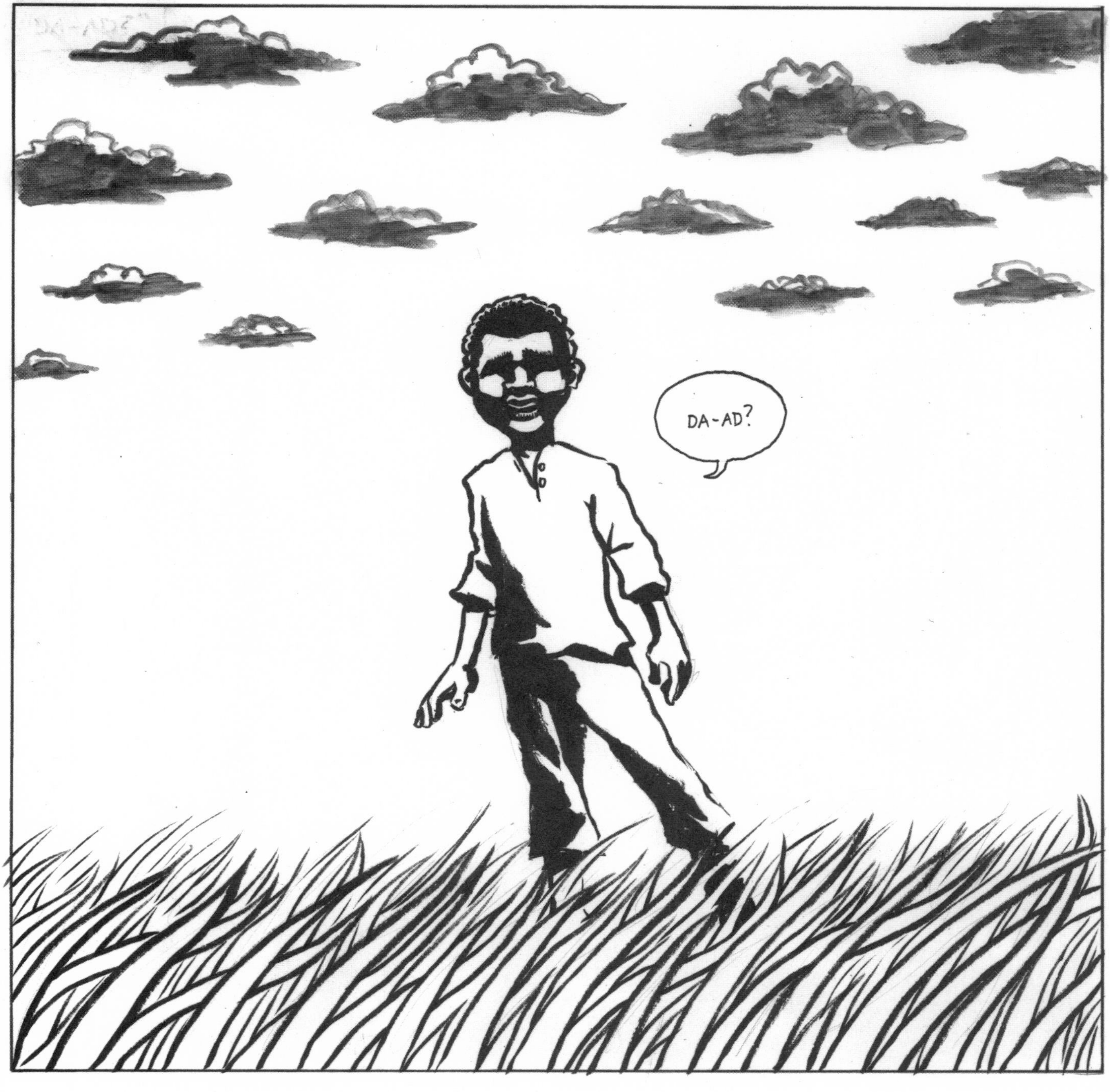
DA-AD?

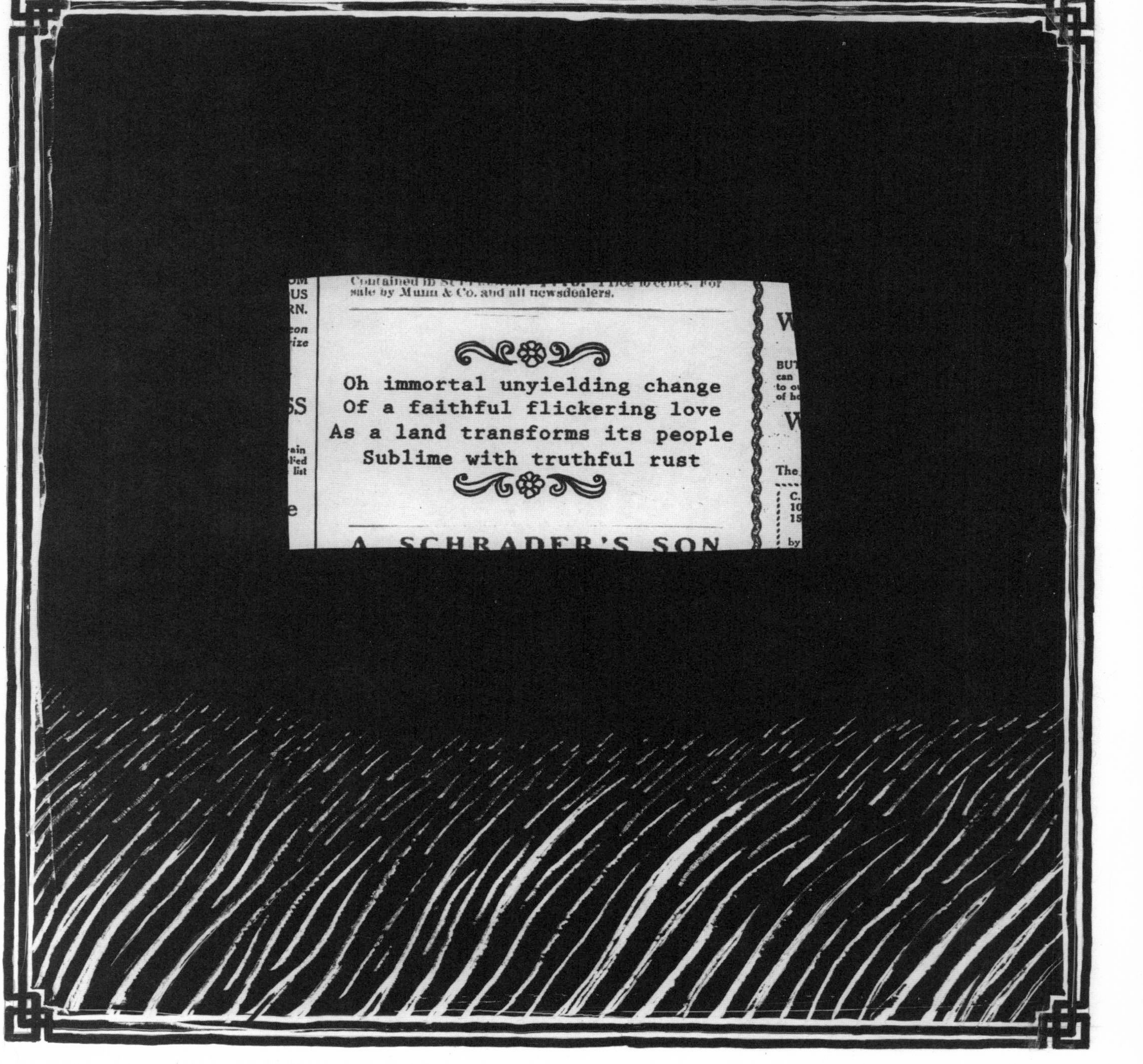

Oh immortal unyielding change
Of a faithful flickering love
As a land transforms its people
Sublime with truthful rust
A. SCHRADER'S SON

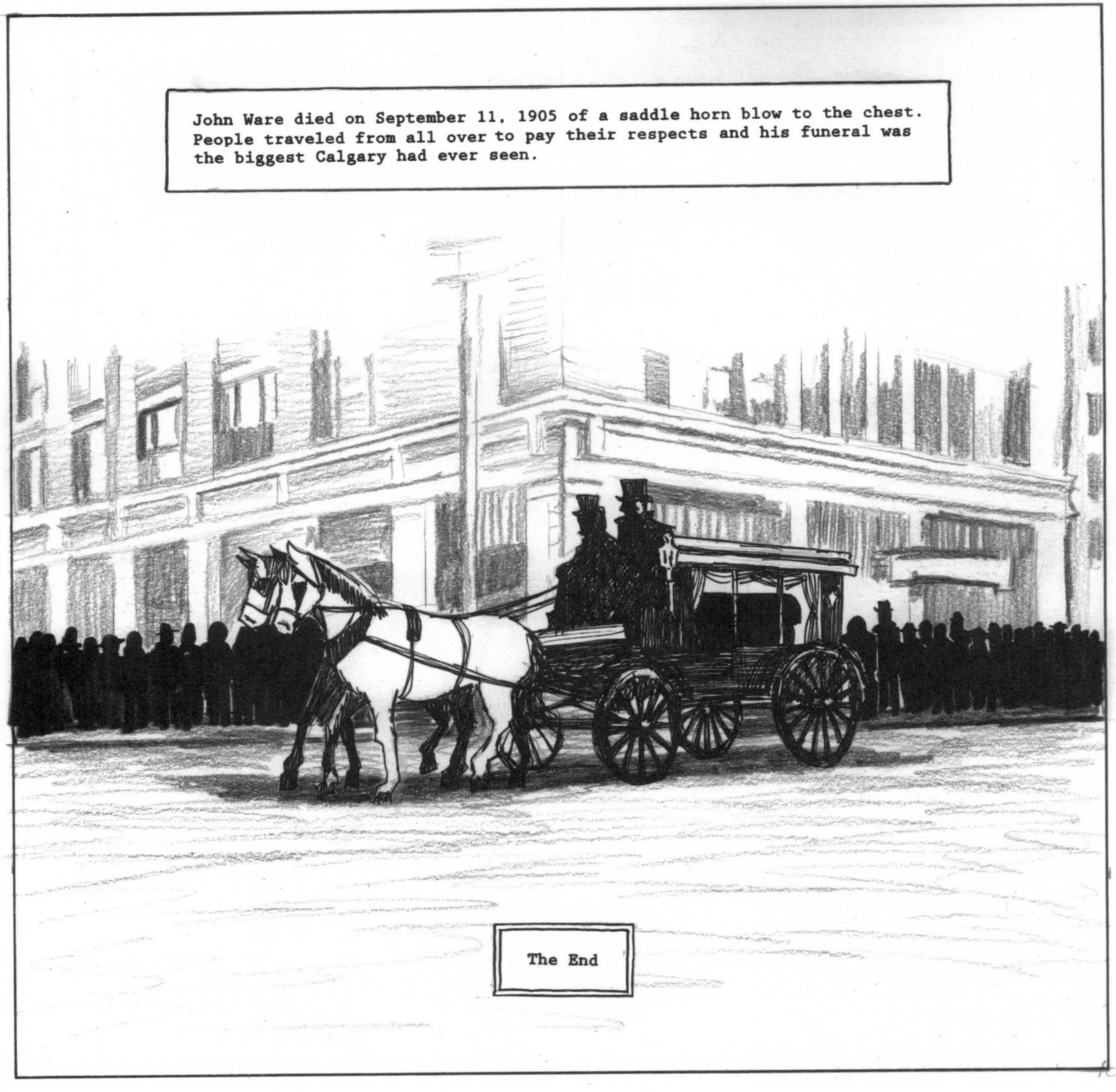
John Ware died on September 11, 1905 of a saddle horn blow to the chest. People traveled from all over to pay their respects and his funeral was the biggest Calgary had ever seen.
The End

NOTES BY JAMES DAVIDGE

While researching this story I was driven by two primary sources; a book and an archive collection. Grant MacEwan's *John Ware's Cow Country* is a very thorough documentation of Ware's life and is based on numerous interviews with people who spoke from first-hand memory. However, even MacEwan admitted that people's tendency to exaggerate and embellish during storytelling made it hard to confirm fact from legend.

The Glenbow Museum archives is a wonderful public resource full of much material from Alberta's early history. Their *Mavericks* exhibition features John Ware and they have amassed an impressive collection of material surrounding the cowboy's life. As well, Harry Sanders (*CBC Radio's* Harry the Historian), one of the archive curators, was of immense help with his detailed knowledge of Calgary's past.

I was also extremely grateful to meet Con Loree, the daughter of Fred Ing who was a friend of John Ware. While she never met John, her tales of her father and those earlier times assisted me in gaining a better sense of those pioneer days. A tip of the hat to my friend, Toby Malloy, who arranged for the interview as Con was her mother-in-law. Sadly, Con Loree passed away before this book reached publication. I wish Con could have seen the images she helped develop, particularly the "Snakes, Ropes & Jokes" strip which was indirectly inspired by her recounting Fred Ing's overzealous fear of lightening (Ing used to insulate his favourite chair's legs with old newspapers) and as well as his colleague's enjoyment of a good prank.

This project would not have existed had Shawn Canning not suggested it. While on a camping trip to Dinosaur Provincial Park, he discovered John Ware's last cabin which had been moved years earlier by the Brooks Kinsmen Club to the campground for permanent preservation and interpretation. He suggested that I create a graphic novel about Ware for which he would compose a musical score. As it turned out, one of my first teaching positions had been at John Ware Junior High. This was at the dawn of Google and I recall one of my first web searches being about John Ware as my curiosity was piqued by a picture of him that hung in my classroom. Shortly after our first discussion, Shawn and I met at my place to begin research on the project. I was living in Ramsay just below Scotsmen's Hill with the Calgary Stampede grounds on the other side. Within a few hours of internet surfing and guitar playing we discovered that John Ware was buried less than a kilometre away at Union Cemetery. On that first trek to his grave, less than a day into our focused involvement with his life, I felt a great exhilaration combined with a growing sense responsibility to do right by Mr. Ware. Shawn confessed similar emotional connection to the material. His soundtrack to the Duchess Ranch of Old John Ware is an exquisite companion to the novel and is available for free download at bayeux.com.

On that note I must acknowledge Bob Prodor, the artist of this work. Using a small grant from the Alberta Foundation for the Arts as a seed of support, Bob has done more than just follow my script when drawing these pages. He has taken ownership and been extremely creative with his interpretations. Many wonderful details are due to his instinct and research.

In contemplating my process, more than a year after I completed the first draft of this story, I confess that my recollection is as equally hindered as the original anecdotes that inspired this tale. My memory is often susceptible to ego and embellishment. As was the story. That being said, I hope you will benefit from this brief explanation of my process.

Page 1

This is the first verse of a poem I wrote while working on the grant proposal for the project. One early idea was to explore geography as character and have the story told from the perspective of the landscape. While John's tales quickly dominated the project, I wanted the settings to feel significant throughout.

Page 2 – 4

I soon realized that the poem was going to take up quite a few pages and it was going to take a while to introduce John Ware. I thought the audience might be intrigued by this simple but telling scene near the end of John's life. The moment establishes that he has become a rancher and a family man without giving away too many details. Mildred is mentioned cryptically. His horse steps into a hole and we are taken back to the dark beginnings of time.

Page 5 -12

Larger immersion into different components of John Ware led me to feel that there was more story to tell than one physical area could account for. However, I still wanted to use my geologic poem as I hoped that the history of the universe might parallel and contrast with John's own odyssey in many diverse and unanticipated ways.

My fascination with big bang moments being depicted in comics goes back to my frequent re-reading of Marv Wolfman and George Perez's *Crisis on Infinite Earths* as a young boy. The first page of this DC Comic had a panel featuring many fiery worlds blasting out of a singularity. Since writing this script I have learnt of a compelling theory that suggests that there never was a big bang and that we have to imagine the universe as a continual and morphing system where time does not exist in anyway we imagine it. I contemplated changing the "explosion of light" panel but felt that I needed to explore the "No-Big-Bang" theory in more depth if I were to represent it in a story and that, darn it all, there's just something about multiple fiery spheres blasting out of a singularity that excites me.

While on a research camping trip to Dinosaur Provincial Park I read quite a bit of William Blake and Percy Shelley. Inspired by their romantic versions of universal history I scratched out my own poetic geologic timeline. My years as a Gr. 7 science teacher, where planet Earth is a main unit of study, had provided numerous moments of contemplation on this topic. Interestingly, I did not write the bulk of this poem in Alberta. Shortly after the camping trip I travelled to Howick, Quebec where my uncle has converted an old church into three simple apartments. Sitting in a front room with light travelling through old stained glass windows was an inspiring local. So was sleeping in a steeple.

Page 13 - 34

The Odyssey map builds on the notion that this is a geographic journey. The little symbols are westernized lower-case versions of the greek letters alpha, beta, gamma, delta and omega. The anecdotes shared here are based on information in *John Ware's Cow Country*. However, the actual moments have been fictionally devised. The newspaper articles on page 21 are inventions of mine to account for further details from the MacEwan book.

Page 35 -36

It is documented that John much preferred the rural areas in comparison to the growing streets of Calgary. He found the township generally unfriendly. Jesse Williams had been recently hung for murder and some use this to explain the cold reception of John Ware. However, Alberta has a history of intolerance towards others and that can't be explained away by one criminal case. Almost every culture ranging from Ukrainian to Chinese can tell tales of mistreatment in early Alberta.

What is clear is that John was a wrangler through and through, and drawn to its outdoor lifestyle. Ranchmen all had comfort and ability with grand beasts and wide ranges. They relied on their own impressive strength and were used to a high degree of isolation.

Page 37 - 42

The "John Ware of the 19th Century" strips are meant as homages to the Sunday edition newspaper cartoons that grew in prominence during John's time. I was re-introduced to samples of these while reading Art Spegielmen's *In the Shadow of No Towers*. The title of my devised series is clearly inspired by *Buck Rogers of the 25th Century*. I liked the idea of creating something that presented a cowboy's life as exciting without the often glamorized gunplay.

Page 43- 44

These poems serve as the swan song of John's life as a bachelor. Fair's Fair Bookstore in the Inglewood neighbourhood of Calgary has a vast, diverse and interesting collection of used books. One day I got to browsing through their various collections of cowboy poetry. Inspired by their simple thoughtful words I went out to the recently erected sculpture garden at 9 Ave and 8 St. Southeast and scratched out these lines with the hope that their inclusion helps communicate the wild freedom and earnest loneliness that many a wrangler testifies to feeling.

Page 45

This is a word for word replica of the original announcement for John and Mildred's wedding. The clip was found in the Glenbow Museum archives. I was immediately drawn to it because I think it conveys the respect the community had for John. I find it worth noting that they never mention Mildred's name which serves both as an example of that era's significant gender bias and the minimal nature of print media in the 19th Century. It is also simply possible that they didn't have that information at deadline.

Page 46 - 52

Tensions grew quickly between the established ranchers and the homesteaders that were migrating from Ontario and elsewhere in increasing numbers. John soon made a decision to move his family. The scene with the belligerent drunk is based on an anecdote of John's daughter Nettie Ware, recounted by Cheryl Foggo in her article "My Home is Over Jordan". It is a fiction that this occurred when John was going to buy the land. It seemed fitting to combine these moments of prejudice and relocation.

Page 53

These deeds of sale are also replicas of items found in the Glenbow archives. I like how this map contrasts with the earlier "Odyssey" map. The earlier map had John travelling great distances with only legends of his feats as markers. Now older, John is travelling a relatively shorter distance leaving behind a trail more of paperwork than adventure.

Page 54 - 58

Much of the material I found on John was notably revering but this story shows that John had a rebellious side to him.

Page 59 – 60

This scene is based on a letter written by Mildred Ware from the archives. John Ware was illiterate and Mildred handled his correspondences. Her father, Stephen Lewis, moved from Ontario with his family to have a go at farming but Stephen's main vocation was constructing spiral staircases. Mildred was an educated woman and she often found rural life a struggle.

Page 61 – 67

This story of the flood and subsequent rebuilding is a well-known testament to perseverance.

Page 68 – 70

The story of the mange trenches is told by many to demonstrate the community minded character of John Ware. It has sometimes been stated that John Ware invented this technique; however it is more likely that this is a misconception due to his involvement with such a large cleansing.

My research time at the Glenbow archives led me to an interesting conversation with a woman that was researching John Ware for a documentary. Her self-admitted tendency towards the nefarious had led her to use certain papers in the archives to hypothesize that John may have had debt problems that her thesis suggested was common to the immigrant experience. She proposed that his later community involvement may have been evidence of repayment. I remember finding her ideas provocative but felt my story being pulled in a different direction.

Page 71 – 77

John's trek to get medicine for his ailing wife certainly helps confirm the great love he felt for her.

Page 78 - 80

In a documentary entitled *John Ware: The Good Neighbour* I heard a recording of Nettie Ware recounting this story. As one of the only tales I heard directly from a Ware family member, it was undeniably deserving of inclusion. It also helped provide a moment of brevity before the impending tragedies.

Page 81 -83

Mildred died of pneumonia in April of 1905. It is most likely a fiction that her death was on the same day as the previous story. I felt the underlying links between "stealing mother's milk" and "a mother's passing" warranted tying the two moments together into one scene.

Page 84 -97

It is well established that John's oldest son, Bob, was with him when he died in September of 1905. The conversation between them is a fiction. It is an attempt to synthesize John Ware's life with themes of character, race and cosmological mystery. I found reading Cheryl Foggo's *Pourin' Down Rain* whose anecdotes of growing up in Alberta's black community helpful in imaging Bob's perspective. I am also indepted to Cheryl for her insightful advance reading of this story.

The dialogue also came about from reflecting on conversations I had with my parents about the world as a young boy. My social understanding often came from my mother and my moral understanding from my father. Although by no means did either have exclusive influence over these areas. My mom taught me much about right and wrong but it is her unbridled passion for Canadian history that I strive to honour with this project. As well, my dad was always very knowledgeable about the world but in contemplating my most pivotal moments with him, I recall calm earnest discussions concerning my troublesome actions that we would have, usually well after my mom had provided the initial reaction, lecture and application of consequences. His practical guidance using logic and anecdotes often had a lasting impact.

John's five surviving children – Nettie, Bob, William, Mildred Jane and Arthur - would have spent most of this time living with their grandparents. While it is probably an incorrect depiction having John's other children also at the ranch I wanted John's last statement to be one showing him be a protectorate for his family. I was admittedly disappointed to learn that none of John's children had any offspring of their own.

Page 98

Re-presenting the verse from the beginning of the book in a different form brings us full circle while also giving a sense of the changing times.

Page 99

The shipping of Ware's body to Calgary for the funeral was paid for by George Lane, one of the famous Big Four founders of the Calgary Stampede and a character in a couple scenes in my tale. I had a brief conversation with George Lane's grandson, also George Lane, and he was able to recall a fond reunion shared between his grandmother and Nettie Ware that he witnessed when he was a young boy.

I wanted this last moment to be a somber celebration of a life well lived, as many funerals have the natural and rightful tendency to be. John's gravesite at Union Cemetery in Calgary is near the top of a large tombstone-ridden hill with a distinct view of the downtown landscape.

Bibliography

Brado, Edward, *Cattle Kingdom* (2004). Heritage House Publishing. Surrey, Canada.

Charon, Milly, *Between Two Worlds: The Canadian Immigrant Experience* (1988).Nu-Age Editions. Montreal, Canada.

Conrad, Norman C., *Reading the Entrails: An Alberta Ecohistory* (1999). University of Calgary Press. Calgary, Canada.

Elofson, Warren M., *Frontier Cattle Ranching in the Land and Times of Charlie Russell* (2004). McGill Queen's University Press. Canada.

Foggo, Cheryl, "My Home is over Jordan: Southern Alberta's Black Pioneers" *Remembering Chinook Country* (2005). Desilig Enterprises. Calgary, Canada.

Foggo, Cheryl, *Pourin' Down Rain* (1990) Deselig Enterprises. Calgary, Canada.

Humdey, Ian, *John Ware* (2006). Fitzhenry & Whiteside. Markham, Canada.

Ings, Frederick, *Before the Fences (Tales from the Midway Ranch)*. Memoir edited by Jim Davis (1980). McCara Printing. Canada.

Leeder, Terry, *Brand 9999* (1979). Dundurn Press Limited. Toronto, Canada.

MacEwan, Grant, *Fifty Mighty Men*. (1958) Western Producer Prairie Books. Saskatoon, Canada.

MacEwan, Grant, *John Ware's Cow Country* (1973). Western Producer Prairie Books. Saskatoon, Canada.

Palmer, Howard & Tamara, "The Black Experience in Alberta" *Peoples of Alberta: Portraits of a Cultural Diversity* (1985). Western Producer Prairie Books. Saskatoon, Canada.

Thomson, Colin A., *Blacks in Deep Snow* (1979). J.M. Dent & Sons Limited. Don Mills, Canada.

Calgary, Alberta, Canada. Her Industries and Resources (1885) Compiled by Burns & Elliott. Reprinted 1974 by the Glenbow- Alberta Institute.

John Ware: The Good Neighbor (1998). Video made by Great North Productions.

Various records and documents on file at the Glenbow Museum archives.